The Last Gentile

By

Cary R. Bybee

Published by Bybee Books
Lebanon, Oregon
U.S.A.

This book is a work of fiction. While I strived to keep history, science, geography, and Biblical truths true and accurate, any resemblance to real events or situations or actual persons, living or dead, is coincidental.

The Last Gentile
Copyright ©2003 by Cary R. Bybee

Published by Bybee Books, January 2004

Edited by Bea Kassees and Tina L. Miller
Page layout by Tina L. Miller
Cover art and design by Steve Gardner
Copyright ©2003 Bybee Books
Cover Photos Copyright Digital Stock, Digital Vision, Corbis

ISBN: 0-9744398-0-0 (soft cover)
        0-9744398-1-9 (hard cover)
        0-9744398-2-7 (electronic book)

Library of Congress Control Number: 2002095843

Previously published in March 2003 by 1st Books Library.
Previous ISBN's:
        1-4033-8656-0 (soft cover)
        1-4033-8657-9 (hard cover)
        1-4033-8655-2 (electronic book)

All rights reserved. No part of this publication may be reproduced, stored in a retrieval system, or transmitted in any form or by any means—electronic, mechanical, photocopy, recording, or any other—except for brief quotations in printed reviews, without the prior written permission of the author.

Printed and published in the United States of America

This book is printed on acid free paper.

Dedicated

To
My lovely wife, Peggy K. Bybee

Other books by Cary R. Bybee:

Deacon's Horn
The Final Witness
The Library Man

Acknowledgements

Bea Kassees of Millennium Christian Shows—Thank you for your tireless dedication to this ministry and your many thoughtful prayers.

Tina L. Miller of Obadiah Press—Thank you for helping us make our work more worthy of God.

Steve Gardner—Thank you for the wonderful cover designs.

Dustin and Melissa Mitsch of Written Communication.com—Thank you for the terrific web site.

Chapter 1 - The Legend

"Lunchtime comes a bit late today," Joseph Bastoni grumbled under his breath. His new assignment to the Vatican was quite an honor for a priest from a small town just outside Appleton, Wisconsin, and especially for one so young. Joseph didn't feel terribly young, but compared to nearly all of the other priests and nuns working at the Vatican, he most definitely was.

As the new guy, Joseph was getting the lion's share of the work lately. All of it was paperwork, of course—newsletters and other correspondence needing to be sent out to the many Catholic churches around the world. It was a constant exercise in Latin.

The Vatican had decided long ago that it would be much easier to correspond with all of the churches from every nation if they used a common language. Luckily for Joseph, this language turned out to be Latin, since that was what he had studied while attending Notre Dame. It was his renowned translation and understanding of old Christian documents of Latin origin, as well as his speaking and writing abilities, that had secured for him this highly esteemed position.

Joseph's new office was not much to brag about. He was beginning to understand the importance of seniority in the Catholic Church. *Well, at least I have a window,* Joseph thought. Peering out of it, he noticed how beautiful the day was turning out. Joseph loved the Vatican City and Rome. It was a mysterious and romantic place brimming with fantastic history and exquisite architecture.

Having had enough of his paperwork for the time being, he decided to take a walk. Actually he took a walk every day about this time. Joseph was a cigarette smoker, and his office was now a smoke-free building. To him, the whole world was becoming a smoke-free environment.

When he made the decision to become a priest, Joseph gave up all hope of a wife and family and any hope of wealth, as well, but the world was going to have to accept him as a smoker. He had given up all he was going to.

On this particular day, Joseph decided to take a stroll into the park. It was within walking distance of his office, and as far as he knew, it wasn't a smoke-free environment, at least not yet.

Standing under a large, old sycamore tree, Joseph enjoyed his cigarette as he shaded himself from the intense August heat. Italy was a very seasonal place, especially compared to Wisconsin. There they had only two seasons to contend with—the hot one and the cold one.

As he leaned back against the bark of the ancient tree, he noticed an old woman sitting on a park bench. Her hair was white as cotton and thin—very thin. Her eyes were black as night, yet bright and full of life. Her skin was wrinkled, reminding Joseph of the cracks that appeared in the earth each year in Africa as precious watering holes dried up into dust.

As the old woman sat there on a small wooden park bench, he wondered who she was and where she had come from. He had been to the park many times, but he had never seen her before.

He watched the lady intently, although he tried not to let her notice. Like the Pied Piper, she began to draw the many children who were playing in the park to her. All at once she started to speak to the children who had gathered around her. "Would you like me to tell you a story?" she asked.

"Oh, yes, Grandmother, tell us a story!" all the children exclaimed simultaneously. The woman motioned with her frail, old hand for the children to sit down on the ground. They responded at once and sat in a semicircle around the bench.

By this time Joseph's curiosity was provoked and, not wanting to miss the story himself, he began to inch his way closer to enable him to hear more clearly. Joseph stood next to an old whitewashed birdbath pretending to be watching the birds as they bathed while he listened intently to the old woman as she spoke.

"A long time ago," the woman croaked with a voice that was like a phonograph, scratchy and high-pitched, "when I was a small child, there was a mysterious man who came into our Sunday mass one Easter morning. Because he came in late, but also because he was dressed in a peculiar way, everyone began to notice him. Near the end of mass, he got up and walked towards the pulpit. His long robe with its gold sash seemed to glow as he walked. Looking the priest straight in the eyes, he requested to speak to the congregation."

The old woman stretched her neck out toward the children, revealing a beautiful jaw line as she did. "Well!" she screeched. "I am not sure if the priest was convinced by the sheer will of the stranger or just caught so far off guard that he gave way, but he nevertheless moved from the pulpit and allowed the stranger to address the people."

Pausing to catch her breath, the woman leaned forward on the bench and looked into the small, anxious faces of the children. After composing herself, she spoke again. This time she spoke with a little more excitement in her voice. "The man began to speak," she said with a very serious look on her face. The children leaned in closer to hear her as she whispered, "'A time is coming,' said the man, 'when the earth will no longer bear the sorrow of the sins of this world. At a time known only by Him, the earth will shake uncontrollably, and the stars will hide themselves. No man will have a place to go and escape the troubles to come, though he will try.'"

The woman pointed her shaky old finger at one of the children saying, "'The mountains will turn to rubble, and the land will waste away.' This is what the strange man said to us on that day."

"He said one more thing," she exclaimed as the children sat quietly slacked-jawed and wide-eyed. "'At this time the Evil One will be living amongst you, yet many of you will be spared.' He paused," she said, "and as he leaned over the pulpit, he said, 'There will be one last one among all of mankind who has been known from the beginning of time. He will be the last, the last Gentile to be saved. Evil cannot harm him. The Lamb protects him, and when he is saved, the saints will be delivered unto

God. At that very moment, the earth will shake as it gives up its dead. Woe unto the many who are left behind, for they will be devoured!'"

"And when the man was finished speaking," she said, "he bowed his head in silent prayer and then walked out of the church never to be seen again."

Joseph had been listening so intently that he hadn't even noticed when the ground started shaking. He was startled into awareness of the brief but powerful quake as the birdbath toppled over with a loud thud. Joseph moved quickly to avoid getting water all over his work clothes, as he preferred to call them.

All the children screamed and ran off. The old woman remained seated on the bench with a serene look on her face as if she were somewhere else at that moment. Not in the least surprised by the quake, she just sat there peacefully.

Joseph stared into the woman's eyes. He wanted to ask her who she was. The old woman stood quickly, catching him off guard. She walked up to him and looked straight into his soft brown eyes. Reaching out, she touched his shoulder. "And you will see all of this, too, my son," said the old woman, "but your path will be a hard one." She frowned and walked away more quickly than Joseph would have thought she could.

Chapter 2 - The Evangelist

It's going to be a big night. Oh yes, we are really going to rake it in tonight, Carl Perkins thought. October 31 was his favorite day of the year. For as long as he could remember, he always got something for free on that day, simply by asking. At first it was only a small piece of candy or a green apple, but now 30 years later, and at the age of 37, Carl was at the very top of his profession. People came from all over the world just to hear him speak prophetic words over them.

They are such desperate people, Carl thought. *No! Wrong choice of words. They're not desperate—they are hopeless, and hopeless people have a tendency to dig deep.* Carl checked his watch as he drew his head back from behind the side stage curtain. He still had an hour before the show. *Just enough time to get charged up,* he thought.

******

Back in his dressing room Carl removed a small vial of white powder from his vest pocket. Applying a small mountain of the drug to the back of his hand, he quickly raised the cocaine up to his nose. With a loud blast from his left nostril, the powder disappeared, and the hand was clean as before. Carl was so attentive to his own private little addiction that he didn't even notice when the door to his room opened.

"You really ought to cut back a little, Carl," said Stephanie. She was the great pastor's aide, and unknown to Carl's wife, she was his lover as well. Steph, as he liked to refer to her, was tall, modestly dressed, somewhat awkward, and yet, quite a beautiful woman. She was also 10 years younger than Carl. He, of course, saw this as a real plus.

Carl stepped forward and wrapped his arms around Stephanie's waist, his diamond cufflinks glistening as he rubbed his hands up and down her backside. Stephanie pulled herself away from him. "I mean it, Carl!" she said. "You told me that you would give that stuff up. It's bad enough that you still haven't told your wife about us like you promised."

Reverend Perkins pulled Stephanie back in again. "I'll quit right after tonight's show. I promise! And you know I can't tell Clorisa about us right now," Carl said while shaking his head. "She would ruin my ministry."

Perkins had no intention of ever telling his wife that he and Stephanie were engaging in an affair. Clorisa was the perfect pastor's wife, as she was not overly educated like Carl. Instead, she was friendly, modestly attractive, and genuine in her compassion for all of the lost souls in the world. Stephanie was a great lover, but Carl had certainly had great lovers before, and he would again as soon as Steph became too much of a liability. If he had learned anything at seminary, it was that a man sometimes has to cut his losses and move on. *Try not to dwell on the past* was his motto. Of course, for a man with no conscience, this was not much of a chore.

"There are a lot of people out there!" Stephanie exclaimed.

"They always come in large groups on Halloween. Scared of the devil, I guess," Carl grinned wryly. His only redeeming quality was that he really wasn't a hypocrite in the true sense of the word. One would actually have to believe in Heaven and Hell and in the God that created them both to be a real hypocrite.

Carl saw these people as opportunities to make money. Oh, sure, he was taking advantage of them, but he reasoned that he gave them back something as well. Hope. After all, if they really believed in God, why were they wasting their time coming to him for miracles and forgiveness? Hadn't they ever read the Bible that they claim to be the Word of God?

Didn't the Bible state that all could come to the Father through the Son and that if they believed by faith, they could ask the Son of God for anything and it would be given to them? Sure, Carl took these hopeless people's money, but in return, for a little while at least, they were no longer hopeless.

Carl had decided long ago after many empty unanswered hours of prayer that there could not be a God because he never heard, felt, or saw any real evidence of God. He nearly blushed as he recalled an earlier time in his life when he thought that maybe there was a Supreme Being.

How many times, as a young man, did he run to the altar when the preacher called? *Oh, yes, the frenzy of a charismatic church can almost make you believe that Jesus Himself is standing at the altar calling you,* he mused.

Carl did not have to think hard about what college to attend when he completed high school. After all, he was the third generation of faithful pastors. "The Perkins family went way back with God," he used to boast on stage. This was probably truer than Carl ever knew. His father and his grandfather were faithful and devout men who spent their lives trying to do God's work. They were also powerful men of prayer who believed that God would eventually hear and answer every need.

Carl never considered any other career, yet when his revelation that there was no God consumed him, he became desperate to find a use for his type of education. A Ph.D. in Christian Theology was not all that marketable, but fortunately for Carl, he had seen many evangelists in his youth. He knew that come Sunday afternoon the offering plate was always passed around to provide subsistence for the poor overworked evangelist. All of them were probably godly men, but that didn't matter to him.

Carl had no idea he would be so successful. However, once he figured out what the people wanted to hear, and having no compunction about compromising the Word of God to please the masses, money began to flow. Having been a relatively poor child raised on his father's pastoral salary, he quickly learned that any pleasure could be attained with enough money, but Carl never had enough money. The richer he became, the less satisfied he was. He had grown up poor, and he despised it. He despised poor people in general. In his sad mind the unfortunate could never make a worthy contribution to this world. For him, however, the only worthy contribution was to himself.

As he became more popular, it became evident that he would need to find additional ways to capitalize on his own good name, so as a result, he began to write and publish books on the End of Time Prophecy. Carl, albeit an unbeliever, was very well versed in the Bible. He had read and studied many additional Biblical sources in preparation for his doctorate.

His books sold like hot cakes, and although they were actually Biblically correct in content, they also included Carl's own slant on each topic. In particular he often repeated in his books the need for people to repent and to begin to obey God by tithing to his evangelistic ministry. It seemed that even with all his education he still failed to understand that forgiveness and salvation are a gift of grace offered to all simply for the asking—no strings attached.

Stephanie stood by the stage curtain observing Carl as he preached. She truly enjoyed watching him. He was a natural, pacing back and forth with a Bible in one hand and a handkerchief and microphone in the other.

On this warm Florida night, Carl was working up a real sweat as he spoke of the sin in our lives that had caused many to become physically ill. "Sin has made you all sick. It's the work of the Devil," he repeated.

Standing in the middle of the stage with a spotlight shining directly onto him, Carl opened his arms wide. "Come to me, my children. Come and repent of your evil ways and be healed."

Stephanie always found herself moved during this part of Carl's sermon. With *Amazing Grace* playing in the background and with Carl yelling out encouragement to convince people to run to the altar, it was like the Lord was really there. It gave her goose bumps, and tears always welled up in her eyes. She knew that Carl had his faults, but after all, hadn't he earned the right to a little private happiness? He had devoted his life to helping others. To Stephanie, Carl was a holy man, appointed by God to evangelize the world.

Carl was walking through the multitudes laying hands on the people as he went by. Hundreds were kneeling at the altar. "Be healed, my son," he said to one. "Repent and live," he said to another.

Stephanie watched this in amazement. She could see the cameraman focusing on Carl as he laid hands on one elderly woman. At that very moment the ground began to shake. Shouts of fear rang out in the stadium, and then the quake stopped as suddenly as it had started. *What an opportunity*, Carl thought as he grabbed his microphone. "God is with us, people," he said. "Repent! Repent! Repent—the Lord is with us."

People began to run to the altar crying and sobbing, begging God for forgiveness. Carl was amazed by his good fortune. Never before had Mother Nature helped him out so much. This was going to be a record moneymaking night. He caught sight of Stephanie by the side of the stage and gave her a big smile. In return she gave him a coy little wave. Stephanie's body was momentarily frozen where she stood as she analyzed the thought that had just consumed her mind at that very moment. She was staring at a man 10 years older than herself who was deceitful, reckless, and married, but it didn't matter. She loved him anyway.

Chapter 3 - The Volcanoes

December 24: The night began to fall on the city of Quito. The sky had an eerie red tint as the sun illuminated the smoke-filled valley. Mount Chimborazo, Ecuador's largest mountain at over 20,000 feet high, had been belching smoke for many months now. Chimborazo was a geological curiosity and, although Mount Everest is said to be the tallest mountain in the world, this is only true if one measured these mountains based on sea level. In fact, Mount Chimborazo from the center of the earth would be considerably taller than Everest.

Geologists had been studying this mountain's sudden volcanic activity for over six months since they first saw signs of life. However, working in the jungle as they studied the huge mountain had taken its toll on the team of specialists. Nearly all of them had been flown back to the United States because of a bacterial infection that supposedly came from the native waters of the region.

Only three geologists, or volcanologists as they prefer to be called, remained. The distinction is one of risk and danger. Volcanologists have been known to get too close to erupting volcanoes. Sadly, they have often paid for this indiscretion with their own lives. The three remaining scientists had completed all of their tests. This mountain may be smoking, but that is about all it is doing, was their general consensus.

There were no traces of poisonous gas or volcanic activity, such as tremors, to indicate an eruption in the forecast. In fact, this volcano had turned out to be a complete disappointment for the whole team. The sum total of their investigations had revealed nothing new. Most of the team was sick, and the accommodations in this region were barely tolerable for a week, let alone six months.

Tomorrow the team would go home. Their job was done, and all they had to show for it was a few inches of ash and some gray smoke. Marcus Walker, the team leader, hung his head in disappointment as he, Tina Glover, and her brother, Tommy Glover, walked back to their truck to store the last of their equipment.

How interesting it is that geologists often get disappointed when the mountains they are monitoring do not erupt. The mere explosive power of the average volcano could easily destroy a large city with considerably more explosive force than the nuclear weapons used during World War II, not to mention the pyroclastic cloud that could move at hundreds of miles per hour while carrying intense heat from super heated gases as a result of the explosion. If that were not enough, the poisonous gas and suffocating ash could destroy every remaining living thing in its path.

Marcus considered all of this, but he couldn't help being disappointed. This mountain would have made a great documentary, which would have brought more grants and more opportunities to study other volcanoes. Looking through his rear view mirror as he drove the team off the mountain, Marcus whispered to himself, "What a dud!"

Back in their hotel room the three geologists packed their gear for the early morning ride to the local airport. The team had requested to be flown out before the 24th of December. However, due to the smoke and rain, the plane could not come in. They would have to spend Christmas day in the air flying home. And in a small commuter plane, the flight from Ecuador to Los Angeles would make for a very long day.

******

In the city of Pompeii it was already Christmas day. The tourists were everywhere, swarming over the rebuilt ruins of the once destroyed metropolis. Pompeii and all its inhabitants had been immortalized in an instant one afternoon back in 79 A.D. Mount Vesuvious' eruption had caught everyone off guard. When the archeologists excavated the city, it became apparent that poisonous gas or suffocation from ash must have killed the city's dwellers before they knew what was happening. Many bodies, still well preserved, were found beneath a mountain of ash. Some were still in their beds while others were obviously in the middle of eating a noonday meal, preserved for the last 2,000 years at the dinner table.

As the tourists gathered around their tour guide, Sofia Carlini, she began to dramatically reenact that fearful event when the entire population of Pompeii was decimated. Pointing in the direction of the small but deadly Mount Vesuvious, Sofia described for the audience the events of that fateful day.

Among the attendance was a young, newly married couple, Steve and Stacy Carver. It was Stacy's idea to come to Rome for their honeymoon. Her father, as a teenager, had been in Rome during the war. He had told her many times the stories of how he met her mother while she was working at the ticket counter of the local train station. Stacy's mother's English was not very good at the time, but it was apparently good enough for Stacy's dad to ask her out to dinner.

This was the beginning of 50 years of marriage, which had just recently and tragically ended when Stacy's mother died of breast cancer. *It happened so quickly*, Stacy thought. The reality was that her mother had known for quite some time that she was dying of cancer, but she didn't want her children to suffer with that knowledge along with her. Only after the chemotherapy had failed to stop the cancer's spread did her mother enlighten the children as to her terminal condition.

Steve knew that their trip to Italy was Stacy's way of trying to remain close to her mother even after her death. Their honeymoon was already full of highs and lows, and unknown to Steve, things were not going to get any better.

******

It was still Christmas Eve at the base of Mount Denali as Mark Hendricks and his friend, Calvin Fraser, began to prepare their equipment. McKinley Park, as Calvin referred to it, was one of the most spectacular sites in all of Alaska. Mark and Calvin had been waiting for months for the weather to improve enough to allow them to climb the face of

Mount Denali. Both men had taken a mountain climbing class at Elmendorf Air Force Base where they were stationed. They were eager to put their newly acquired skills to use.

Calvin was a short and stocky black man from Palo Alto, California. When he was a small boy, he used to stroll past Stanford University and stop to stare at all the young adults walking busily from building to building. He made up his mind at a young age that he wanted to attend Stanford. However, coming from a moderately poor family, he needed help to pay for his tuition. He could clearly remember the day he got his acceptance notice from the university. He had spent many long hours studying to prepare for college. He could also clearly remember the day he saw how much the tuition was for a single year of schooling. He never told his parents about the cost of attending the school of his dreams. Instead he joined the Air Force ROTC program, promising Uncle Sam six years of active duty as payment for his education. Calvin thought it a small price.

As it turned out, Calvin had a knack for engineering, and after college he was admitted into the pilot program. He loved the thrill of flying. In fact, he loved the excitement of anything dangerous. Unknown to Calvin, he was about to get the thrill of his life, but would he live to talk about it?

Mark Hendricks was a much less serious person than Calvin. Life was a game of chance, and to Mark, that's what made it so entertaining. He grew up in a small Texas town called White Settlement. The only thing his town could boast of was that Lee Harvey Oswald had once lived there.

Mark was habitually bored. He required constant entertainment, and the more dangerous, the better. This was the reason he joined the Air Force after graduating from the University of Texas at Arlington.

He had always been fascinated with flying, and by the age of 16, he was a fairly good pilot. As a child he flew every chance he could with his uncle on his small package delivery route. Today Mark was not going to be bored. In fact, this kind of entertainment he could probably live without.

******

Tina Glover was the first one of the three scientists to feel the earth shake. Rolling out of her cot as quickly as possible, she went straight to Tommy's bed to wake him. By this time Marcus was stumbling around trying to put on his pants.

"Oh, my God! Oh, my God!" Marcus shouted. "It's right below us!"

"What's below us?" Tommy yelled as he tried to be heard over the groans of the mountain.

Tina and Marcus both ran to the cabin's front door. Tina got there first and threw open the door.

It was barely 5:00 a.m. on Christmas day, and it should still have been dark, yet it wasn't. Looking directly west of their cabin, Marcus could see the glow of fireworks coming from Mount Chimborazo. He turned around in the cabin doorway, bumping into Tommy as he did.

"I need my shoes!" he shouted.

"Where are you going?" Tommy inquired. Marcus looked at him with a scornful, incredulous look as if to say—do you really need to ask?

Tina began to put on her shoes too.

"Oh, no you don't!" said Tommy. "He may be crazy enough to go to an erupting volcano, but you're staying with me."

Tina knew that he meant what he said. She looked at Marcus, who only glanced at her and shook his head as he ran out the door and climbed into their truck.

******

Peter Metler looked at his wristwatch. *I can be there before 6:00 a.m.*, he thought with a smile, *and I hope they have a long runway.* Over the years Peter had been hired to fly into many remote places. Some had reasonable runway accommodations, and others were not so good. Peter was on autopilot as he poured himself another cup of coffee.

"It's not exactly Starbucks," he spoke aloud, laughing to himself as he sipped his own home brew. *Fifteen more minutes and I'll take her off autopilot, turn west, and fly her in*, he figured.

A moment later the plane began to shake, spilling hot coffee all down

Peter's arm. "Ouch!" he yelled as he dropped the coffee and grabbed the controls. Things were getting pretty bumpy, which is sometimes expected around the equator. This, however, was pretty extreme. "Time to find a lower altitude," he said audibly.

******

Tina and Tommy were scrambling to pack up all they could carry. "The plane should be here around 6:30," said Tommy. Tina was still angry with Tommy and was unwilling to acknowledge his statement. Tommy didn't care. She'd get over it and at least she would be alive.

"We're going to have to walk to the runway, Tina," he said. "So we'd better leave now." It was only a mile or so away, but time was running out.

"Fine!" said Tina with frustration in her voice. "Let's go," she growled as she walked past her brother through the doorway.

They were stunned to see so many people outside watching the mountain begin its final struggle against the pressure building underneath its crusty surface.

"Why are these people still here?" Tina asked. Tommy could hear the concern in her voice. "Don't they know that when this baby blows, they may all be killed?"

With concern for the innocent natives of Quito, the brother and sister team began to urge the people to evacuate the area before it was too late.

"Take what water and food you can and leave right now!" Tina shouted. The people did not understand the grave situation in which they found themselves, but as the ground below them began trembling again, this time with more intensity, fear hit the people, and they scattered in every direction, quickly running away from the mountain.

"I guess they heard you," said Tommy as many panic-stricken people collided with them.

"Good!" replied Tina. "At least they'll live, even if they won't have a home when they come back."

******

Peter approached the landing strip with a slow fly-by, hoping to see a long, paved runway but expecting a short, dirt road. Tina and Tommy were at the edge of the runway as he passed by. They waved to him and he dipped his wing in acknowledgement of having seen them both.

As Peter turned the plane to approach the landing strip, his attention went to the spectacular fireworks display coming from Mount Chimborazo. "Dear Lord!" he shouted. "What the heck is going on here?"

Looking down Peter noticed people running away from the city. At this point he pulled back on the stick. He needed to think things over before he landed.

Tina yelled at Tommy, "He's not going to land!"

"Yes, he will," said Tommy with little confidence.

******

By this time Marcus had driven to the science station that they had abandoned only a day earlier. All of his equipment had been packed away. *What a shame*, he thought. *If I only had my equipment, or at least my video camera...*

Marcus stood on the edge of a cliff, staring at the mountain. *How come we didn't detect this?* he wondered. At that moment the earth began to shake violently and the mountain belched a huge, fiery cloud of dense, black smoke. Realizing the mountain was not just going to let off a little steam, he quickly turned to head back towards the truck when suddenly the shaking of the earth knocked him to the ground. Panic and fear filled his body as he realized that his own curiosity and fascination with this mountain had now put him into incredible danger.

Abruptly the earth stopped shaking. There was an eerie silence that lasted for as much as 10 seconds. Marcus got to his feet and was racing back to his truck when suddenly there was a tremendous explosion.

The top of the mountain just simply disappeared into a cloud of fire, smoke, and gas. The shockwave from the explosion reached him before he could even get the truck door open. Marcus never fully comprehended the massive force that ripped his body to pieces.

******

Flying at 17,000 feet, looking over his shoulder, Peter was amazed by the site of the explosion. Looking ahead from the cockpit, he gave the plane full throttle and mumbled, "Giddy up!"

In the back seat sat Tina and Tommy. Tina was crying, having realized that Marcus could not have survived the eruption.

"I didn't think you were going to land," said Tommy.

"I thought about it," said Peter, "but hey, it's Christmas!"

******

The ground only shook once as the group of visitors stood next to their tour guide. Sofia paused, surprised by the small tremor. When it was over, she wryly remarked to the group, "Special effects are at no extra charge." The crowd laughed nervously, and Stacy gripped Steve's hand a little tighter.

It was a lovely day in Pompeii, probably much like that day back in 79 A.D. There was a slight easterly breeze blowing right past Mount Vesuvious. Had the tourists and Sofia not had their backs turned towards the deadly little mountain, they would have seen a puff of grayish white smoke emerge from deep within. Furthermore, had they not been looking in the other direction, they would have seen a noxious cloud of deadly gas lift off the small mountain and head straight toward them.

Sofia Carlini was pointing out the great detail in which the city was rebuilt. "Let's now move to the traditional dining room for some lunch." The crowd followed her into a very old, white building without ever looking back, all except for Steve and Stacy who thought it would be fun to run off unsupervised and explore Pompeii.

Steve and his bride skipped away, laughing as they moved from the dining hall that held the other 15 members of the tour group. They walked down the center of the main street of Pompeii hand in hand admiring all the bleached white buildings and old pillars.

Suddenly, as Stacy and Steve rounded a turn, they found themselves looking straight at a grayish white cloud moving very fast and low towards the ancient city.

"What is that?" Stacy asked. Steve was not sure, but he had read much on Pompeii before their visit. He had heard speculations that most of the city's dwellers were killed by poisonous gas. *Did it look like this?* he wondered. Where it came from, he hadn't a clue. Grabbing Stacy's arm, Steve led her back to the dining room as quickly as possible.

They entered as the group was just starting to eat. Sofia knew that the two honeymooners had not come in with the rest of the group, and as they appeared now, she smiled, remembering her own honeymoon. *Too may years ago*, she thought.

Steve walked up to Sofia. "There's a cloud outside," he said. The tour members began to laugh, but not Sofia. She knew better than most about the deadly gas clouds coming out of both Mount Etna and Vesuvious in past centuries, killing entire villages.

"How far away?" she asked quickly. The sincerity of her voice, heavily laced with her Italian accent, caught the attention of the tour group. This was the effect she was hoping for, not truly believing any real danger was possible, but just as eager to add a little drama to the tour.

"It was maybe a mile or so away," he replied with fear beginning to show in his youthful face. Stacy maintained her grip on his hand as the two sat down at the table with the rest of the group.

No one will ever really know for sure if what happened next was a mistake on Sofia's part or if it would not have mattered in the slightest. Sofia got up and went to the exit door of the dining hall. She opened the door to look out, hoping to see a rain cloud heading away from Pompeii. Instead what Sofia must have seen was something like dense fog, for as soon as she opened the door, the deadly mist was all around her head. Choking horribly on the poisonous gas, Sofia was dead within a few seconds.

Everyone in the dining room screamed and began to run, but there was no place to go. Mercifully, they all died within seconds of the poison entering their lungs. Steve was still clutching Stacy's hand when the rescue party came on the scene three days later after the all clear had been given.

******

Mark and Calvin had been climbing the mountain for about four hours. It was tough going but exhilarating, especially for Calvin who really took in the beauty of it all. Alaska was wild, rugged, and full of splendor. Mark seemed more interested in the task at hand. It seemed that throughout his life he rarely stopped long enough to appreciate the beauty of this world.

Far below the ledge where the two climbers were presently navigating was a crystal clear view of the base of Mount Denali. In the distance the smoke trail of a train moved slowly towards the mountain. It was right on time and full of passengers who had paid dearly to come and see the largest mountain in America, even if it wasn't really in America.

December was not normally a good month to climb or even to visit Denali, as the risk of a snowstorm was too great, but for some reason, this year's weather had been extremely moderate, so the officials in the Alaskan government had authorized a limited number of days for mountain climbing.

As Calvin continued to climb, he suddenly felt a presence around him—an unexplainably strong force. "Mark," he said, "do you feel that?"

"Feel what? I'm half frozen and tired—I feel that."

"No!" said Calvin. "It's not that."

Mark continued to climb while Calvin paused to look around. Suddenly a soft voice spoke to Calvin, not that he could hear it with his ears really. It was more like the voice talked directly to his mind.

"Who are you?" he asked in fear.

"Turn back," said the voice.

"What?" he asked. "Turn back! But why?"

"Turn back now—quickly!" the voice whispered into Calvin's mind.

By this time Mark was a good 80 yards away from Calvin. "What about Mark?"

"This is his time. Let him go," said the voice.

"I can't leave him," said Calvin. "I won't leave him."

"You must!" said the voice. "It is not your time. God has a different plan for you. Climb down now!"

Heading down was a lot faster than going up. It probably took Calvin less than an hour to get to the bottom. Calvin had tears in his eyes as he reached the base of the mountain. He never looked back at Mark, but in his heart, he felt like he had abandoned his friend. He reached Mark's car and took the spare key from the visor. Without bothering to store his gear, he simply got in and drove away. He could hear the whistle of a train as he drove alongside the tracks.

"Take comfort," said the voice. "Your obedience has saved you."

At that very moment Calvin heard a great explosion, and shortly after that the ground beneath his vehicle began to shake violently. Calvin slowed to look back at the mountain. He could see a huge black and red cloud rising from the top. At the same time he could see a tremendous amount of white powder filling the air all around the mountain.

"Turn away and drive faster!" said the voice.

Calvin began to cry aloud as he sped away. "I'm sorry, Mark," was all he could say.

******

Mark hadn't noticed Calvin missing for quite some time. When he did finally realize that his climbing buddy was nowhere to be found, he began to descend, believing that Calvin must have fallen into a ravine. Approaching the location where he had last spoken to him, he stopped and looked out at the valley below. In the distance, Mark could see his partner driving away in his Jeep. He was stunned. What in the world was Calvin doing?

The ground started shaking where he stood. Looking up, Mark could see the snow coming even before he heard the blast. Within seconds he was swept away by an avalanche, propelling him down the mountain at over 200 miles per hour. Mark crashed into a large rock as he tumbled down the slope. His neck was broken, and mercifully, he died quickly.

The avalanche continued down the mountain and directly into the path of the train below Mount Denali. Many of the passengers saw it coming. Some were screaming, but none could get away. The train was thrown from the tracks as if it weighed nothing. The train tumbled down a steep ravine and was quickly covered in 20 feet of snow. The survivors of the train wreck probably had as much as an hour's worth of usable air before succumbing to the disaster.

Chapter 4 - The Affair

On January 3 the snow in London was incredible. Four feet in three days, and now the temperatures were dropping to all-time lows throughout England. Pastor Perkins had been disappointed by the turnout at his revival meetings during the last few days. "It's the weather," he cursed. However, Carl was an eternal optimist, and he was sure that tonight, his last night in London, was going to be a huge success.

Carl looked at his watch and decided it was time to go to the convention center. "Steph," he called, "time for me to go."

Stephanie came walking out of the bathroom looking completely unready to leave for the revival service. Her hair was not yet fixed, nor was she dressed in anything other than a hotel bathrobe. Carl looked at Stephanie with apparent annoyance. "Why aren't you dressed?" he inquired.

"Carl, I'd like to stay in tonight if you don't mind. I'm not feeling very well," she said. He was obviously disappointed but agreed that, since she wasn't dressed in the first place, she may as well stay in the hotel. Carl had been spending too much time with her lately, and he was already beginning to grow tired of her. As he turned to leave, she kissed him goodbye, showing her affection openly.

******

I have three hours, Stephanie thought. *Three hours to put this all together.* She had been planning to surprise Carl for days with a romantic candlelight dinner and a night of romance. She, too, began to fear that Carl was growing tired of her. Stephanie had ordered dinner to be prepared and delivered to Carl's room.

She, of course, had her own room. Carl was a very discrete person, never leaving too much for reporters to write about. It just so happened, however, that Carl and Stephanie had adjoining rooms.

The next two hours went by in a blur as she prepared for Carl's return. Stephanie was dressed in a very seductive evening gown; her hair was also fixed attractively as she allowed it to hang over her shoulders. The dining table in Carl's room was nicely set, and the champagne was already chilling. Stephanie hoped that Carl would have a big crowd tonight. He'd been in such a bad mood because of the weather and subsequent poor turnout.

There was a knock at the door. *Could the food be here already?* she wondered. Stephanie opened the door and, to her surprise, there in the doorway stood Clorisa, Carl Perkins' devoted wife. Stephanie was stunned. Clorisa was supposed to be in Los Angeles minding the mansion that Carl had purchased five years earlier.

"Expecting someone else?" Clorisa asked with a frown of obvious disapproval.

"Well, yes! I mean no! What are you doing here?" she inquired.

"Are you surprised to see me, Stephanie? After all, this is my husband's suite, is it not?"

"Yes, of course! But I thought…"

"You thought I was home being the ever faithful wife while you were here being the unfaithful secretary."

Clorisa walked past Stephanie into the living room. "Nice place you two have here," she observed.

"It's not my room," Stephanie offered.

"Well, of course not! Yours would be the room next door if I've guessed correctly."

Clorisa continued to walk through the suite into the dining room. She stopped at the dining table and adjusted one of the napkin holders. "Lovely setting," she quipped.

By this time Stephanie was past the point of surprise and was rapidly moving into the arena of anger. "Yes, well, this is our last night in London and things here haven't gone too well for Carl, so I thought I would surprise him with a nice meal."

"Well, your formal gown is a nice touch, dear," Clorisa sneered.

That was the final straw. Stephanie could take no more. "What do you want, Clorisa? Do you want me to say that I'm sleeping with Carl? Is that it? Well, it's not that cheap. Carl and I love each other."

Clorisa turned and looked directly into Stephanie's eyes. She paused for what seemed like an eternity to Stephanie. Tears began to well up and run down Clorisa's flushed cheeks as she walked to the sofa and sat down.

"Come over here," she said. Stephanie didn't want to move, but she couldn't help herself. It was like Clorisa was pulling her to the sofa.

Clorisa spoke more gently to Stephanie. "I know that you love Carl, and I know that you think Carl loves you."

"He does!" Stephanie's retort lacked an ounce of confidence.

"No, Stephanie, he does not love you, or me." Stephanie was surprised at this. "In fact, Carl doesn't love anyone or anything but himself."

"That's not true," Stephanie argued. "Just look at all the good he does and all the people he helps."

"Yes, he does many good things for people. But he is unaware that he really does help others. He only thinks he is helping himself," Clorisa accurately surmised.

Stephanie was amazed to hear Clorisa say these words. She had always seemed so mild and removed from all of Carl's activities. Stephanie's own heart knew the truth. She had often wondered if Carl really cared for the people or just for the money and fame.

"Carl's ministry does get the Word out to many people, and that is important. Even if he does not believe what he preaches, God's work gets done all the same," his wife said sadly. "Furthermore, time is short until Christ's return, and the gospel needs to be preached to the entire world."

Stephanie was moved by the sincerity of this woman, "Why have you come here?" she asked.

Clorisa stared into Stephanie's pretty eyes. "For you!"

"For me! Why?"

"God revealed to me a couple of days ago that He had a special plan for your life and that you needed to repent of your sinful lifestyle," Clorisa said gently.

Stephanie was stunned with this blunt but caring, loving manner in which Clorisa was speaking. "The life you are living is not what God has planned for you. You were a true believer once, Stephanie, and you will be again."

Stephanie began to cry aloud. "I am so sorry!"

"I forgive you, Stephanie." Clorisa lifted the young woman's chin. "Now let's pray to the Father to forgive your sins and ask Him to cover them with the blood of the Lamb."

Both women held hands and prayed earnestly to God for forgiveness. They cried and hugged each other. Stephanie got off the sofa and looked at Clorisa. "I'll be packed and gone in 15 minutes."

"Where will you go?"

"Home—back to Chicago," said Stephanie.

Carl was going to be surprised by who was coming to dinner.

Chapter 5 - The Attack

Zach Miles was about as ordinary as a middle aged, depressed, disillusioned, divorced man could be. Sitting in the living room of his downtown Chicago apartment, he stared at the pictures of his son, Timothy, and his ex-wife, Valerie. Zach knew that he was going to spend another holiday alone.

Well, at least it's not Christmas this time, he thought.

Zach didn't care much for Easter anyway. It wasn't always that way though, he recalled. His mind drifted back to that sunny morning in April when he was nine years old and having the time of his life running all around the back lot of the People's Church of Chicago.

Zach, his two brothers, and his parents had gone to church there for as long as he could remember. Perspiration started to form on Zach's slightly receding forehead as he began to remember that tragic day.

The Easter egg hunt was over and the Miles family was heading out to the parking lot to get into their car for the short ride home. A wonderfully prepared holiday dinner would come shortly after. Young Zach was standing in the center of the parking lot looking into his basket full of colored eggs trying to determine how many of the little decorated trophies he had found. His family had not noticed that he had stopped in the middle of the entranceway to the church.

Turning and looking back over the top of the family car, Zach's father, Jack, saw his son standing in the road. At that same moment, Jack saw a large dark green sedan turning into the church parking lot. The car picked up speed as it headed straight towards Zach. Jack yelled to his son as he ran across the parking lot and into the path of the sedan. Both he and the speeding car reached his son at nearly the same time. Zach lifted his eyes in time to look head-on at the approaching car. Staring into the bright red eyes of the driver, he was suddenly frozen with fear as he dropped his basket of eggs. Just then, out of nowhere, came a large black man who grabbed Zach and pulled him out of the path of the car.

What happened next he didn't like to think about, but it couldn't be helped—the memory was too vivid.

He could, as if it were yesterday, clearly recall the automobile racing recklessly through the parking lot. In fact, it appeared to speed up as it approached Zach and his father. He could remember his father flying over the hood of the green sedan and crashing into the car's windshield.

Jack rolled off the hood and onto the pavement while the car sped away, never to be seen again. Zach could recall his mother's scream. He could see Leo Thomas, the family pastor, kneeling over his father.

There was something else he could remember as well. It was something he just could not forget. While he was lying there, clutched in the arms of the powerful black man, he had a sense of warmth and strength all around him. Even now after so many years had gone by, Zach could recall the sensation of peace, coupled with a unique smell. What was that smell? It wasn't familiar to him. It was indescribable, like no other smell he had known.

Zach got up and ran to his father. Jack looked up at his young son and smiled weakly. Then he closed his eyes for the last time. The man who had saved Zach disappeared through the crowd never to be seen again. Many people inquired about who he was, but none recognized him.

******

How long has the phone been ringing? Zach wondered. "Hello," he said. It was Valerie. Zach thought she might call. Valerie had a knack of knowing when he was depressed, which was most of the time, especially during holidays and on weekends.

Zach preferred to work his life away. If he had his way, he would have worked seven days a week—and as a news reporter, he often got his wish.

"How are you?" she asked.

"Fine," he lied, though not convincingly.

"Would you like to come over for dinner? Timothy's here!"

Dinner was tempting, but Zach didn't feel like getting into another argument with his son. Timothy was all of 10 when Valerie and he had split up. For years he had hoped his mother and father would reconcile, but after three years of separation with no improvements on Zach's part, Valerie finally filed for divorce.

That was 14 years ago, but Timothy still held his father responsible for breaking up his happy family.

"No, thanks!" decided Zach. "I've already eaten." That, too, was a lie and, of course, Valerie well knew it. She could always tell, though it did not happen very often.

"Well, then, how about just coming over for a little visit?" she urged.

Zach paused, caught off guard. "I have a long day planned tomorrow, so I'd better just stay in and get some sleep."

Valerie's voice began to show signs of disappointment. "Zach, you and Timothy can't avoid each other forever."

"Not tonight, Valerie," he begged.

"All right," said Valerie. "Good night then."

Zach hung up the phone more depressed than ever. *Maybe I should have gone.* He did, in fact, miss both Timothy and Valerie very much.

Zach never remarried after he and Valerie divorced. She was the only woman he ever loved. She, on the other hand, had met a man from the small church she attended and, after courting for quite some time, she finally consented to marry him. Zach could remember the day that she called and asked to have lunch with him. When they met, he could tell that Valerie had something on her mind.

"What's going on with you?" he inquired.

Taking a deep breath and holding most of it in, Valerie said in a very low voice, "I'm getting married." Zach knew that she had been dating for a while now. He didn't like it at all, but he understood that he had no right to say anything. Zach looked into her lovely brown eyes. She was still as beautiful as the day they met on the campus of Iowa State University.

She had been a new freshman, he a 20-year-old sophomore. They met at the campus bookstore. Zach was working as a clerk to pay his way through journalism school. She needed a used book for Western Civics. As soon as Valerie stepped up to the cash register and his eyes met her soft brown eyes, the magic began.

"You're what?" Zach asked dumbfounded.

"I'm getting married!" Valerie restated.

Zach was speechless. He had known this day would come, but he hoped it wouldn't. His voice croaked, both with emotion and surprise, "When?"

Valerie could sense the pain in Zach and began to cry. "I'm sorry, Zach, but—"

Zach interrupted her. "For what? You can do whatever you want. After all, you're not married to me anymore. Well, I had better get back to work."

"Work, work, work. Just keep hiding behind your work, Zach, never mind facing up to life!" Valerie was enraged.

Zach knew he was treading on thin ice. Whenever her tone reached this level, he understood it was time to shut up. "Do you love him?" he asked quietly.

"Do you really want to know?"

"Yes," he nodded.

"Then yes! I do love him." The words were like a knife in Zach's stomach. "I love him very much!" Only this time she said it to convince herself, not Zach.

"I hope you'll be happy," he said, his voice lacking sincerity.

"I was happy, but you ruined that!" she cried.

This really caught Zach by surprise. Unfortunately at this point he went with his instincts, poor as they were. "I'm not the one who wanted to join that stupid church. I'm not the one who was always bringing up Christianity."

"I just wanted you to get saved and submit your life to Christ," she said.

"You just wanted me to change, but I didn't. I won't!"

Something inside Zach knew she was right, that she was not the one who needed to change, that it was he.

"Okay, Zach. Go back to work and hide. I've said what I came here for." With that she had gotten up quickly and left the restaurant.

And Zach had sat there wondering how he could have gotten into that same old argument. Religion and God—that's what they always fought over. That was what had pushed him out of Valerie's life. He had no desire to go to church. What had church ever done for him but take his father away? Zach knew there was a God, but he didn't like Him. He was still very angry with God for letting his father die.

He and Valerie had tried to live together in separate worlds. She was active in church and had a tremendous prayer life. He figured that he was a good person and a hard worker who took good care of his family. He didn't need some god to tell him how to live his life.

As time went on, Valerie began to urge Zach more and more to make peace with God. This just pushed him further away from God. In fact, it began to push him away from her as well. Soon they began to fight over just about everything.

Zach was under conviction, and he knew that it was wrong to be angry with God. He knew that his bitterness toward God was being taken out on Valerie. Yet he was unwilling to give up his anger.

Sadly, he and Valerie had finally separated. They both agreed that it was the best thing for Timothy and, unless they wanted to begin to hate each other, it was the best thing for them as well.

As it turned out, Valerie never got married. She said it was because she and her fiancée just felt like it was not meant to be, but the reality was that Valerie was still very much in love with Zach and always would be.

Now, years later, she and Zach lived separate lives but stayed in constant contact with each other. In fact, though they only lived five miles apart, the two of them seemed destined to live lonely, sad lives separated by a single, huge disagreement—God!

******

Still sitting in his living room, Zach thought about calling Valerie back and going over to her house for Easter dinner. He just couldn't bring himself to pick up the phone and instead decided to go out and get something to eat. No sense in starving! He often ate out, largely because of always working so late, and then also, he was a poor cook in general.

The easiest thing to do was to eat fast food. Valerie would, from time to time, drop a dish of food by Zach's place. She would always say that she made too much, but Zach knew that she worried about his health, and his eating habits had always bothered her.

******

Steve Ellington was a high school dropout by the time he was 15, and now at the age of 20, he had been living on the streets for 3 years. The drugs had really begun to take a toll on his mind and body. Sitting at the end of a dimly lit alley, he had smoked up the last of his crack earlier that afternoon. Now he was wondering where he was going to get money to buy more drugs. Often Steve would steal whatever he could and then sell it to buy drugs. Sometimes he even resorted to male prostitution to raise the cash. That was his least favorite thing to do, and since he was now so thin and sick from the AIDS virus flowing through his veins, it was unlikely that he could even turn a trick. He couldn't even sell his blood anymore like he used to. In fact, it was the Red Cross that had informed Steve, over a year ago, that he was HIV positive, and now he was going downhill in a hurry.

The streetlight over Steve's head flickered as he looked down the alley towards the street. He saw a shadowy-looking man, tall and very thin, standing in the middle of the entranceway. The man was dressed in black clothing, and even his head was covered with a black derby. Steve thought he had seen the man before—was it on the streets or in other alleys like this one? How many times? He suddenly felt a cold shiver as the man turned toward him. The stranger's face wasn't visible, as his coat collar was turned up over his chin and mouth, but his eyes…his eyes…they seemed to flicker as they looked directly at Steve.

"What do you want?" Steve grumbled nervously.

The man didn't answer but started walking toward him, boot heels clicking with every step like a pendulum as it sweeps to the left and then to the right.

"Who are you, a cop?"

Click, click, click…Steve was afraid, too afraid to run. Instead, out of his coat pocket he pulled a large knife he had stolen from his father just before running away from home. He thought it would be good protection.

The dark figure stopped directly over Steve as he sat in the corner among the trash and empty boxes looking up as terror filled his body. The knife shook violently in his hand.

The man in black opened his coat to reveal his grotesque and hideous face—an evil, lifeless face, barely recognizable as human. Indeed it was a demon's face. Steve began to cry aloud as the demon grabbed him by his chin, forcing his thumb into Steve's mouth. He pulled the young boy off the ground and stood him up.

"You'll do just fine," his deep and frightening voice said while his evil eyes looked into Steve's very soul. The knife dropped out of Steve's hand and fell to the ground with a clank. Slowly the evil creature started to dissolve. Steve's posture began to straighten and shake.

He tried to scream, but nothing came out. Soon the look in his dim blue eyes was the same as the look in the eyes of the demon that, by now, had completely disappeared, dissolved.

The demon had entered Steve and was now in control of his mind and body. He had been there before. Many demons had been there before, and each time entering was easier.

The new and somehow taller Steve bent down and picked up the knife, then walked out of the alley as the overhead light flickered, suddenly going black.

******

Zach entered the kosher deli that was located at the bottom of a 60-story building. Just behind him entered a tall, strongly built, black man. Zach went directly to the counter where a very heavy bald man stood wearing an apron speckled with mustard, mayonnaise, and oil. The shopkeeper smiled and greeted him, "Hey, Zach! No Easter dinner for you again this year?"

Zach gave the man a pathetic smile. He was glad that at least his favorite sub shop was open on Easter. *I guess this guy doesn't celebrate this holiday either,* he thought.

The room was small and bright. The walls were painted white with old newspaper articles plastered throughout the restaurant. Everything else was made of chrome except for the bright red seat cushions covering every chair.

In the middle of the deli sat two Chicago police officers. They were enjoying a couple of pastrami sandwiches and hot coffee.

The man who entered after Zach stood just behind him looking up at the menu board. The door opened again, and in stepped Steve, only not exactly Steve anymore. His eyes met the eyes of the large black man and locked into place for a few seconds.

Zach, being completely engrossed in deciding which sandwich best fit his less than festive holiday, was totally unaware of the danger that was quickly coming to him.

Suddenly Steve dashed past the black man and grabbed Zach around the neck. Reaching into his pocket, he pulled out the large hunting knife and drew it up to Zach's throat. "Give me all of your money," he said to the heavy shopkeeper.

Steve turned his hostage around toward the black man. Both he and Zach looked into the face of the man who seemed very calm and nonplussed, as well as vaguely familiar to Zach. However, he wasn't exactly in a position to fully evaluate this thought. Steve tightened the grip on Zach's throat. By this time both police officers were standing with guns drawn and pointed directly at the youthful would-be robber.

"Let's calm down and talk about this," stammered one of the officers, still trying to swallow a large bite of pastrami sandwich that he had been thoroughly enjoying before being so rudely interrupted.

"Here's your money! Take it and let him go before someone gets hurt!" shouted the shopkeeper. He pushed a brown sandwich bag containing all his cash across the counter toward Steve. Zach could feel the blade under his Adams apple being pressed so hard it was beginning to break the skin, and blood began to trickle down his neck.

"Take the money!" Zach repeated.

Steve was still looking at the black man when one of the officers bumped his chair, making a loud screeching noise as it rubbed against the chrome on the table. Steve turned briefly to look in the direction of the two police officers. Suddenly and swiftly the large black man grabbed Steve by his knife arm and pulled him off Zach.

Surprised, Steve stepped back from both Zach and his rescuer. Then, as rage filled his eyes, he lunged at Zach with his knife fully extended. At the same time the black man grabbed Zach and pulled him to the floor. Simultaneously both officers fired gunshots into the young boy's chest. He was knocked back against the chrome rail. Hanging on by one arm, he dropped the knife.

Slowly his eyes began to change back into their original, pale blue color. Looking past the officers to the outside window, he saw the tall, thin demon, dressed in black looking directly at him through the window. An evil, monstrous grin covered his face as if to say, "I'll see you later—in Hell!"

Steve crumpled to the floor and died without making a sound. Somewhere in Idaho, his mother was kneeling beside her bed praying to God to bring her son home.

Zach sat on the floor as the black man loosened his grip. Instantly, he was filled with a sense of déjà vu as if this had happened to him before. He had the same feeling of warmth and peace. There was something else—a memory even more powerful! What was that smell? It was unrecognizable, and yet it was so familiar. Where did it come from?

Zach looked over at Steve who lay motionless in a pool of blood. Both police officers were checking him for signs of life. *He looks so young*, Zach thought. *What could have driven him to this pathetic ending?* Zach looked back expecting to see the man who had saved his life standing over him, but he wasn't there. Zach was stunned! The man couldn't have left so quickly and quietly without being seen by him or any of the others standing in the room. Once before Zach's life had been saved. He had never met that person either.

******

Standing at the end of the block, hidden in the shadows, was the stranger that Zach was looking for. The large, black man knelt on the cool, damp ground and lifted his eyes toward Heaven. "Father, I give You praise and thanksgiving for helping me defeat evil one more time."

A soothing glow surrounded the man as a soft, gentle voice spoke, "I am well pleased with your work, Philip. You are a true and faithful servant." Philip bowed his head in reverence and awe of God.

Chapter 6 - The Earthquake

It was 6:13 p.m. Easter Sunday in Portland, Oregon, and it was rainy as usual. There were very few travelers on the roads, and the Burnside Bridge was clear of all but two motor vehicles. In the first car sat John Carpenter with his lovely wife and three daughters. They were heading back home to Salem after a pleasant Easter supper with his parents.

Karen, his wife, was holding onto half an apple pie sent home with them by John's mother. She was a tremendous baker, and Karen had given up trying to match her years ago. She graciously accepted the pie as they left for home.

Behind the Carpenter family, driving too fast in her small, white car, was an 18-year-old girl named Christy. She had just come from an Easter youth service at her church. She was listening to worship music and singing loudly as she drove across the bridge.

Suddenly the bridge began to roll and sway like the waves of the Pacific Ocean on a stormy day. John tried to control his car as he began to slow down. Christy also hit her brakes in an attempt to stop her speeding vehicle.

In an instant the middle of the bridge collapsed. John stood on the brakes, but it was hopeless. The bridge had disappeared 15 feet in front of his car, and he couldn't stop. The Carpenter family, car and all, went sailing off the bridge with all of them screaming until their car hit the concrete pylon 50 feet below and exploded into a tremendous ball of fire.

Christy shrieked and turned her steering wheel as hard as she could. As she stood on the brakes, the car began to rise up on two wheels. She screamed again as the car rolled over. The bridge was still shaking, and another huge section of concrete fell to the ground completely smashing the Carpenter's car.

Christy's vehicle came to a rest at the edge of the new opening on the bridge. The back of her car was literally hanging in mid-air as the top of the car rested on what was left of the Burnside Bridge.

She wrestled with the seatbelt until it finally released, dropping her against the headliner. Quickly she scampered out of the shattered driver's window. Christy struggled to stand up against the buckling bridge. She crawled along the railing until she got to the on ramp of the bridge. Suddenly the quake stopped. Christy turned to look at what remained of Burnside. The section that her car was resting on fell away, and her car disappeared from sight. She cried aloud briefly and then began to wonder if her dad would buy her a new car.

The earthquake hit Portland just above the 45th parallel and registered 8.3 on the Richter scale. Earthquakes of this size just didn't happen in Oregon. Typically they didn't happen anywhere. The city was ill prepared for such a disaster. Since a good portion of the homeowners built their dwellings on the hillsides, most of the houses disintegrated before the quake was even finished with its intense fury. Before the day was over, thousands of lives were lost to this tremendous disaster. The city was in ruins with fires and destruction everywhere.

******

Following the 45th parallel out into the Pacific Ocean, some 5,000 miles away and 11,000 feet below the water's surface, the floor of the ocean began to crack. Large fissures appeared along parallel lines some 70 miles long as hot gases bubbled up.

At the ocean's bottom, deep within the earth's core, pressure had been building for eons, pushing up against the massive tectonic plates. These plates acted in many ways like the skin of a human body, preventing internal organs from moving around and spewing out altogether.

As the pressure increased, the massive plates began to move around, creating cracks and fissures in the earth far above, yet over two miles below the ocean surface.

Described by simple physics, it is impossible for two objects of equal size and mass to occupy the same space at the same time. Thus, as these tectonic plates began to move in an eerie primitive dance trying to find an unoccupied area of low pressure to rest from their wandering, they began to slide over each other. Worse yet, they began to bump into each other with incredible, hardly imaginable force due to their tremendous size.

While the hot gas continued to escape from the ocean floor, two of these massive plates ran into each other and were both hit by a third equally gigantic plate. The result of this historical collision would be remembered for the rest of human history. A shockwave of incredible magnitude tore the ocean floor wide open, creating a trench perpendicular to the Marianas Trench and surpassing its depth of over 35,000 feet.

The shock wave continued to travel up at hundreds of miles per hour. When it reached the surface of the Pacific Ocean, it created a fantastic water display. Large fountains of saltwater miles long extended above the ocean surface for hundreds of feet and, as the moonlight hit these jets of water and hot gas, all the colors of the rainbow began to run the distance of this spectacle. Reds and greens, blues and yellows danced back and forth for miles along the side of the water fountain. It was beautiful but deadly!

The fountain began to diminish as if it were being pulled back into the trench from where it came. For miles the surface of the water began to concave and waves began to form, crashing over into the channel made as the water was pulled back down into the earth's core.

Slowly the sea began to swell again, rising higher and higher…higher and higher, until it was over 100 feet high. This incredible wall of water bent to the west and began to roll forward, gaining momentum and size as it went on.

******

Tsunamis were rare, but not completely uncommon, for the island of

Japan. There had been small tsunamis crashing against the shores even during this most recent decade. But what was coming now had never been seen before. At least no one had ever lived to tell about it.

Honshu, the largest of Japan's four main islands, had an excellent tsunami detection system. Having been battered by so many of these monstrous waves throughout history had motivated the islanders to take precautions. From the small islands of Yaeyama, Miyako, and Amami-Shoto to the island of Kyushu, alarms were sounding a warning that a tidal wave was imminent.

Yasuki Sutani was in charge of the overall evacuation plan. It was his job to determine how far and how fast people should be evacuated. Yasuki had just received the data of estimates of this particular tsunami. His mouth dropped open as he read the characters off the page. Lifting the phone, he called his first of seven contact point supervisors to instruct them.

Takao Nagata was from the island of Miyako, the first island that would be hit. "Takao, this is Yasuki. The tsunami is confirmed."

"How big?" Takao inquired.

Yasuki drew a deep breath and spoke softly. "Takao, it is approximately 200 feet tall."

Takao paused for a moment. Regaining his composure, he asked, "How long?"

"Forty-five minutes or less," said Yasuki.

"Thank you, sir. I must prepare."

"Good luck," said Yasuki sadly. He knew there would not be enough time for Takao and his island.

Yasuki continued making calls to each supervisor. "Turn every train north, empty every school, and take the women and children first," he instructed each of them. Finally all the calls were completed except for one. Yasuki lifted the phone to call his wife. Fortunately, she and his two sons lived north of Tokyo. He was sure that his hometown was far enough away to be spared. Just two more days and his rotation in Osaka would have been up. He would have come home to be with his family for the next month.

Iroku answered the phone. She had heard all the news reports, and she expected her husband would call her when he could. Yasuki tried to mask his fear and sorrow as he spoke to his wife.

"How are you, honey?" he asked. "How are the kids?"

Iroku could sense his attempt at composure. She began to understand that this was his farewell phone call.

"How big is it?" she inquired.

"Too big," he said softly.

Iroku paused, "I love you!"

"I love you too. Kiss my boys for me."

Iroku began to quote Psalm 23 over the phone. Yasuki joined her at the second verse, "'He maketh me lie down in green pastures...'"

With this, Iroku began to cry. She and Yasuki had met at a small Christian church in Tokyo during their college years. They were saved together and eventually married in that same church. Eleven years and two young children later they were saying goodbye for the last time.

"'...And I will dwell...'" Yasuki continued.

As he spoke these last words to his wife, the line went dead. Iroku screamed into the phone, "Yasuki! Yasuki!" Dropping the phone on her lap, she began to cry uncontrollably.

Yasuki could see a great wall of water coming directly toward the 12-story building he occupied. The wave was full of debris as it sped his way. To him, it looked like the entire Pacific Ocean had been turned on its side and dumped right on the island of Honshu. The wave was as tall as the building that housed Yasuki, and it was moving fast—too fast!

******

Okinawa was a very traditional island, as were the numerous small islands that surrounded it. Today tradition went out the window. Every person that had a boat was in it heading southwest as fast as possible. There just wasn't time to try and get to the island's high ground.

Fights and other violence had broken out throughout Okinawa as people tried to buy or force their way onto any boat that would float. All of the people on the main island knew the size of what was coming. They knew that anybody left behind on the small island would not survive.

Panic fueled violence, and many people were already dead as a result. Even the island police were fighting to save their own lives and the lives of their families. Who could blame them? What would be the point of maintaining order in a community that was soon to be washed away by a 200-foot tall tidal wave?

******

Tomoya Nishizaka was 17 when he joined the Japanese Navy during World War II. He had survived Midway with a year in the hospital recovering from severe burns after a carrier explosion. Tomo, as his friends and family called him, was a proud man of substantial wealth. He had earned his money the hard way. He worked for it. Tomo started with a small fishing boat in need of great repair, but over time he was so successful at fishing that he bought a second boat out of his profits. He eventually had a small fleet of fishing boats.

He also employed hundreds of the island's locals. His business had grown and extended to include the largest fish-packing factory on the island. Even throughout his years of great success, Tomo never lost his compassion for the people. He was loved and well respected by all who knew him.

On this particular day, Tomo would become a legend for all time. His advisors had urged him to leave by plane right away. He looked at his advisors in disgust. "I will not abandon these people," he said sternly.

"In less than an hour there won't be any people!" said one of his aides.

"Then we had better work fast," replied Tomo as he walked toward his front door. People were already swarming outside the old man's home in hopes that he would have the wisdom, kindness, and resources to help them escape. Tomo looked back at his advisors. "We have two large commercial jets and three smaller commuter planes. Fill them up with as many of these people as possible."

"What about pilots?"

"Find them!" he yelled. "We also have seventeen 35-foot boats in the bay. Fill them up with people and head them southwest at full speed!"

"People!" Tomo shouted at the top of his voice. "Listen to me. Do not panic and we will all survive. I want all of the men on my left and all of the women, children, and grandparents on my right." Tomo motioned with his hands, and the people moved quickly to their proper location. There were even more people than he had thought. There were literally hundreds or maybe even thousands. It was apparent that there would not be enough room for any of the men. "Grandparents, please move over here with the men." Again the people quickly complied. This time the numbers of women and children were more manageable.

Tomo stepped back toward his advisors, turning to look at them and away from the crowd. "We will not have enough boats and planes for everyone. None of these men or grandparents will escape this island alive. I want each one of you to break these women and children into groups and move them to the planes and boats right away."

"I have located four pilots, but I can't find a fifth," said one advisor.

"Tomo, you can fly the plane," said another advisor.

"I will not leave this island," he said sternly while looking over his shoulder at the people standing calmly by. Then, stepping over to where the men were lined up, he asked, "Is there a pilot among you?"

Tomo stood waiting as the group of men milled around. Finally a young man around 25 years of age stepped through the crowd. Tomo looked at him square in the eyes. "You can fly a jet?" he asked suspiciously.

"Yes," the man answered.

"What is your name?"

"Izuho Saeki," said the young man. Tomo was a cautious man by nature, not quick to judge or to trust.

"What's the landing speed for a Gulf Stream?" Tomo asked quickly.

"It depends on wind shear, but in general about 100 knots," replied the man.

Tomo looked the young man in the eyes. He knew he had the power of life or death in his hands. If Izuho stayed with the rest of the men, he would die unless God intervened, but Tomo didn't believe in God, so Izuho would die unless he let him go. "This is your best day!" decided Tomo. "Go with them. Leave now!"

Tomo turned and faced the crowd. "I want all those on my right to go with these men behind me. All of you on the left stay with me and wait for further instructions." He supposed that some of the men and grandparents realized what had just happened, but he also knew that many others would assume that if he was still on the island, then there must be a plan for the rest. Surely he wouldn't stay on the doomed island and die with all these people. So they all stood by Tomo watching as the women and children marched away. There were tears and waves, but no hugs goodbye. There wasn't time for this. In 30 minutes this island would be washed as clean as a plate after dinner.

******

Twenty minutes passed, and the crowd started to get restless. "When do we leave?" they asked. "How do we get off the island?"

Tomo faced the crowd of men and grandparents. "Friends, I do not have a way off this island for you. I only had enough boats and planes for your families." The group was quiet as Tomo pronounced their death sentences. Over his shoulder, not too far in the distance, they could already see the tsunami coming. It was tremendously large and moving fast.

One of those gathered began to yell at Tomo, "You must have a way off! Surely you would not stay here and die with us."

"Die with you, I will!" He began to sing an old Japanese folk song, and soon all of the others were singing along with him. Tomo could hear the deafening roar of the tidal wave coming up behind him. He turned to face death head-on. He was a brave man.

******

Overhead Izuho turned his plane sharply to the right where he could see the tidal wave consuming the island of Okinawa from the east. "Thank you, Tomo! And may your god have mercy on your soul," Izuho whispered.

******

The island of Taiwan was not nearly as prepared as Honshu had been. There were no detection systems to warn the people. By now the entire country had heard of the tsunami that destroyed a large part of Japan's smaller islands. They knew it would take Okinawa with it, as well, but according to the local experts, it would bypass Taiwan and hit Shanghai instead. Tidal waves usually have predictable paths with very little deviation from the course of travel.

All of this allowed Taiwan to breathe a sigh of relief. They had dodged a major bullet, for which they were in no way prepared.

******

Sitting in the air traffic control tower some 80 feet high, Jared Wong watched as night fell on Taipei. All aircraft had been rerouted to the most northern part of Japan into the Yellow Sea. Obviously, this was not intended to avoid an aircraft to tsunami collision, but it was necessary to allow rescue workers to fly into Honshu using only Tokyo's Kansai air traffic control for direction.

Jared was grateful that his island was not going to be washed away but was sorry for those who had died and those that would soon die off the coast of China.

If he and the experts in Taiwan had only known one other little bit of information, things might have turned out somewhat differently for them. The experts had calculated the direction and speed of the tsunami. They even took a guess at how tall it would be when it got to Shanghai.

What they didn't realize was that right behind this killer tidal wave was a small, but growing, swell. Spawned by the monster that destroyed

Okinawa, its path was a little different from the one the experts in Taiwan were tracking. Fueling itself on the currents created by the primary tidal wave, this smaller tsunami was increasing and moving in a hurry on a path just southwest of the first wave. Many of the slower boats leaving Okinawa would not survive this wave.

If the experts had known about the second tsunami, they would have known exactly what Jared was staring at through his air traffic tower windows. The sun was behind him as he looked out of the tinted glass. There was no mistaking the receding tide and the large gray swell moving directly towards Taipei International Airport.

There wasn't a person in Taipei who expected to see a 100-foot wall of water come rushing into their city. Hundreds of thousands of people would be dead by morning. The oceanographers had been sure the killer wave would miss Taiwan completely. How wrong they were!

Chapter 7 - The Plan

It was 4:00 a.m. and Zach was awake. Counting up the time, he figured he maybe had slept for three hours. He turned on his coffee maker and headed into his bathroom. "May as well take a shower," he mumbled. "Maybe it will help. It sure couldn't hurt."

Flipping on the bathroom light, he was spooked as he saw his own reflection in the mirror. *Still a little jumpy*, he thought to himself. Moving closer to the mirror, Zach could clearly see the red line just below his Adam's apple, a reminder of what had happened last night—that it was, in fact, real and not just a bad dream. *Probably leave a scar*, he thought.

Showered and dressed with a hot cup of coffee in hand, Zach sat down in his chair to watch the early edition of the Chicago news. Turning to his favorite channel, he was suddenly staring at a horrible scene of mass destruction.

The news reporter, a young Japanese woman, was standing on a ledge overlooking the Japanese coastline. All up and down the coast were huge piles of rubble, homes, cars, and other unrecognizable items that were completely destroyed.

"The death toll on Honshu alone is estimated at 3 million," she said as tears rolled down her face. Zach was so engrossed by all he was seeing that he didn't even realize that he was spilling his coffee on his pants until the heat of the brown liquid finally penetrated his clothing. "Ouch!" he exclaimed as he set his cup down on the table and leaned closer to the television. "My God, what happened?"

The news station switched back to the Chicago broadcaster who spoke into the camera. "In case you are just tuning in this morning, that was a live report from our affiliate in Japan. A tidal wave struck all four of

Japan's major islands and many of its smaller ones just a few hours before sundown. The experts have calculated the size of the tsunami to be over 200 feet tall. It is estimated to have killed nearly 3 million people on Honshu alone. It will be weeks before the death toll of the surrounding islands can be calculated. Needless to say, it will be horrific! If not for the heroic work of the Japanese emergency reaction team based in Osaka, all of which are presumed to have died in the disaster, the death toll would have been twice as high."

"In local news," the reporter continued, "two Chicago police officers shot and killed a young man yesterday at a downtown kosher deli at approximately 7:00 p.m. The age and identity of the deceased is not yet known. Apparently—" said the reporter as he began to elaborate.

Zach grabbed the remote control and switched the TV off. He already knew the rest of the story.

After changing into a dry pair of pants, Zach slipped out of the apartment and headed down the street to his office. His work was exactly one and a half miles away. In the spring and summer he usually walked the distance. He enjoyed the opportunity to collect his thoughts and begin to prioritize his day. Zach would generally see many familiar faces on the streets and in the shops along the way.

They all knew him. He was kind of a local celebrity. As a news reporter, he reached into the homes of many of these people. Recently, however, Zach had left his anchor position and moved into a special segment position primarily working on exposés. He now only reached into their homes once a week, but it was usually with something interesting, unlike the constant stream of bad news he had been used to.

Zach was fed up with reporting the evening news. It was always the same thing: death, murder, and other crimes. He had been about to quit altogether when the station's young producer, Scott Turner, presented Zach with the opportunity to host a weekly talk show.

"Will it be a Jerry Springer or a Larry King type of show?" he asked his boss.

"It will be a Zach Miles kind of show," Scott had retorted with a smile.

Scott was Zach's boss and, except for the fact that he hadn't hit puberty yet, Zach figured Scott was okay. In the news business it is not uncommon for the producer to be a little young. After all, the news business was always looking for a fresh perspective on otherwise old news.

It was not yet 5:30 a.m. when Zach walked past the kosher deli where his life was nearly extinguished. The lights were out, and the room was dark. He paused for a minute to reflect. How sad it was for that young man to lose his life in such a senseless way.

Who was the man who saved me, he pondered, *and where did he go? He couldn't have just disappeared, could he?* Zach continued up the street to his office. With the exception of a couple of homeless people and a street sweeper driving slowly down the block, he saw nobody. That was all right with him. He really didn't feel like talking yet this morning.

******

Entering the main lobby of the huge office building, Zach met a security guard. "Good morning, Mr. Miles. In early today?"

"Good morning, Bob," said Zach as he tried to avoid a conversation by moving directly to the elevator. Stepping in, he pushed the number 17 and stood back against the rail for the quick trip up.

As the elevator doors opened, a steady stream of moving bodies greeted Zach. It had always amazed him how busy this office was compared with the rest of the world. This morning, even at 5:30 a.m., was no exception. As Zach stepped off the elevator, many eyes focused on him. *They know,* he thought. Zach walked across the room toward the private office that came with his new job. He could feel everyone watching him as he strode the short distance.

Zach entered the small but comfortable room. On the wall hung a handful of small pictures: one of his mother and father, both of whom were no longer alive, and another of Zach's two brothers in military uniform. There was also one picture of Valerie and Timothy. His wife and son were standing in front of the Vietnam Memorial in Washington, D.C.

Zach was never a soldier, but both of his brothers were, and both of them lost their lives somewhere in Vietnam. The news of Zach's oldest brother's death had reached him and his mother only 14 days before the news of his second brother. He could remember the expression on his mother's face as the Air Force colonel handed her the confirmation notice. Her life left her at that point. Seven years later, shortly after Zach and Valerie were married, she had a massive stroke and died while still asleep in her bed. A neighbor and close friend became concerned when she wouldn't answer her door, so the neighbor called the police.

Valerie was pregnant with Timothy at the time. Zach took the news terribly hard. There weren't any living members of his family anymore. Valerie and his son were all he had in the entire world.

******

Zach had been in his office exactly two minutes—just long enough to sit down and turn on his computer—before Scott rolled through the door without knocking. Courtesy wasn't one of Scott's strongest points.

"Stand a little too close to your razor blade this morning?" Scott asked. Zach ran his hand over his throat. The pain was still there when he touched the cut. Obviously not everyone in the building knew what happened to him last night—at least not yet.

"I guess you've heard about the tidal waves by now?" Scott asked with a frown.

"Yeah, I saw it on the news this morning. Japan really got hurt!"

"Not just Japan, but Okinawa, Taiwan, and Shanghai too, not to mention the huge earthquake that leveled Portland, Oregon, last night," Scott added.

Zach realized that he was missing some of the facts—indeed most of the facts. Scott understood by the expression on his face that Zach was unaware of the many disasters that had plagued a large part of the world overnight.

"Where have you been? Haven't you been watching the news?"

"No," said Zach. "I was a little busy."

"Well, come with me. There's someone I want you to meet." Scott turned and left abruptly. Zach followed not far behind. Scott led him into his own office which was much nicer than Zach's, and it had windows. On each wall was a picture of Scott shaking hands with important people like Dan Rather, Joe Montana, and of course, ex-President Bill Clinton. Behind his desk was a trophy case full of awards and silver plated trophies.

This guy is an overachiever, he thought.

"Have a seat." Scott picked up the phone and dialed quickly. "Can you come to my office now?" he asked.

Scott hung up the phone, lifted a piece of paper off his desk, and turned toward Zach. "Do you have any idea how many natural disasters there have been this year?" Before Zach could even begin to reply, Scott began to list some of them: "Quito, Ecuador, volcano eruption. Over 30,000 people dead, half a million homeless. Alaska's Mount Denali, the roof blows right off and an entire trainload of people are killed. Pompeii, a floating gas cloud kills a tour group and many of the locals. Pompeii! Portland, Oregon, has an earthquake 8.3 on the Richter scale, thousands are dead or missing. Turkey has an earthquake that kills tens of thousands. Greece has two earthquakes this week, and they haven't had an earthquake in over 100 years. Mount Etna blows its top. There have been months of blizzards and flooding throughout Europe—they're going to starve this year. Drought in the Midwest—we're going to starve this year. Now tidal waves have completely destroyed Okinawa, Taipei, Shanghai, and a big chunk of Japan. Millions of people have died in the last five months alone!"

Scott paused for effect and, by the look on Zach's face, it was working. Of course, he knew about most of the disasters minus the most recent horrible events, but he hadn't stopped to put any of it into perspective.

Scott backed up to his desk and leaned against it for support. He dropped the paper on a pile of other papers undoubtedly full of equally bad news. Reaching across to his bookshelf, he lifted a large, black, leather-bound book. Scott walked over to Zach and dropped the book onto his lap. "Zach, do you know God?" he asked with a grin. Zach wasn't sure what Scott was leading up to, but he didn't like it. He and God were not on speaking terms, and this young overachiever was pushing the wrong button.

Just then there was a knock at Scott's office door. "Come in!" The excitement in Scott's voice was evident. Zach turned in his seat as the door swung open. In walked Stephanie Miller. Since leaving Carl Perkins' ministry team, her hair had grown out some, and she was still somewhat awkward in her demeanor, but she was just as beautiful as ever.

Her appearance had obviously not escaped Scott's attentive eyes, for his posture straightened up as soon as she entered the room. Being from the old school, Zach stood out of courtesy.

"Zach, meet Stephanie Miller. Stephanie, this is Zach—our star news reporter."

Stephanie extended her long, thin hand towards Zach. He almost blushed as he shook it. He had eyes, too, and recognized the new face was extremely attractive. He also noted that she was about the same age as his own son.

"How do you do?" he asked too harshly. So much activity so soon this morning had his anxiety level rising quickly.

While he and Stephanie stood in the doorway, Scott picked up the book now lying in the chair previously occupied by Zach. Turning quickly to a bookmarker, Scott ran his finger down the page until he found what he was looking for. "Luke 21:11," he said firmly. "And there will be great earthquakes, famines, and pestilence in various places and fearful events and great signs from Heaven." Zach stared at the Bible in Scott's hand as he closed the book. "Christians around the world are saying that these recent disasters are signs of the end of the world and the coming of Jesus Christ. What do you think, Zach?" Scott asked as if he thought Zach would really have an answer.

Stephanie turned and looked at Zach as he stumbled for the right words to say. "I think its nonsense. Christians are always claiming that the end of the world is coming soon, and they're always wrong!"

"So you don't believe that what the Bible says will truly happen someday?" Stephanie inquired.

Zach was offended by the question. *How dare she even ask me that question?* he thought. *She doesn't even know me.* Zach looked Stephanie in the eyes and asked, "Who are you anyway?"

"Good question," said Scott, finally sensing Zach's anxiety about the whole topic. "Stephanie has recently been hired by us as a research expert. Her specialty is religion."

Stephanie smiled as Scott spoke. "Actually it is in Christian Theology."

"What's the difference?" Zach muttered, thinking Stephanie wouldn't hear him.

"The difference is significant," assured Stephanie.

Zach was surprised by her rapid response and came back quickly himself. "In what way?" he asked.

"Well," Stephanie explained, "religion is a man-made set of traditions and beliefs, whereas theology is the study of God's Word in and out of context."

Scott was amused by this brief debate. "Thanks for clearing that up for us, Stephanie. Now both of you have a seat. I've got some things to talk about."

Stephanie and Zach were comfortably seated side by side as Scott sat behind his large oak desk. "I'd like to do an exposé on the end of the world." Not waiting for either employee to chime in, he continued, "and I'd like you two to work together."

Stephanie looked intently at Scott while Zach began to squirm in his chair. He liked working alone and had no desire to investigate any of this religious stuff. *I'm not religious,* he thought.

"Do you really think anyone will be interested in a show on religion?" Zach queried.

"Theology!" corrected Stephanie.

"Whatever!" Zach countered.

"What I want is a show with differing viewpoints that the audience can embrace," Scott said sincerely. "A debate on whether or not these most recent disasters are a sign of the end of all mankind. We'll bill it as *End of Time Prophecy—Fact or Fiction, by Zach Miles.*"

Stephanie turned and looked at Zach inquisitively.

Sounds like Jerry Springer after all, Zach thought.

"Miles? Zach Miles? Was that you last night?" she asked incredulously.

Scott looked at Stephanie, dumbfounded. "What are you talking about?" Zach had wanted to avoid this turn of conversation, but he knew it would have to come up sooner or later.

"Are you the one who nearly got killed last night?" Stephanie asked with little tact. Scott's interest perked up as he leaned forward over his desk.

"It was nothing—really!" Without thinking, Zach rubbed his hand over his throat until he noticed Scott staring at the cut on his neck.

"What happened, Zach?"

Zach sighed. "Nothing."

"This morning's paper said that you were nearly killed and that one man was shot to death!" marveled Stephanie.

"You can't believe everything you read," Zach replied with a smirk and a bit of journalism humor.

Back in his own small but comfortable office, Zach leaned in his chair. The restless night was catching up with him. This new assignment was also weighing heavily on his mind. *I can't do this story,* he thought. *It is a waste of everyone's time. The end of the world? Come on!*

The phone awakened him abruptly from his own thoughts. "This is Zach," he said allowing the weariness to show.

"Hello, Zach," said Valerie. Her voice was soft and lovely, and he wanted to see her more than anything right at this very moment. "Are you okay?" she asked.

She knows too, Zach thought. "Yes, I'm fine!"

"Are you hurt?"

"No, really. I'm fine!"

"What happened?" Valerie asked, not out of curiosity, but out of loving concern for her ex-husband.

Zach told her the entire story minus the part where the black man suddenly disappeared. Valerie listened patiently as the details unfolded.

"That's about all," he concluded.

"I'm so glad you're not hurt." Her voice was so full of emotion it gave Zach goose bumps and a lump in his throat. He still loved Valerie very much.

Trying to break the tension, Valerie said loudly, "See, you should have come over to my house for dinner."

"How right you are!" Zach laughed.

"As always!" she said with a cute little giggle. Zach always enjoyed her sense of humor, and he especially liked hearing her laughter.

"Zach, Timothy is very upset by this entire thing. I think he realized how close you came to death. I still have some leftover Easter supper, and I want you to come over tonight after work. Don't you try to say no to me!"

He knew she meant what she had just said and, in his heart, he wanted to be nowhere else but with her and Timothy tonight.

As the day rolled by, Zach began to consider his new assignment and how he was going to pull it all together. He was painfully aware of the fact that he needed Stephanie's help to make it work. After all, he hadn't spent much time reading the Bible or attending church over the last 30 years or so. He had no information to make this work, and he certainly didn't know whom the real religious experts were. *Theologians,* he corrected himself.

Zach picked up the phone and dialed the operator. "Research, please." He and Stephanie talked on the phone for a few minutes before Zach finally said that he needed her help to pull this off.

"I'm at your disposal," said Stephanie. "Maybe we can work on this over dinner."

"Sure," he said without thinking. "That will be fine."

"Where should we go?" Stephanie asked.

Suddenly Zach remembered his promise to Valerie. "Actually I'm supposed to have dinner with my ex-wife and son tonight." He felt embarrassed at forgetting his dinner plans. He also felt badly for leaving Stephanie out of the picture.

"Well, then, I guess I'll see you tomorrow," she said disappointed.

Reacting on impulse, Zach said, "How about coming with me tonight?" After all, he was sure that Valerie wouldn't mind.

"Are you sure?" she asked.

"Yes, of course!" Zach made a mental note to call Valerie as soon as he was finished talking to Stephanie. In reality, he wasn't sure how Valerie would take it if he walked in with a surprise guest, especially one so young and beautiful.

"Your car or mine?"

Remembering that he had walked to work, Zach responded, "Let's take your car."

******

Pulling into the driveway of the small but very cute house, Zach began to reminisce. He and Valerie had hunted throughout Chicago for a fixer-upper that they could afford. "This house has character," Valerie had remarked as they toured through it with the help of a local realtor.

It's also 15 minutes from work, he thought to himself.

Zach and Valerie had such an enjoyable time fixing the place up. Valerie painted and papered the nursery while he painted the house and built a small deck in the backyard. Together they landscaped the front. Zach had no idea that Valerie knew so much about plants and flowers. He guessed that she must have learned this while growing up on her parents' dairy outside Burton, Iowa. This house had a lot of memories, and Zach was glad that Valerie didn't want to sell it after the divorce.

Zach stepped onto the porch with Stephanie only a couple of feet behind. Before he could even reach the front door, Valerie stepped out and threw her arms around his neck. She kissed and hugged him tightly. Looking into Valerie's face, he could see tears glistening in her eyes and was moved greatly. Rubbing his hands gently over her rosy cheek, he whispered, "I'm okay."

Discerning this was more than just a casual hello, Stephanie stood back until Valerie was finished hugging Zach. She was a bit surprised by the love she observed between these two. After all, hadn't Zach told her they were divorced? Stepping back from Valerie's grip, Zach turned toward Stephanie. Temporarily unaware of her presence, he was now struck with a sense of embarrassment.

"Valerie, this is Stephanie Miller."

Valerie smiled at Stephanie. "Nice to meet you."

"Likewise, I'm sure." Stephanie replied. She could sense the kindness in Valerie.

"Please come in and make yourself at home."

The front door led directly into a small, cozy living room that had been decorated in a tasteful country fashion. There was a woven rug covering the hardwood floor. Two glass lamps flooded the room with soft, white light. There was a fireplace with a huge mahogany mantle, and just above it sat a rather old, large picture of Jesus Christ. In the center of the room, right where Zach had left it, was a light brown, very comfortable-looking, soft leather chair. He wanted to take the chair with him when he moved out, but for some reason, Valerie wouldn't stand for it. She said it went with the house; he suspected she had an ulterior motive for keeping the chair.

Zach headed straight for the old chair and sat down in it. He instantly felt an inner peace that had been eluding him for quite some time. Looking around the room, he took note of every little change, though there weren't many.

The only addition that he discovered was the picture of Jesus, and even that wasn't new. It was just out of place. Valerie had found the picture at a garage sale and brought it home. She had proudly displayed her treasure before Zach and suggested it be mounted over the mantle. He had taken one look at the picture and cringed inwardly. "I think maybe the dining room would be a better place for it." After all, it was the place he visited the least. Valerie had sensed his disapproval over the picture and avoided another argument by hanging it where he had suggested.

Looking at the picture now, Zach wondered how anyone could believe that Christ really looked like this. Wasn't Jesus supposed to be Jewish? Then how did he get blonde hair and blue eyes?

The air was full of delicious smells. Oh, how Zach missed Valerie's cooking. *No fast food for me tonight,* he gratefully thought, as he looked towards Stephanie and Valerie who were now sitting on the sofa getting acquainted with each other.

"Have you and Zach been working together very long?"

"Oh, yes!" Stephanie had a delightful laugh. "About 12 hours now." They joined in laughter as suddenly the front door opened and in walked a handsome, young man about six feet tall, with dark, curly hair and mellow brown eyes.

"Hi, Timothy," smiled Valerie as Zach pushed himself up and out of the comfortable chair.

"Hi, Mom," Timothy's eyes panned the room looking from Valerie to Stephanie to Zach, back to Stephanie, and finally back to his dad.

Timothy focused directly on his father. "How are you, Dad?"

Zach wanted to move the five feet to his son and throw his arm around him, but all he could do was to say, "I'm okay. How have you been?"

"Fine. Busy! How's the job going?"

"It's okay."

Stephanie was amused as she sat back and watched this father and son game of charades. *What is going on here?* she wondered. Looking to Valerie for understanding, she noticed the tears streaming down her cheeks. There was obviously some history here about which she was unaware. Moreover, this was a most unusual family. There seemed to be an endless amount of love and affection, but it was also quite evident that there were separate walls built up around all three of these people.

"Come on, you two. It's time for dinner." Valerie rose from the couch. Understanding the cue, Stephanie stood as well.

Entering the dining room, Stephanie lingered awkwardly, not knowing exactly where to sit. "Zach," Valerie said, "don't you think you should introduce your guest?"

Being so engrossed in seeing Timothy, Zach had once again simply forgotten all about Stephanie until now. "Forgive me," he said. "Timothy, this is Stephanie Miller. She works at the station with me."

Timothy smiled at Stephanie and pointed her to a chair at the table.

They all sat down for a delicious, belated Easter dinner. "Are you a news reporter too?" he asked.

"No. Nothing that glamorous," she looked Zach's way with a grin. "I'm a research aide for the network."

"Really!" he said. *Besides being beautiful, she's also smart.*

"Yes, I'm a theologian!" she said with a little too much pride.

Timothy looked at his father, whose expression was one of despair. "What does a theologian do?" Valerie asked.

"I research Biblical facts, analyze new information, and answer questions about God."

"Are you a Christian?" Valerie was most interested.

"Yes, I am!" Stephanie's answer was cheerfully enthusiastic.

Zach tried to ignore the conversation by staring at his food. Interestingly enough, Timothy did the same. He was listening, however, as she spoke. He knew she had to be too good to be true—so attractive and smart—but a Christian! That was an area Timothy couldn't overlook. He and his father both had a grievance with God. His anger came as a result of seeing his happy family split in half over religion. He had spent so much time as a young boy praying to God, imploring Him to fix his family's problems. "Please don't let my mom and dad get a divorce." Timothy used to plead nightly to God. His prayer went unanswered. In retaliation, Timothy decided if God didn't have time for him, then he didn't have time for God.

Poor Timothy spent most of his young life angry with both his earthly and heavenly fathers.

******

Once again adjourning to the living room, all four adults sat back comfortably sipping on cups of coffee. "Dad, do you feel like telling us what happened yesterday?" Timothy piped in.

Zach didn't want to talk about it, but he knew that his son really wanted to know. He briefly described the events of the previous night, trying to play things down as much as possible. When he was finished, the room was silent for a moment until Timothy finally spoke up, "I'm glad you're okay, Dad."

At this Valerie rose. "I'll get some more coffee," she said as she headed quickly into the kitchen. Zach followed her, knowing by the tone in her voice that she was upset.

Standing over the sink unaware that Zach was behind her, Valerie spoke a soft prayer to God, thanking Him for protecting the man she loved. Wiping her eyes with the back of her hand, she suddenly felt Zach's presence and turned around.

An outstretched hand holding a white handkerchief greeted her. Zach smiled sympathetically and appreciatively to Valerie. She was still a very beautiful woman. He wanted to kiss her, but he knew better. It had been too many years since he and Valerie had a physical relationship. Being celibate was difficult at first for Zach, but over time he became accustomed to it. Oh, sure, there were moments when desire overwhelmed him and he wanted to go to Valerie. His pride prevented him from pursuing those thoughts to fruition. He wondered now if Valerie struggled as he did with the absence of a physical relationship. Maybe, but he doubted it.

While still sitting in the living room, Stephanie tried to make conversation with Timothy. "So what do you do for a living?" she broke the ice.

"I'm a contractor," Timothy replied shyly. *She really is a nice girl. Too bad she's a Christian,* he thought to himself.

"Really—a contractor! How did you learn to do that?" Stephanie found Timothy quite attractive, and she wanted to get to know him better.

Timothy and Stephanie spent a few more minutes getting acquainted with each other before Valerie and Zach returned. Stephanie found Timothy humble but charming and, unlike Carl, with whom she had been infatuated, he seemed very sincere. She was, quite understandably due to her huge mistake with Carl, very leery. She didn't ever want a lifestyle like that again and yearned for the simple and pure things of life.

As the evening drew to its inevitable closure, Valerie queried Stephanie about the project she and Zach were working on. Stephanie looked over to Zach to see if he wanted to try to explain. Realizing that he had no intention of taking the ball, she explained. "Have you noticed all the horrible disasters that have plagued the world this last year?" A confirming nod from both Valerie and Timothy allowed her to continue, "Well, we've been asked to find out why these events are happening and what they mean."

"What they mean?" Timothy interrupted. "How can a disaster mean anything?"

Valerie chimed in. "You mean like the end of times?"

Stephanie was surprised but delighted that Valerie understood. "Exactly! The Rapture."

Timothy looked to his father for confirmation. Zach just rolled his eyes up to the ceiling in opposition to the entire concept.

"Well, how are you going to find the answers to all of this?" Timothy asked.

"I don't know," Zach was resigned. "I guess we'll start to figure that out tomorrow."

Chapter 8 - The Preacher

Zach struggled against the weight of the man as he was pulled to the ground. Looking into his face, Zach was horrified by his gruesome, distorted features. He began to suffocate as the evil creature tightened his grip on Zach's throat. He could see the horrid man's eyes flicker as they pierced his dying soul. Zach struggled with the creature one last time with all his might, and suddenly he was free.

Sitting upright, he opened his eyes to a pitch-dark room. Covered in perspiration, Zach reached over and turned on the nightstand lamp. Nearly two weeks had gone by since the attack at the deli, yet he still continued to have nightmares. In his dreams he was never in the same location, though he always had the same evil character trying to kill him.

Zack rolled out of bed and walked into the bathroom. Turning on the light, he bent towards the sink and twisted the knob on the faucet. He splashed cold water on his face, hoping the shock of the icy water would clear his head. He stood and looked into the mirror closely. He was dismayed by his weary appearance. "These dreams have to stop!" he said aloud.

******

It was not yet 6:00 a.m. on Saturday morning, and Zach was already showered and ready to go. He and Stephanie had been working non-stop over the last couple of weeks. They had developed a plan of attack that they hoped would enable them to present the local public with enough information to draw their own conclusions. Of course, Zach was still opposed to the whole thing, and he certainly hadn't changed his mind on whether or not Jesus was coming back soon. *But,* he thought, *if I have to do this show, then I want to do it well.*

Stephanie and Zach had broken the task into manageable pieces. Stephanie provided the necessary Biblical research questions and recommended the best experts to get for the show. Zach completed the research on the most recent disasters and created a list of survivors to be interviewed off camera. Since Stephanie was inexperienced at interviewing, Scott, their young station producer, decided that Zach would pursue and question the experts on end time prophecy while Stephanie would do the off-camera interviews of the disaster survivors.

Stephanie was much relieved because of this, as the first name on the list of experts she gave to Zach was Carl Perkins. It had been nearly four months since she had walked out of Carl's life. Stephanie knew that she and Carl were past history, but she did not relish the idea of seeing him again. Additionally, she was working hard to rid her mind of all the memories she and Carl shared. She had repented of her sins, and she knew that she was forgiven, but this didn't necessarily take away the pleasant memories she had. This required a change of heart in order to see all that she did as adulterous and to hate it. She was definitely over Carl. It turned out she was more infatuated with the charismatic personality than with the Reverend Perkins for whom she felt no fondness. For that she was very grateful.

Zach, on the other hand, would have preferred to interview the list of survivors and stay away from the religious experts altogether. But he understood Scott's concern and eventually agreed with his decision.

Stephanie's list included two other experts. The first was Lisa Taylor, a Professor of Divinity and author of numerous books on Bible prophecy. Stephanie had studied under Lisa in many of her undergraduate classes and held her in high regard. The final name on the list was Joseph Bastoni, a renowned scholar of ancient writings still held sacred by the Catholic Church.

******

Out the door and on the street, Zach had decided to drive this morning even though it was a beautiful April morning. Looking at his watch, he saw it was only 6:30 a.m. Stephanie wasn't due into the office until 8:00. She nearly had to beg Zach to let her sleep in. "It's Saturday!" she complained. "How about letting me sleep in until 7:00 a.m.?" Zach knew he had been working the young lady pretty hard. He understood she wasn't up to his pace yet, but she had hung in there pretty well so far.

"Okay," he finally agreed. "I'll see you at 8:00 sharp!"

Zach also knew that Stephanie had been seeing Timothy nearly every night since they had first met at Valerie's house. He was glad about this. He was beginning to like her very much. He also liked the fact that Timothy had been coming by the news station often. It was good to have more time with his son, and it now seemed as if they were finally getting along the way he had always hoped.

Driving around the city seemingly without purpose, Zach's car rounded a corner off the main highway and slowed as he passed near a modest but well-maintained building. In the front of the building was a large sign that read: *People's Church*. In small letters below the sign was the name: *Pastor Leonard Thomas*. For some reason Zach felt compelled to pull into the driveway.

He stopped the car at the edge of the parking lot facing a large wooden cross. The weather-faded cross had been suspended against the side of the building with three large stakes, one on either side of the crossbar and one at the base of the longer of the two pieces of wood. Zach supposed this was more for theatrics than functionality.

Sitting in his car just staring at the church, Zach suddenly felt a cold shiver, so he reached over and turned his heater up. He began to drift in and out of thoughts from the past. So many things had happened to him at this church. First his father was killed. *No, that's not correct,* he thought. First he was baptized. His mother was so proud. Zach could still remember how his big brothers teased him and frightened him all week prior to his baptism. "They're going to drown you," they would say, "and everyone is going to watch as Pastor Thomas holds your head under the water until you quit kicking and all of your air is used up."

Being the youngest, he often got picked on by his brothers, but this right was given to no one else. If any neighbor kids tried to bother or hurt Zach, his brothers, Danny and Steve, would jump in and put a quick end to the assailants. Oh, how he missed his brothers and his mother and father too.

Suddenly Zach was startled by a knock on his driver's side window. He turned abruptly to see an average height but very slender black man wearing a blue jogging suit. The man was balding at the temple and gray all around. Zach hit the power button and lowered his window. He looked up at the man who was now smiling brightly.

"Hello, Pastor Thomas."

"Good morning, Zach!" said the pastor with a slight southern drawl. "What brings you here this fine morning?"

Zach was embarrassed. He didn't really know why he was sitting in the church parking lot at 6:30 a.m. on a Saturday. Not able to even come up with a response, he just shrugged his shoulders.

"Would you like to come in for some coffee?"

"No, thanks, Pastor Thomas. I really need to get going."

"Zach, call me Leo."

"Okay, Leo. I have to get to work," he said, stretching the truth.

"I haven't seen you for quite some time, Zach. How long has it been?"

"Since Mom died," Zach responded.

"That's right," Leo reminisced. "Your mother was a wonderful woman—a godly woman too. Come on in, Zach, and share a cup of coffee with me." Turning and walking towards the side entrance of the church, it was apparent to Zach that Pastor Thomas wasn't going to take no for an answer. He wished he hadn't come to the church this morning. He was also angry with himself for not being able to resist Leo's influence. Regardless of Zach's age, Pastor Thomas was still an authority figure to him, and he was taught as a youth not to disobey authority figures.

Zach got out of his car and locked the door behind him. Church parking lot or not, this was still Chicago. He followed Leo as a child follows behind his parents or maybe like a child on his way to see the principal after tugging on the braided hair of the little girl in front of him. Leo moved quickly for an old man. *Maybe that jogging suit is for more than show after all,* Zach surmised.

Leo was much more informal than Zach had remembered. Zach soon realized that he really didn't know this man at all. On Pastor Thomas' desk sat a worn Bible with little pieces of different colored sticky notes hanging out everywhere. It was obvious to him that the owner of this Bible spent a great amount of time reading and taking notes.

Leo grabbed a thermos off the corner table and headed across the room to a small closet. Digging inside he soon came out with a stack of Styrofoam cups. "Brewed it myself this morning before I came in," he said proudly. Pouring hot coffee into a cup, he handed it to Zach. "Sugar's on the table," he said, "but I don't have any cream."

"Black is fine."

"It's one of my favorite colors." Leo chuckled heartily. Zach got the joke and laughed cautiously.

"Have a seat, Zach. Let's talk."

"I really need to get to work." Zach was resisting.

"What for? It's not even 7:00 a.m. Besides, it's Saturday. Sit down."

There is no point in fighting this, Zach thought as he complied with Leo's request.

"I read about you in the paper a couple of weeks ago," Leo frowned. "That was a close one!"

Zach nodded.

"Seems like someone is always trying to kill you," he said lightly, but his eyes said more than that to Zach. Zach had a question for the pastor, but he wasn't sure he wanted to enter into a philosophical conversation with the old man.

"Yeah, I still remember that terrible day when your father died. Jack was a good man and a good father too. In fact, I've buried every member of your family. So many tragedies!" he said, shaking his head with even more emphasis this time.

What's this guy's point? Zach wondered. *If he's trying to cheer me up, it is not working.*

"Yeah, your whole family except for you," Leo mused. "It seems like maybe God has His angels protecting you."

Zach looked at Leo. The idea hadn't crossed his mind until now. The thought seemed absurd to him. *Why would God protect me? We don't even like each other.*

"You know," he continued, "they never did find the man that saved you that day. He just sort of disappeared. You ever run into him over the years?"

Could it have been the same man that saved me in the deli? Zach pondered. *And how did Leo know that I might well have seen him just two weeks ago?*

"No!" Zach was emphatic. "I've never seen him since." He looked at his watch, and it was after 7:00. "Well, I really need to go. Thanks for the coffee."

"You're welcome, Zach. Now before you go, why don't you ask me the question that brought you here?"

How does he know I have a question? he marveled. "What question?" he calmly asked.

"There's always a question when someone comes to see me. Since you were here at 6:30 a.m. on a Saturday, I figure you have a really big one!"

"Well," Zach hesitantly replied. "I do have one question."

Zach adjusted in his seat and looked directly at the floor as he spoke. "Do you think the Rapture will happen soon?" Leo was surprised by that question. He was even more surprised that Zach Miles was interested in such things. Zach cleared his throat and looked up at Leo who sat smiling in wonder of this whole scene. "What I mean to say is that I'm doing an investigative report on all of the recent disasters that have plagued the world. As a part of this story, I've been asked to investigate the remote possibility suggested by some Christians that the world is coming to an end."

"And so it shall," Leo beamed, "in God's own good time!"

"When is God's time?" Zach asked somewhat sarcastically.

"No man knows the hour or day but the Father in Heaven. All we can do, Zach, is to watch for the signs foretold in the Scriptures, and, most importantly, we can make sure that we are ready to meet the Lord when He does come."

Leo stood and walked directly to where Zach was sitting. "Will you be ready to meet with Christ when He comes, or will you be passed over for God's judgment?"

"What judgment?" Zach asked, his anxiety level rising dramatically.

"The tribulation has been set aside for those who do not believe in Jesus Christ. The wrath of God will be poured out on everyone who does not ascend to meet Christ in the air during the Rapture."

"Do you believe this stuff?" Zach asked cautiously.

"Yes, Zach, I do believe, just as I am sure you do too!"

"I don't know what I believe," Zach said as he stood to leave.

Leo held his hand out to Zach to say goodbye. "How long will you be angry at God?" he inquired.

"Until He can give me a good reason for taking my family away from me," Zach admitted as he shook Leo's hand briefly.

******

Back at the news station Zach, Scott, and a tired Stephanie sat in Scott's office preparing to review the plans they had made for the upcoming show. "Well," said Scott, "lay it on me. What's the plan?"

Stephanie shuffled through her papers trying to organize her thoughts. She and Timothy had spent the better part of the night sitting in a park on the edge of Lake Michigan, so her mind was not focused on the job at hand. Between the two of them, there were so many things to talk about. It seemed to Stephanie the more time she spent with Timothy, the harder it was to say goodnight to him. She was learning a lot about his life and Zach's as well. The one thing she hadn't fully understood, however, was why Timothy had never considered marriage. In fact, she was surprised to learn that Timothy had never even dated seriously. *This is a strange family,* she pondered.

Finally organized, Stephanie began to lay out the details for the coming weeks. "We plan to air three separate interviews with disaster survivors. Then we will turn to a panel type of question and answer session with Zach and our three experts on Bible prophecy."

Scott sat back for a second to absorb the plans laid out before him. Looking in Stephanie's direction, he said, "Tell me about the survivors you are going to interview. Who are they, and do we have footage of each disaster? What questions will you ask?"

Stephanie took a deep breath and looked in Zach's direction. *I shouldn't have stayed out so late,* she thought to herself. "Well, the first interview is with a couple of geologists that were at ground zero during the Mount Chimborazo eruption. There were three actually, but one of them got too close. These two, interestingly enough, are brother and sister."

Stephanie looked to Scott for approval, but it was too early to tell so she continued. "The second is a Japanese man who was hand selected to fly a planeload of citizens out of harm's way only minutes before Okinawa was completely destroyed by a 200-foot tall tidal wave. His story is remarkable!"

She was desperately trying to get a rise out of Scott who now demanded, "Continue!"

"Finally we have an interesting story of an Air Force pilot who was on Mount Denali just before it erupted. His partner was killed, but interestingly enough, he said he was told by an invisible voice to leave the mountain before it exploded."

"I gather his friend didn't hear this voice?" Scott asked suspiciously.

"Yeah, well, the military apparently didn't buy this story either, because this guy's new address is Leavenworth, Kansas."

Scott leaned up and smiled brightly at Stephanie while trying to control his laughter. The mental picture of Stephanie interviewing this guy who hears voices, and especially from within a military prison, was just too much for Scott. He began to laugh openly. Stephanie didn't get the joke. Zach did, but he didn't think it was very funny. "Oh, come on you two. Lighten up! This assignment isn't going to kill you."

Leaning back in his chair again Scott looked to Zach. "Okay, Zach, what's your plan?"

Zach shifted slightly in his chair. "I have three guest speakers planned for the show, but before I bring them on, I'd like to go and interview them."

"Why?" Scott asked even before Zach could finish. Scott was starting to annoy Zach a little bit, and he knew it. In fact, he enjoyed it.

"I can't just bring these people on my show without knowing how legitimate they may or may not be," Zach remarked impatiently. "What if we wait until they get on the show and find out they are nuts or something?"

Scott nodded. "Seems reasonable to me. Where are you going first?"

"We have one local expert. I thought I'd start with her," said Zach.

"Good!" said Scott. "A local expert will help to balance the show. What's her name?"

At this Stephanie proudly piped in. "Her name is Lisa Taylor, and she is extraordinary."

"You know her personally?" Scott queried.

"Yes, sort of. She was one of my professors at college."

Without acknowledging Stephanie's comments, Scott turned back to Zach. "Who's next?"

"Well, I thought I'd go to Rome and interview a priest that Stephanie recommended—Joseph Bastoni."

"Do you know him too?" Scott asked Stephanie with indifference in his voice.

She wondered what difference it would make but answered, "No, I never met him, but he is renowned as an expert in Bible prophecy."

"Who's the third one?" Scott asked without taking his eyes off Stephanie.

"He's an evangelist living in L.A. Carl Perkins is his name."

"Yes, I've seen him on television. He's pretty good!" said Scott. He liked the idea of having such a well-known figure on the show. Stephanie was just glad Scott didn't ask her if she knew Carl as well. "We'll make this guy the center of our show as the leading expert of the bunch," said Scott.

"When are you leaving for Rome?"

"A week from tomorrow," said Zach.

"Mother's Day." Scott looked at his calendar. Zach made a mental note to buy some flowers and a card for Valerie before he left for Rome.

******

Nearly noon that same day Stephanie and Zach were putting the final touches on their plans for the show.

It's shaping up into a pretty good show, considering, Zach thought.

"I'm hungry!" Stephanie said boldly.

"Yeah, me too," agreed Zach. "Let's get out of here and grab some lunch. I feel like Italian today. How about you?"

Stephanie laughed. "A salad will be just fine with me."

"Why do women always order salads? If I wanted to graze, I'd eat the plant on my desk!" Zach's grin brought Stephanie a much needed laugh.

Standing in front of the elevator, waiting for it to make the climb up to the 17th floor, Zach began to think about his conversation with Leo Thomas. It was hard not to like Leo. He seemed so genuine and honest to Zach, but the part about rising in the air to meet Christ was a bit much.

The elevator light came on and, with a chime, the door opened. To everyone's surprise, Timothy was standing in the elevator smiling. "Hi, Stephanie! Hi, Dad!"

Zach couldn't help but notice Stephanie's face light up as she made eye contact with him.

"Hi!" she said brightly.

"Hey, Timothy, you're just in time. We're going to lunch. Have you eaten?"

"No, not yet."

"Feel like Italian?" Zach ventured.

"Sure. Sounds okay to me," Timothy smiled cheerfully.

If nothing else, Chicago definitely had the best Italian food in North America. Zach and his two companions sat at an umbrella table outside the restaurant.

"Stephanie tells me you are going to Rome," Timothy directed to his dad.

"Yeah, next week," Zach said. "And then out to Los Angeles a few weeks later."

"Who is it you are going to see in L.A.?" he asked.

"Some evangelist guy named Carl Perkins. Have you ever seen him on television?" Zach knew the answer before he asked.

"No!" Timothy's answer was a bit loud and perhaps a little too quick.

Zach assumed he might actually have seen him but also knew that his son was as opposed to God as he was. He wasn't sure that he liked that fact, but he supposed that his son had his own reasons just as he had. It concerned him somehow. *What if Pastor Thomas is right?* He hated to think of his son tormented for an eternity because of—because of what—me? He didn't like the answer, so for Zach the only solution was not to think about the question.

"Me either! But then again I don't spend much time watching television."

Just the mention of Carl's name made Stephanie a little nervous. She was forgiven for her sins, and she knew that emphatically, but she couldn't help feeling guilty, especially around Timothy. Stephanie wondered what he would think about her having an affair with a married man—in particular a pastor some 10 years her senior—which made it sound worse.

Wanting to change the subject, Zach asked Stephanie, "So what do you think about my son?" Timothy was instantly embarrassed, looking away to avoid eye contact with Stephanie.

"I think he's a lot like his father!" she smiled and winked at Zach. It was Zach's turn to be embarrassed.

"See what you get for asking," Timothy said.

"Actually," Stephanie turned toward Timothy, "I'm quite pleased with him so far."

Timothy blushed and smiled back at Stephanie.

Trying to break up this mushy scene, Zach asked Timothy how his mother was doing. Though he knew his dad had been over only two days earlier, he obliged him with the news that she was fine. "She only has four more weeks before summer break." His mother enjoyed the three months off each summer. She looked forward to working in her yard or just sitting back and reading something besides school papers.

"Oh, I almost forgot, Stephanie," Timothy remembered. "The reason I came down to the station. I have two tickets to tonight's basketball game. Do you like basketball?" He couldn't imagine anyone living in Chicago and not liking hoops, even though the Bulls without Michael Jordan were like cupcakes without frosting.

"Yes, of course, I like basketball, but when is the game?"

"It's at 6:00 this evening."

Stephanie looked towards Zach with a pitiful but hopeful expression on her face. "I don't know, Timothy. I'm not sure I'll be done working in time."

Zach got the hint and smiled. "Well, I think we've done enough for the day. Besides, I've got something I need to do."

Zach ate his lunch quietly listening to Stephanie and Timothy as they made small talk. They seemed like a good match for each other. Zach hoped that somehow Stephanie could help Timothy regain trust in personal relationships, especially after watching him and Valerie mess things up for so long. Perhaps they could develop a lasting relationship, and who knows, maybe they would even get married and have grandchildren for him and Valerie to play with.

Leaving the restaurant satisfied, Zach decided to drive over to Valerie's for a brief visit. He wasn't sure why, but lately he felt the need to spend more time with her.

******

The house smelled like chocolate chip cookies—Zach's favorite. Valerie stepped into the living room. Her hair was pulled back off her shoulders, and she was wearing a pair of brown shorts and a tee shirt. Her look reminded Zach of when they were first married. Depression began to set in as he considered what a mess he had made out of his marriage to such a kind-hearted and great-looking woman.

"I thought you would be over today. Would you like some cookies? I made your favorite—chocolate chip!"

Zach began to perk up. "Sure. Got any milk?"

Valerie smiled as she walked back into the kitchen. Zach sat in his favorite chair, and soon he began to feel that usual sense of peace fill his spirit. Looking up at the fireplace his eye caught the picture of Jesus as before. "So You're coming back soon?" he asked quietly.

Valerie walked up beside Zach's chair with a plate of cookies and a tall glass of milk. "Did you say something?" she asked.

Startled, Zach looked up at her. "No! Well, not really."

"How has your day been?" Valerie asked as she sat on the sofa.

Zach looked at Valerie and with a mouth full of cookie mumbled, "It has been a pretty good day. I had lunch with Timothy." This pleased her very much. She had been praying for so long that Zach and Timothy would work out their differences, and now it was beginning to happen. "Stephanie was there too!" he muttered.

"Timothy told me he was spending a lot of time with her. I'm glad! She seems very nice," Valerie smiled.

Zach agreed with a nod and took a long drink of milk adding, "I saw Pastor Thomas today." Surprise and confusion came over Valerie's face. Not wanting to keep her in suspense or build up her hopes that he had become a Christian or something silly like that, Zach spoke up. "I went to talk to him about Bible prophecy for our show, that's all."

Valerie wasn't fooled, however, and could tell there was a little more to it than that. "What did he say?"

"He said Christ is coming soon." Zach grinned antagonistically at her.

She ignored his theatrics and pushed on for more information. "And what else did he say?"

"He said that nobody knows when Christ will come back. He also said that if you are not selected to go with Him, you will have to stay and face the wrath of God."

"Not selected!" said Valerie. "God doesn't choose you. You have to choose Him. He gives us the choice."

The conversation was starting to annoy Zach, so he added with disgust, "Well, you'll be glad to know that God has His angels protecting me from harm."

Valerie didn't understand what he was talking about, but she knew that the conversation was over all the same.

Chapter 9 - The Priest

May 8: Zach had spent the better part of the week trying to schedule a meeting with Lisa Taylor. It began to look like she was ducking the interview, but he was persistent. Finally on Friday he got his chance. Zach was nervous but well prepared for the interview. He had hoped to get Lisa to come down to the news station—his comfort zone—but Lisa declined and instead insisted that he meet her in her office on campus.

Zach and Lisa were to meet at 11:00 a.m., not a time he preferred. He was afraid that Lisa would try to use lunchtime as an excuse to hold the interview to a half hour or less.

Entering the foyer outside Lisa's office, Zach was met by her secretary. "Dr. Taylor is on the phone, but she said to invite you in anyway. Oh, by the way, Lisa has a lunch date, so you'll have to keep your interview brief." There it was, just as he had predicted.

Lisa's office was stuffy and not just because of the air quality. Diplomas and numerous awards framed in polished silver and glass hung on the walls. On the far wall was a massive bookshelf full of books, and a large, fake fig tree stood in the other corner. Lisa sat behind her huge, neatly organized glass desk while talking on the phone. Looking up as Zach entered the room, she waved him in and pointed to a neatly padded chrome chair.

Zach took his cue and sat down facing her. He took pride in his ability to tell what kind of people he was dealing with by their mannerisms and style of dress. Lisa was dressed in a navy blue business suit with large silver buttons all down the front. Looking around the sanitary room there seemed to be chrome everywhere. *What's the deal?* he wondered. *This lady's stainless.*

Sitting up attentively he watched and listened as Lisa spoke on the phone.

"No, I would rather do my next book signing at Walden's," she said. "I'm not interested in Wal-Mart."

Zach found all of this a bit boring. There in front of him in the middle of this hygienic room was a somewhat large, not overly attractive woman working out a book deal over the phone. He sat patiently waiting for the interview that had taken him nearly a week to schedule, one in which he was only going to be allowed to ask questions for the next few minutes.

Finally Lisa finished her conversation and hung up the phone. Sitting upright, prim and proper, she extended a hand and said, "You must be Zach Miles?"

Rising, Zach shook Lisa's surprisingly firm hand. "Yes, I am. It's a pleasure to meet you, Ms. Taylor."

"Likewise," she replied.

Trying not to draw any premature conclusions, Zach couldn't help but wonder what Stephanie saw in this lady. She seemed very self-absorbed and militant.

"So tell me, Mr. Miles, what can I do for you?"

Zach began to explain once again the reason for the interview. As he did, he noticed Lisa fiddling with some papers on her desk. Eventually she began to write on her calendar. *She's not interested in what I have to say at all,* Zach thought.

Just then her phone rang. "Pardon me, Mr. Miles, but I need to take this call."

Zach sat another five minutes before continuing his conversation with Lisa. His verdict was in. He didn't like her one bit. Finally getting around to the main purpose of the interview, Lisa spoke up, "To answer your question, Mr. Miles, do I think the end of the world is coming as indicated by these disasters, and do I see a relationship between these disasters and the Rapture? Frankly, I don't. In either case, no!"

"Do you think Christ is coming back soon?" Zach asked.

"I see no signs of that happening," she said plainly. "Now as far as being a guest speaker on your television show, we may be able to work something out, but I have some stipulations."

"Continue," said Zach.

"Well, I've never seen your show, so I'm not sure it's the kind of a show that I'd like to be a part of. Nevertheless, I'll give you the benefit of doubt." Zach's anger began to well up as Lisa continued. "My agent can work out the cash details for my presence on your show and also my latest book promotions."

"Promotions?" asked Zach.

"Yes!" Lisa went on. "If I'm to do your program, then I'd like to promote my new book on the coming of Christ."

"But I thought you said that He wasn't coming."

"That's right. He's not!" said Lisa with confidence.

The phone rang again, but this time before Lisa could pick it up, Zach stood and extended his hand. "Thanks for your time." Lisa looked at him with contempt and surprise. Mindlessly she shook his hand as he turned and walked out of her office.

Back in the foyer Zach looked at Lisa's secretary and smiled. "She can go to lunch now!" he said as he passed by.

Driving away from the university Zach began to wonder if all of his interviews were going to be like this one. He couldn't wait to see Stephanie again so he could ring her neck. Zach remembered that he was to meet Valerie, Stephanie, and Timothy for an early Mother's Day dinner at Lowry's Steakhouse. He'd get her then!

******

Across town Zach turned the corner in view of the People's Church. As he drove by, he saw Leo mowing the lawn. He sped up in hopes that Leo would not see him drive by, but that didn't work. Waving frantically, Leo motioned for Zach to turn into the parking lot. *I wasn't fast enough,* Zach thought. Stopping the car near the exit of the church, he rolled down his window. Leo stepped away from his mower and walked towards Zach.

"Good afternoon, Zach."

"Hello, Leo, how are you?"

"Fine as wine! Are you hungry?" In fact, Zach was starving, but lunch with Leo was not what he had in mind. "I brought in some fried fish I caught last week. Come on in and have some with me."

Leo walked off toward the office. Zach was determined not to follow behind him again, but before he could say a word, Leo spoke up as he walked along. "I have some pictures of your family I want to show you." Leo really was a good fisher of men. He always knew what bait worked best.

Zach parked the car and followed him into the church once again. There was enough fish for four people, and it smelled wonderful. Zach loved pike. "Expecting some company?"

"You never know," Pastor Thomas said lightly. He fixed Zach a plate of fish, fresh cantaloupe, and bread. "Sit down, son. Here you go. Try this." Zach took a bite. It was delicious!

"Good, ain't it?" Leo grinned. He made himself a plate and sat on the edge of his old desk. Reaching behind his back, he lifted up an old box and handed it to Zach. Putting his plate down, Zach took the box and, out of anticipation, his hand shook noticeably as he did.

"Found these when I cleared out that closet the other day. I thought you might like them," Leo said.

Zach sat staring at the gray cardboard box. It was old—very old! Slowly he lifted the lid and, as he did, brittle pieces of cardboard began to flake off. He looked deeply into the box for a minute or so before he lifted his eyes towards Leo. "When were these taken?"

"Over the years," Leo smiled.

Zach looked down into the box and took out a picture of his parents. They seemed different to him—much younger than he had ever remembered. They both seemed so alive and happy. His father was holding a baby, perhaps a month or so old. "That's you. We had just dedicated you. I can still remember how proud your parents were on that day." The image on the old paper began to cloud and, for a second, he did not understand why he could no longer focus on the picture. Suddenly a large drop of water fell from his face onto the photo. Quickly he realized he was crying. Zach hoped Leo hadn't noticed as he wiped his face with his sleeve. Putting the faded memory back into its crypt, he closed the lid without looking at another picture.

"Those belong to you, son. Take them home and enjoy them," Leo said softly. He had noticed Zach's emotions, and he understood the pain that still lived in his heart. Zach held onto the box as if he had just found a great treasure worth a fortune—and to him, he had.

Finishing his lunchtime meal with Leo, Zach was surprised by how relaxed he was beginning to feel around the old pastor. It was as if Leo had a special ability to bring calm out of calamity. Zach was really starting to like the man quite a bit.

"Any luck on your story yet?" Leo inquired.

"I had my first interview today." Zach's obvious frown told the story.

"Didn't go too well, I gather?"

"No, it did not! Not well at all!"

"Maybe it'll get better next time." Leo smiled thoughtfully.

"I hope so. I have to fly to Rome for the next interview, and if it turns out like this last one—" He just shrugged his shoulders and looked down at his feet.

"Well, what went wrong with today's interview?" Leo asked.

"Do you know Lisa Taylor?"

"You mean Dr. Taylor from over at the university?"

"Yeah, that's the one!"

"We've met," said Leo with a disgusted look on his face.

Zach was surprised by Leo's show of anger. It seemed that the good minister did have more emotions than just calmness after all.

"I tried to talk to her this morning, but she was more interested in promoting her newest book than she was about my interview. How do you know her?"

"We had a little run-in a while back."

"Really!" Zach was pleased that Leo had an intolerant side after all.

"Lisa was a youth pastor in my church for one summer many years ago. She was doing an internship for the university and had a good heart—full of optimism."

"Opportunistic maybe," Zach said flatly.

"Yes, well, she wasn't always that way. The summer started off just great. Lisa had developed a street ministry and she, with our own teens, went out every day sharing the good news to neighborhoods all around."

The thought of Ms. Taylor caring enough to walk the streets of Chicago preaching about God just didn't seem to fit the Lisa that Zach had recently come to know.

Leo seemed to drift away into thoughts from the past. Soon he spoke up again. "Slowly Lisa began to spend less and less time out on the streets with our youth. She began to come in late and leave early. Finally I confronted her with my concerns. 'What's happened to all of that enthusiasm?' I asked."

"What did she say?" Zach asked.

"At first she said that she was uncomfortable walking through the neighborhoods witnessing. I could understand this. After all, she was young, and it can be intimidating to talk about Jesus to total strangers. But I felt there was more—something else underneath it all. The more I questioned her," said Leo, "the more I began to understand. It was not the ministry of Jesus Christ that bothered Dr. Taylor. It was the people. She simply didn't like the people. Oh, not just the black ones. She didn't much like any of them." Leo shook his head and, with a sigh, said, "The day after I confronted her she quit. Since then she has been teaching and writing books on how to spread God's Word and minister to others."

"Some do and some teach, I guess," said Zach.

"Yes, and many do both very well. I suppose that Lisa is doing work for God even if she could care less about all His people."

******

Spending the afternoon with Pastor Thomas was a pleasant surprise for Zach. He now understood why his parents were always so faithful in attending this church on a regular basis. The afternoon went by quickly, and Zach knew it was time for him to leave. *I wish I could spend more time with this guy,* he thought to himself. *He really isn't all that bad for a minister.*

An additional thought occurred to Zach as he looked at the wiry bright-eyed old man. Maybe Pastor Thomas would be a good fit for his upcoming show.

"Leo, how would you like to be a guest speaker on my upcoming show on Bible prophecy?"

"The one you are researching on Christ's return?" Leo asked.

"Yes, you can take Dr. Taylor's place as my local expert." Zach was really getting enthusiastic about his new idea. "You'd be great on the show. I'm sure you would."

"Let me ask you a question," said Leo. "Why are you doing this show?"

Zach looked at Leo inquisitively. "I've already told you. My station manager wants me to do a piece on these recent disasters while focusing on the prophecy of Christ's return."

"Yes, but why are *you* doing this show?" Zach looked confused as Leo continued. "I know you, Zach," he said. "If you didn't want to do this show, it wouldn't happen."

"I don't have as much pull as you think," Zach said plainly.

"Maybe so, but if you didn't want to do this show, you'd have found a way out of it."

Zach paused. It seemed he was caught off guard by this statement. *Why am I doing this show? I could get out of it if I wanted to. How is it that this old man can see right through me so easily?*

"Is it possible that you wonder yourself whether or not the end is coming soon?"

Zach didn't like the question. It meant that he had to consider the reality of God. This was a thing he did not like to do, not in the least.

Leo had a way of pulling the truth out of Zach even when his very instincts resisted.

"I suppose I am curious like many others. There have been a lot of incredible disasters this year. That much is for sure."

"But the idea of a God out there somewhere in control of everything bothers you?" Leo exhorted with frankness in his voice.

"The fact that some people believe that God is responsible for all of these disasters is what bothers me," said Zach wearily.

This whole conversation was starting to strain him. Zach understood that Leo was more than a match for him. He knew that he was not sure what he believed. That made it tough to defend his position, especially against a man of such simple faith in a God he'd never be able to even prove exists.

Leo, on the other hand, knew that Zach felt vulnerable. He seemed to understand just how far he could push him before he would have to ease up a bit or risk alienating himself. "When is your show scheduled?"

"Sunday, July 10," Zach half-heartily replied.

"Morning or afternoon?"

"Afternoon."

Leo turned and looked at Zach. The old man's eyes were as black as coal yet full of compassion. The wrinkles in the corners of his face deepened as he smiled at Zach. "Okay, I'll do it, but don't expect great insight from me. I'm not a theologian. I'm just a simple minister." He extended his hand towards Zach. "I'm glad you came by, and I hope you enjoy your pictures." Zach had forgotten about the box still clutched tightly in his hands. Releasing his grip from it, he shook Leo's hand.

"I'll look you up when I get back from Rome and we can prepare for the show."

"That'll be fine, Zach. I hope your next interview will be better than your last one."

"Me too!" exclaimed Zach enthusiastically.

"Be safe, young man!" Leo smiled brightly.

******

Zach had just enough time to go home and take a shower, but first he thought he'd run by the flower shop to get a nice bouquet of spring flowers for Mother's Day. Valerie loved flowers, and he would enjoy seeing her beautiful smile as he gave them to her over dinner. Pulling his Explorer into the turning lane, Zach waited for the opportunity to cross the intersection. *This has turned out to be a pretty good day all in all. Maybe I won't choke Stephanie. But I still don't see what she ever saw in Lisa Taylor,* he thought to himself.

The coast now clear, Zach started to turn left through four lanes of traffic when suddenly a large yellow truck that had been stopped at the signal bolted through the red light heading directly towards his green Explorer. Zach hit the brakes hard. From his far left, a small white sedan pulled across in front of his car and directly into the path of the speeding truck. The white car spun in a complete circle as the yellow truck hit it broadside. The collision was so forceful that the front tire of the old truck broke cleanly off at the spindle that previously held it in place. Zach could see the tire and spindle in full flight heading in his direction. As the sedan spun around one last time, however, the rear quarter panel hit and redirected the tire's flight back towards the truck. The tire shattered the truck's windshield. The driver never saw what hit him as the attached spindle tore through his chest, and the onlookers never saw the red eyes of the driver turn briefly back to green just before they closed for good.

The sight of the tire smashing through the truck's windshield and through the chest of the unfortunate driver caused Zach to look away in disgust. As he turned around again, he observed the white sedan driver's door was wide open. Staring hard through the slightly tinted rear window, he tried to see the condition of the driver whose sacrifice undoubtedly saved his life. He couldn't see anyone in the car. *Maybe he is lying on the floor,* Zach thought. By this time many people were climbing out of their cars, moving in the direction of the injured vehicles. A few gathered around the truck while others moved towards the white sedan. Zach climbed down out of his undamaged vehicle. There was no need to look in the truck—he knew the fate of the driver.

Zach walked over to the driver's side of the sedan. By now there were half a dozen people standing staring with mouths wide open. *It must be a horrible sight,* Zach thought as he observed the expressions of the onlookers. Zach moved to a position to enable him to look inside the car. What he saw was not what he expected in the least!

"Where did he go?" one observer asked.

Another commented, "Someone had to be driving this car."

The car was empty. Zach didn't know what to think. The driver couldn't have walked away from this wreck without being seen.

"Boy, you sure are lucky!" said a middle-aged woman as she looked at Zach. "That truck was heading right at you when this white car cut him off. If it wasn't for this car, you would be dead!"

He began to shake as the scene replayed in slow motion in his mind. How was it possible that he had escaped from the accident unhurt or, worse yet, dead? How was it possible that no one was driving the car? With a single thought running through his mind, he turned and walked away from the lady and back to his Explorer. *I need to go home.*

Forgetting about the flowers, he held tightly to the steering wheel as he headed home. *A shower is what I need,* he thought in sheer desperation. *All this will make sense after my shower.*

Putting his box of family pictures on his bed, Zach stepped into the bathroom and turned on the hot water. He stood under the showerhead for at least 10 minutes with the vision of the flying tire being redirected into the chest of the driver of the truck continually flashing through his mind.

Sitting on his bed after his shower, Zach tried to fit the pieces of the last couple of weeks together. Up to this point his life had been average, if not downright boring. Except for all the family tragedies he had faced in the past and his divorce—which he considered more of a formality than a reality—he really led a pretty ordinary life.

But now twice in as many weeks he had come face to face with death and somehow survived. He decided not to tell Valerie or Timothy about the car wreck. In fact, he decided not to think about it at all.

******

Too late for flowers, Zach decided to stop at the grocery store and at least get Valerie a Mother's Day card. He entered Lowry's five minutes late. "I'm supposed to meet my family here," he told the hostess.

"Yes, Mr. Miles, your family is already here," she smiled and pointed in the direction she wanted him to follow.

She seems too young to know me from my news show, Zack thought. *How did she know my—*

Before Zach could even finish the thought, the young, energetic girl spoke up. "Your wife described you, but she said you'd be holding flowers."

"They were all out," he said sarcastically, but his humor was lost on the hostess.

Following the girl up the stairs, he noticed a large vase of flowers and, without missing a step, he grabbed a few of them. Shaking off the stems, he followed the young lady to his seat. Zach sat down between Valerie and Stephanie. Sliding the card and flowers over towards Valerie, he kissed her on the cheek and said, "Happy Mother's Day!" She held his hand in both of hers as she smiled brightly, which was just what he needed at that moment.

Turning to Stephanie, he growled at her in a low voice, "I met your friend Lisa today."

Stephanie perked up with, "How'd it go? Isn't she great!"

Zach began to question whether he really knew Stephanie or not. How could she refer to this rude, self-absorbed, self-righteous woman as great? "That's not the word I would use exactly."

Stephanie could sense his hostility towards Lisa and was confused. "So tell me, when was the last time you saw Lisa?" Zach asked inquisitively.

"It's been about eight years or so, I guess. Why?"

"Oh, no reason," Zach sneered.

Stephanie knew he had more to say, but she figured he was done with Lisa for now, if not forever.

The conversation shifted to Timothy and work. Zach always liked to hear what life was like in his son's world. He often wished he were a carpenter like Timothy. They had spent many hours together over the years working in Zach's shop, which now belonged more to Timothy than to him.

It seemed the only way he and Timothy could communicate was by working on projects together. They had made birdhouses together at first, then later, as Timothy's expertise improved, they began larger jobs—redoing the deck, making a new fence. Both of them relished and missed this time together.

Timothy continued to pursue construction work during and after high school. Zach tried to get him to go to college, but he refused. It wasn't that he didn't want to go to college. It was simply that Timothy knew it would hurt his father if he didn't go. Later, however, he did put himself through a trade school and eventually got his license as a general contractor. Timothy could still remember how proud his father was when he got his contractor's license. It was quite a surprise to him, as he really didn't think his father cared about what he did for a living. Timothy knew he judged his father too harshly, but it was an old habit that died hard.

"Dad, can you take Mom home after dinner?" Timothy asked. "Stephanie and I are going to a show." He obviously had strong feelings for Stephanie as he now spent nearly all his free time with her.

Zach hoped Stephanie felt the same towards his son, and he really thought she did. It occurred to him that they were a very unlikely couple. She was well educated and worldly as well as a professed Christian. Timothy must have it bad for her to overlook these things without feeling out of place. With a grin and a wink, he agreed to take Valerie home.

The night turned out very pleasantly, and the prime rib was awesome, as usual. As Timothy and Stephanie rose to leave, Timothy picked up the check. Zach took it from his hand, "No, Son, this one's on me."

"Dad, I'll take care of it."

"Not tonight, Timothy. It's your mother's special day, and I'm paying."

Timothy nodded. He knew it was the right thing to do. "Dad, have a good trip to Europe." Timothy extended his hand. Zach stood and took hold of it. He wanted to hug his son, but he knew better.

"Take care of these two while I'm gone," said Zach with a smile.

"I will Dad. Be safe, okay?"

"Call me when you get to Rome," said Stephanie as they began to walk out.

******

Zach and Valerie drove home in near silence through the dark streets of Chicago. Considering the day's events, his time with Pastor Thomas was a very enjoyable surprise, but the car wreck—what was that? He shuddered and wondered how he could be so lucky once again to avoid injury or death. *And what about the driver of that white car?* he wondered.

"What's on your mind?" Valerie inquired.

"Oh, nothing really. I was just thinking about my day." He smiled as he looked towards Valerie.

She reached over and lovingly ran her fingers through the hair on his brow. He had always been the love of her life, divorced or not. She knew something was going on in his mind, something he was not willing to share with her—at least not yet. "You come in when we get home. I want to give you a haircut before you go traipsing around Europe making us Americans look like bums."

Zack laughed. How could he ever live without her? *You do every day, you idiot!* he answered himself. "You take good care of me."

"Somebody has to," she laughed.

"Do you suppose there are other divorced people who behave the way we do?" he asked.

"I doubt it. Most people who behave the way we do are still happily married." The sorrow in her voice came through.

"What happened to us?" Zach asked softly.

"I don't know, Zach," she mused. "I guess we just couldn't find a compromise. We were hurting each other so often that it seemed we needed to do something to save our love for each other."

"Yeah, I guess you're right, but I wish things were different."

"Me too!" she sighed. Valerie prayed nightly for Zach to come back home. *All in God's good timing,* she told herself.

******

Haircut complete, Zach stood to leave. Valerie hadn't said more than a dozen words since they got home. "Valerie, are you all right?"

As she looked at Zach, tears began to well up in her eyes. "I'm okay," she whispered, though she wasn't. She felt that life was getting ready to change. She didn't know what or how, but she could feel it every time she was around him. It was as if they had a destiny to fulfill, something that Valerie feared greatly. All she wanted was her husband back in her life permanently.

He put his arms around her and hugged her tight. "What is it?"

"I don't know, but I feel like something bad is going to happen. I don't want you to go to Rome."

"Don't you worry about me. I'll be all right."

"How can I not worry about you?" she sobbed. "I love you!"

Zach lifted her face to his own and kissed her tenderly. Passion filled his body as she kissed him back. Standing in the living room of his previous home holding his ex-wife—the only woman he would ever love—Zach was filled with remorse. He knew that he would not be able to consummate his relationship with her, and he knew who was to blame.

******

During the long plane ride over the Atlantic, Zach filled the hours by looking at the many family pictures he had brought with him, thanks to Pastor Thomas. So many family events! Some he could vaguely remember; others he was far too young to recall. It was apparent to him that his parents put a great deal of time into family activities, especially those involving their church. His emotions were compounded by his sorrow over his deceased loved ones and his own guilt at how poorly he had managed his own family.

What kind of family memories did Timothy have to look back on? Not many were positive, he was sure of that. *If there is a God,* he thought, *then why has He done all of this to me?*

******

Father Joseph Bastoni had agreed to pick Zach up at the airport, but the details were a bit vague. He hoped the good Father had some way to make himself known. He had no idea what he looked like, knowing only that he was a priest which, in Rome, wasn't hard to find.

Moving through customs was chaotic and slow as usual, but he finally made it through to the terminal exit. Among thousands of other travelers Zach stood on a dirty floor looking out in hopes of spotting a single identifiable feature, like his name written on cardboard in the hands of a priest dressed in black.

His eyes caught a medium-build man of a little less than average height walking towards him. Since he was wearing Levi's and Nike shoes, it wasn't possible he would be the priest. Stepping up to Zach, Joseph smiled brightly and extended his hand. "Mr. Miles, I presume?"

"Yes," Zach said, though still not convinced this man was Joseph.

"I am Joseph Bastoni."

Zach shook the man's hand noting a good firm grip. He looked at the man who seemed friendly enough, but where were his vestments? Aren't priests supposed to wear these clothes whenever they were in public? It seemed a bit unorthodox to Zach.

"Have a good trip?" Joseph asked with a friendly smile.

"Yes, fine," though he was still suspicious something was wrong with this picture.

Intuitively Joseph spoke up, "I'll bet you expected to see me in my work clothes?"

Zach nodded and smiled lightly.

"I took the day off," he grinned. What Joseph really wanted to say was that he felt embarrassed by his vestments and that lately he had had doubts about being a priest, and even more, he had doubts about the reality of God. Joseph, however, had no one to whom he was free to confide these thoughts. He had to endure this personal crisis alone because a priest wasn't supposed to act like a man with fears and doubts and confusion. At least that was what he told himself.

This statement put Zach at ease. *Well,* thought Zach, *this guy seems okay so far.*

"I'll bet you're tired," offered Joseph.

"I could use a shower and short nap for sure," Zach responded.

"Okay then. Let's get you to your hotel." He bent down and picked up one of Zach's bags and walked off with Zach close behind. *So far so good. Maybe he won't be one of those Lisa Taylor types.*

"What hotel are you staying in?" Joseph inquired as they walked to the parking lot.

"The Castillo in downtown Rome," Zach said. "Do you know of it?"

"Yes, I've seen it before," Joseph said without enough inflection to indicate whether or not he approved of the hotel.

The hotels in Rome were not all that impressive from the outside. Everything was covered in a hazy carbon dioxide black. The buildings, statues, even the bark of the local trees wore the exhaust stains of the numerous automobiles that crowded the city streets.

The Castillo hotel was a little more than a block away from the main train station and in plain view of the Basilica, one of the annexed Vatican buildings. Zach knew nothing of this hotel. His travel agency had booked it based solely on rate and availability.

"We've got a 45-minute drive," Joseph said as he tucked Zach's bags into the small trunk of his Fiat.

"Really!" Zach was surprised. "How far away is it?"

"About seven miles or so," said Joseph.

"Seven miles in 45 minutes?"

Joseph laughed. "It's a little harder to get around Rome than Chicago, but not much."

******

Room 214 of the Castillo Hotel was a standard Italian hotel room with a twin bed, a small television, and a mini-bar. There was only one thing out of the ordinary with this room—there were two naked hotel employees rolling around on top of the bed. This sort of thing had been going on daily for months between these two. Apparently Ricco—the tall, dark, married desk clerk—and Mary, the shapely but homely hotel maid—had come up with the lofty goal of having sex in every room of the hotel. To date they had made considerable progress by nearly completing the first two floors of the five-story building.

Suddenly as things between Mary and Ricco began to heat up the door to room 214 swung open and in stepped two horrid-looking beings dressed in black clothing. Although distinctly male, their features were grotesque. One of the creatures slammed the door behind him, thus getting the full attention of both Mary and Ricco.

Mary looked at these two demons as she reached for a sheet to cover her bare skin. Their faces were full hideous grins as they headed toward the surprised couple. Mary looked into their red, glowing eyes and began to scream, as did Ricco, but their efforts were pointless. Within a few seconds the demons had moved to a position just above these two indiscreet hotel employees.

Each demon, with a tremendous amount of strength, lifted both Mary and Ricco off the bed and up against the near wall. Holding the two lovers by their necks above the floor, each demon began to look deep into his victim's eyes. They both began to kick and squirm frantically to no avail. Shortly both demons were gone, disappeared into their victims' bodies.

The new but somehow less human versions of Mary and Ricco stood naked staring at each other fondly with evil grins on their faces. Next door in room 215 Philip knelt next to the bed in prayer. Beside him, also kneeling, was another large, handsome angel of light complexion. "Lord," besieged Philip, "we ask You to guide Barthemaus and me as we prepare to do battle against evil once again."

******

Joseph left Zach off at the entrance of the hotel. "Sorry, but they never have parking in front of these hotels. How do you feel about dinner later tonight?"

"Sounds fine to me."

"All right then." Joseph smiled handsomely. "You get some rest, and

I will pick you up at 7:30."

That's a bit late for dinner, Zach thought to himself.

"Europeans eat pretty late," said Joseph as if sensing Zach's thoughts. "We won't even find an open restaurant until 8:00 this evening."

The bellhop met Zach as he entered the hotel lobby. "Please allow me to take your bags," said the old man with a heavy accent. Zach wasn't sure the man had the strength to lift his bags, but somehow he managed.

Stepping up to the counter, Zach was met by a tall, dark clerk. "May I help you, sir?" Ricco asked in a sugary voice.

"Hello. My name is Zach Miles, and I have a reservation."

"Yes, of course. May I take an imprint of your credit card, please?"

"This guy is just too friendly." He could feel Ricco staring at him even though he worked busily behind the counter.

"All right, Mr. Miles. Your room is upstairs to the left—number 214. Enjoy your stay."

Zach reached out to take the room key from the clerk. "Thank you…" Zach looked at the man's nametag. "…Ricco."

Ricco snapped his fingers and, at this, the old bellhop lifted Zach's bags and began to walk to the elevator. Zach wrestled one of the bags from the elderly man. "He won't die on account of me," he said quietly to himself as he followed the man into the lift.

******

Unpacked, Zach decided to skip the shower until later. "I'll just take a short nap, but I had better set the alarm just to be safe." He fiddled with the radio alarm, trying to set it. Finally he gave up and called downstairs.

"May I help you?" Ricco asked.

"Yes, can I have a wake-up call in two hours, please?"

"6:00 p.m., of course. No problem. Can I do anything else for you, Mr. Miles?"

"No, that's it. Thanks."

That guy wouldn't last a week in Chicago. He's too friendly! Zach stretched out on the bed in the cramped little room and was asleep within just minutes after his head hit the feather pillow.

******

Mary met Ricco in the stairwell just below the second floor. Room 214 was conveniently located just over the first floor crawl access used by plumbers and air conditioning and heater repairmen. Mary handed Ricco a large laundry bag full of solvent-soaked towels. Taking a key out of his pocket, Ricco unlocked and opened the heavy fireproof door. The soaked towels leaked through the bottom of the laundry bag as he hoisted it into the crawl space. The smell of solvent was strong in the small confined area.

"I'll go through here while you go up and prop your laundry cart against his door."

Mary nodded and pushed her cart down the hall and into the elevator.

Slowing his crawl, Ricco positioned himself just under Zach's room. Setting the soggy laundry bag down, he began to remove the towels one by one. Kneeling and taking his time as if he were a perfectionist, Ricco wrapped each towel carefully around the water pipes under the floor. Finally he wrapped the last two around the heater duct just as Mary entered the crawl space.

"The door is blocked. He has no way out," she said.

Earlier Mary had bolted the window shut, and even if she hadn't, the window was far too small for Zach to climb through. Ricco smiled as he pulled a silver-plated lighter from his front pocket.

Philip crept silently down the stairwell and into the vestibule area. Standing next to the small trap door he could hear Mary giggle with delight as she watched Ricco light each towel in succession, starting from the furthest point back below Zach's room and working his way back towards Mary. The fires were beginning to rage, and the smoke filled the crawl space. The heat was intense, and Ricco began to hurry up his ritualistic process.

Mary began to cough and rub her eyes. "We'd better get out of here," she choked.

"Two more towels." Ricco coughed also.

This plan is so simple, he thought to himself with an evil heart full of pride. Mary had blocked the door and bolted the window while he had set what he thought was an ingenious fire right below Zach's room. And just before he and Mary had met under the stairwell, he had gone to the main control panel and switched off the smoke detectors. Oh, sure, the sprinklers would kick on when the heat got high enough. By that time, however, it would be too late for anyone who was unlucky enough to be stranded in this hotel. They would be dead by smoke or fire—Ricco didn't care which, although he preferred they die by fire.

His plan was perfect except for one very minor detail. With a thud the fire door to the crawl space entrance closed and cut them off from any outside light and oxygen. The flames of blue and orange were dancing hungrily as they consumed the bottom of Zach's room. Mary turned and looked at Ricco in terror just as Philip turned the key that locked the door into its rightful place. Ricco screamed in anger as he recalled the small but suddenly crucial error in his plot to kill Zach. The key was still in the door.

Upstairs Zach began to choke and cough as he slept. His room was filling rapidly with dense gray smoke. The wall next to his bed suddenly turned black as the fire on the other side began to consume the wall from within. Zach's breathing intensified, and his mind screamed for his body to wake up, but it was already too late for him. He had by now received more smoke than was necessary to knock him unconscious.

Barthemaus pushed the cart out of the way to gain access to Zach's room. He pounded on the door and called out Zach's name, but there was no response. "Father, give me the strength," he prayed aloud. Inside the room fire had now broken through the wall and was spreading across the carpet and onto the bedspread that partially covered Zach's upper body.

There was a tremendous crash as Barthemaus pushed his way through the thick, fireproof door that held Zach prisoner. Stepping through the flames as if they were not even there, the large angel bent over the bed and scooped Zach up into his massive arms. As he turned to leave, Philip met them by the door and led the way out of the room and down the stairwell.

Along the way Philip heard the screams of two children. Moving towards the sound, Philip burst through a nearby door and disappeared into the dark, smoky room. Soon after he emerged clutching the frightened children. He continued his run through the hall, with the children in his arms, to the stairwell where he met up again with Barthemaus and an unconscious Zach. The light-skinned angel looked at the two small girls in Philip's strong arms and smiled. "God has given us a bonus!" said Philip.

Exiting the hotel the two angels sat Zach and the children against the side of the building. "Two more things," Philip said as he ran into the smoking building. Walking over to the electrical panel, he flipped the switch and the smoke alarm system instantly began to scream out a danger warning.

Four blocks away on a control panel at the city fire department a light indicator went on, informing the attendant that there was a fire at that location.

Next Philip went up through the dense, smoke-filled stairwell directly into room 214. The room was entirely engulfed in flames, but he scanned it carefully until he saw what he was looking for. Sitting in the middle of Zach's smoldering suitcase was the little gray box. Philip walked through the fire as if it were not even there and grabbed the small package. Turning, he walked back through the fire towards the stairwell.

******

Zach awoke slowly to the sound of unidentifiable people speaking Italian. Looking out over the top of what appeared to be some plastic gadget strapped to his face, he could see the backs of two of the strangers. They were wearing white outfits. He just couldn't comprehend what was going on. *Is this a dream?* He asked himself. *Maybe, but why does my chest feel like it is on fire?*

Joseph moved closer to Zach and lifted his hand. "Can you hear me,

Zach?"

Zach tried to focus his eyes on the blurry vision of Joseph, but it was difficult.

"You're in a hospital, Zach. There was a fire. Do you remember anything?"

Zach shook his head slowly, indicating that he had no memory of a fire or even how he ended up in this hospital.

"You're lucky! You are going to be all right." Joseph smiled and patted Zach's hand. "You just rest and I'll stay with you for a while."

******

Birds were singing outside in the trees as long golden beams of sunlight penetrated through the window. Zach sensed warm light on his face and the smell of smoke in his nostrils. He stretched and began to look around the room. *How did I get here?* he wondered. In the corner of the room hunched over in a small, padded chair still sleeping was Father Bastoni. Father seemed like the wrong word to describe this guy. Zach was moved by the fact that this man he barely knew had obviously spent the night there watching over him.

"How are you feeling this morning?" an elderly nurse, dressed in an outfit that looked like it came straight out of the 50's, asked softly.

"Hungry," Zach grinned.

"That's a very good sign," the nurse added as she began to take his blood pressure.

Joseph started to stir and, rising back in his chair, he stretched and looked towards Zach.

"Good morning." Zach was first.

"Well! Good morning to you!" Father Bastoni looked very relieved. "How do you feel?"

"He's hungry!" the nurse chimed in.

"What happened?" Zach had to know.

"What do you remember?" Joseph asked.

Zach thought hard for a couple of minutes. He did have some vague memories, but he didn't know if they were real or just a dream. "Not much, I guess," he said.

"There was a fire in your hotel." Joseph frowned.

That would explain the smell of smoke in my nostrils, he thought. "How did I get out of there?"

"Well, that's where it gets a little sketchy," said Joseph. "The police stated that you and two little girls were carried down the stairs and out of the hotel by two unidentified men."

Zach tried hard to focus his memory. Looking directly at Joseph he asked, "Was one of them black?"

"Oh, you're starting to remember?"

"No," he mumbled.

Joseph was confused. "The report says that one of the little girls described the two men as tall and strongly built—one white, the other black."

Zach leaned back on his pillow and closed his irritated eyes. *What is going on here?* he asked himself. An additional thought tapped his brain like a bolt of lightening. "My pictures!" he cried with anguish.

Joseph smiled at Zach and bent down beside his chair. Turning toward him, Joseph had a small gray box in his hands. "I hope you don't mind, but I looked at a few of them."

Grateful, though stunned, Zach asked, "How did these pictures survive the fire?"

"The doctor said you had these wrapped in your arms when they brought you in here."

Zach just shook his head. He couldn't remember a thing. "I need to call my wife," he said aloud.

******

Checked out of the hospital by noon, Zach now sat in the passenger seat of Joseph's car thinking about his earlier conversation with Valerie. He was glad he called her. She had been so worried because it had been an entire day since he had left Chicago and not a word.

"Are you okay?" she asked with concern.

"I'm fine."

"Why didn't you call me?" she asked, her voice quickly turning from worry to anger.

Debating not telling her the truth, he said softly, "There was a problem."

"What problem?" she demanded.

Are we still married? he thought. *It sure feels like it!*

"There was a fire in my hotel."

"Dear God! Are you okay? Where are you now?" She had the worry back in her tone.

"I'm fine! Just a little smoky, I guess. I'm in the hospital."

Zach consoled Valerie for another 15 minutes before she would finally allow him to hang up the phone.

Zach and Joseph drove through Rome. "I think maybe you'd better just stay with me for the rest of your visit."

How does a priest live? he wondered. "Sure, that's fine with me, but I need to buy some clothes."

"I'll tell you what. Let's go back to my office for a few minutes. I have a brief phone conference, and then we'll go shopping. I know some great places!"

This guy is full of surprises, thought Zach. *A priest that knows great places to buy clothes!* It appeared to Zach as if Joseph was living in two worlds at the same time.

******

Vatican City was a wondrous place. Zach stared at all the buildings in amazement. The architecture was tremendous and very old. "You work here every day?" He couldn't take his eyes off the large old buildings.

"You get used to it after a while."

"Really?"

"No, not really," Joseph admitted. "It's pretty spectacular!"

Having parked the Fiat a good block away, Joseph and Zach hiked to the furthest building down the block. Joseph pointed to a second story window facing directly out towards another old slate gray building. "Not much of a view, is it?"

Zach laughed lightly. Walking up the steps Zach observed three fairly heavyset priests as they walked out the front door. They were all dressed in black flowing outfits. One of them, the eldest, had a red sash across the front of his vestments. He looked so earnest and holy to Zach.

Joseph stopped where he was and faced the senior man. "Good morning, Cardinal!" he said brightly. Joseph was grateful that he was now wearing his proper attire. The last time he got caught out of uniform he took a severe tongue lashing.

"Good morning, Joseph! Who's your friend?"

Joseph turned briefly toward the other two men and nodded out of politeness. They returned his nod just as cordially. "This is Zach Miles, a reporter from the United States—Chicago, to be more precise."

Zach smiled at the large, colorful man. "How do you do, sir?" He was as polite as he knew how.

"Quite fine! Thank you," replied the Cardinal. "Miles—that's a good Irish name, is it not?"

Zach nodded. "That's right."

"And Zach—short for Zechariah, the last prophet from the Old Testament," added the Cardinal boldly.

"Second to the last. Malachi was the last Old Testament prophet, I believe." Joseph tempered his correction with a smile.

"You may be correct," said the large man with slight indignation in his voice. The three priests walked past Zach and Joseph as they continued their climb down the steep brick steps.

Zach looked at Joseph in amazement. "You're kind of bold, aren't you?"

"It's one of my weaknesses. I was hoping that when I turned 40 this would improve, but now I am 41 and still too brash." A frown of self disapproval covered his face.

Joseph's office was not unlike Zach's own. It was small—too small—but Joseph did have a window even if he didn't have much of a view to brag about.

"Have a seat. I'll only be a few minutes." Joseph left the room as Zach sat in an old, leather winged-back chair. Looking around the room Zach noted a lot of Green Bay Packers stuff: hats, pendants, and even an autographed photo of Reggie White hung proudly on Joseph's wall. He also had numerous pictures of what appeared to be family members. In fact, there was one picture of Joseph standing next to a man who, although taller than Joseph, looked just like him. *Must be his brother,* Zach surmised.

Joseph reentered the room with a small piece of paper in his hand. "I just need to make one quick call and then we're out of here." He sat down behind his large walnut-stained desk. This was his favorite part of the room. Picking up the phone, he dialed the number written on the piece of paper.

Zach sat back and observed passively. Joseph looked very stately sitting behind the large desk with the phone up to his ear. *Kind of like an ambassador,* he thought to himself.

"Mr. Carlo Ventini, please." Joseph looked over to Zach and smiled as he waited on his call. "Mr. Ventini, this is Father Bastoni returning your call…Yes sir, I'm sorry. There was an emergency yesterday…No, I'm fine. It was a friend of mine, but he's okay now." Joseph winked at Zach.

This guy is smooth, Zach thought to himself.

"Tonight?" said Joseph. "Well, I have company from the United States staying with me for a couple of days…Really? Okay, if you don't mind then, I'll bring him with me…No, 8:00 p.m. is fine. See you then."

Joseph hung up the phone and turned to Zach. "I hope you don't mind, but we've been invited to a formal dinner with the agricultural minister of Europe, Mr. Carlo Ventini." Zach had heard the name before but couldn't recall where. "If you're not up to it, I'll understand."

"Did you miss a meeting with him yesterday because of me?"

"Don't worry about it, Zach. It's not a problem. Besides, I couldn't just bring you to Rome and roast you the first day, now could I?" They both laughed heartily until Zach began to cough up some residual hotel smoke. "How about a small sherry to help your throat?"

"You drink?"

"No, but it's allowed in the Catholic Church. I only keep it for guests. You might be surprised. Some of these Italian priests can really drink it up when they want to."

Zach declined the sherry and stood to leave. "Well, if I'm going to a formal dinner, then I definitely need some new clothes."

"All right, let's go get some," Joseph said with excitement.

Joseph and Zach spent the better part of the day shopping through many of the smaller clothing stores in the city while getting to know each other. Zach found out that Joseph became a priest more to please his mother than as a calling from God.

"My brother is a doctor, and I get sick at the mere sight of blood," he grimaced, "so I couldn't really think of what else I could be. My mother always hoped I'd become a priest, so after college it just seemed like the thing to do."

Zach couldn't help but think there was a little more to the story. *This guy is all-American—ruggedly handsome, outgoing, and intelligent. There's a potential politician in this priest,* he was sure.

Zach had a question in his mind that he wanted to ask, but he was afraid it might be too personal. He decided to take the chance anyway, "How do you survive without having a woman in your life?"

A large grin filled Joseph's handsome face. "You're married, right?"

"Yes—I mean, no. I mean not anymore." said Zach. It would be too hard to explain to Joseph his relationship with Valerie.

"Well, then, how do you survive?"

Not very well! Zack thought to himself. "I see your point, but at least I did have a woman in my life."

"Yes, well, so did I." Joseph offered no further explanation.

There it is, Zach thought. *Plain as day—a woman had jilted the guy and, as a result, he had become a priest.* Zach was proud of himself for figuring out why Joseph was what he was.

******

Sitting on the sofa at Joseph's small but nicely decorated apartment, Zach fiddled with the collar of his new suit. *These Italian clothes are nice but a little stiff.*

Joseph called out from the other room, "Feel free to call your ex-wife and give her my number if you'd like."

Good idea! he thought.

Zach spoke to a much happier Valerie this time. "I'm staying with a priest. Can you imagine that?"

She laughed until tears filled her eyes. "No, I can't!"

Their conversation was brief but satisfying. Valerie felt better knowing that Zach had met a nice person to help care for her man. She really wanted to be there to do it herself, but that wasn't possible. "Lord," she prayed silently, "bring him back home safely. And Lord, please let me have my husband back for all times."

As Zach hung up the telephone, Joseph stepped out of his bedroom. He was dressed in a black suit with a white collar under his chin. This was a much more formal set of vestments than the ones he had worn as they shopped throughout Rome. Zach had almost forgotten that Joseph was a priest and all of a sudden it was a little intimidating to be in his presence. Joseph seemed to be aware that Zach was now a little uncomfortable.

"I tried to buy this in leather, but they didn't have my size." He smiled at Zach. At this they both laughed heartily. Laughter is the medicine needed to put people at ease, and Joseph understood this well enough.

"We still have an hour before we leave, so if you want to ask me some questions on Bible prophecy, now's your chance." With all the excitement of the last day or so, Zach had nearly forgotten the reason he came to Rome in the first place. He felt instantly guilty that he hadn't focused on his assignment sooner. He also felt guilty for not calling Stephanie by now. He was sure, however, that by this time Valerie would have told her about the fire.

"Okay, let's do it!"

Joseph sat in a small recliner next to Zach. "Shoot," he said as he kicked the footrest up and reclined in the chair. Zach hadn't noticed

Joseph's bare feet before, and now he was very amused at how casual this man really was.

First Zach gave his usual pitch on how his boss was making him do this and about the many disasters around the world. Joseph understood that Zach felt uncomfortable talking about this issue. In fact, he was beginning to understand that Zach was uncomfortable talking about God altogether.

"You know," said Joseph, "we had the worst winter on record this year throughout Europe. In fact, it was so cold and snowy all the way through April that it has destroyed nearly all the early crops and prevented the planting of the later crops as well."

Joseph continued. "One of the reasons I am meeting with the agricultural minister over dinner tonight is to help the church spread the word about how we as a family of European nations will cope with this near total disaster."

Zach had heard of the miserable weather problems that plagued Europe this year, but he had no idea it was this bad. "What will Europe do for food?" Zach inquired.

"That's the million-dollar question," said Joseph with a sorrowful look on his face.

The scene finally set, Zach asked the big question of Joseph. "My boss wants to know if these disasters are a sign of the end of the world."

Laughing, Joseph said, "Your boss wants to know, Zach? The whole world wants to know!" Joseph reached over to the small coffee table and opened the drawer. Zach was sure he was going to pull out some proof of the coming rapture, but instead Joseph pulled out a pack of cigarettes. Taking one out and lighting it with a wooden match, Joseph turned his attention back to Zach. Seeing the look of surprise on his face, Joseph spoke up. "I know smoking is frowned on in America these days, but here in Europe we all still smoke."

Joseph continued with the conversation, puffing away as he went. "There is strong evidence in the Bible to support the concerns of Christians that there will be a time of numerous disasters and ultimately the return of Jesus Christ Himself. However," he continued, "the Bible also lists conditions that have to be met before His return."

"Such as?" asked Zach.

"Well, the big one is that the Antichrist and False Prophet must be living among us before this happens. There must be a peace agreement between Israel and her neighbors—which seems unlikely to happen any time soon."

Zach was impressed with Father Bastoni's knowledge of prophecy.

"There also needs to be a temple or something like it built on the site where King Solomon had built his temple to God. This is to allow the Jews a place to worship prior to the desecration, and a few other little things are supposed to happen as well."

All of this before Christ returns? Zach pondered. "Then why are so many Christians sure He is coming back soon?"

"It's all a matter of interpretation," said Joseph. "You see, many Christians believe that a Rapture will happen before the fulfillment of all these things that I have told you about," Joseph went on. "Their belief is that God has not appointed them to God's wrath. They say that this is supported by God's Word in places like 1st Thessalonians and even in the book of Revelation itself."

"Do you believe in a Rapture?" Zach asked frankly.

"I am not convinced that there is a basis for it," said Joseph. "Throughout the Bible God's wrath appears to me to have been poured out on the righteous and the unrighteous all along."

Zach liked Joseph's more scientific approach to understanding the Bible. There didn't appear to be any emotions driving his comprehension.

"How about you, Zach—what do you think will happen?" Joseph asked with a serious and inquisitive look on his face. Zach figured it would come around to this question sooner or later. It always did.

"I'm not a religious man," said Zach, "and I think disasters are a part of life."

"You might be right," agreed Joseph. He thought that Zach might not be telling the whole truth about what he did or didn't believe, but he had learned over the years not to push this issue too much. Joseph had his own doubts. The Catholic Church was full of faithful, God-fearing, God-serving men and women, but for him it was also full of traditions and rules that for some reason he just could not ever get past, at least to the point at which he could focus in on a personal relationship with Jesus. Many others had done this successfully, so he was not sure what held him back.

******

Joseph and Zach pulled under the carport as the valet stepped out to meet them. "Park it in a safe place," Joseph said with a laugh as he handed the keys to the young man. His priestly salary just did not afford much in the way of luxury, such as the many Jags strewn throughout the parking lot.

The restaurant was impressive to say the least. The floor was a green marble with etched carvings of a great Roman battlefield. The ceiling was covered with many large crystal chandeliers, and every 12 feet or so stood a massive pylon extending from the floor into the ceiling. The tables were finely decorated with crystal glasses, china coffee cups, real silver utensils, and linen napkins. Zach was glad his old clothing burned up. He would not have had anything nice enough to wear in this place.

Over in the center of the room at a very large table sat six elegantly dressed people—four men and two women. One of them turned towards Joseph and Zach as they walked in. A balding, heavyset, somewhat short man of maybe 40 years of age rose and began to wave his hand towards them. Zach followed Joseph nervously over to the table. The man extended his hand to Joseph saying, "Father Bastoni, I presume? I am Simon Koch, Mr. Ventini's aide and assistant agricultural secretary."

"It is a pleasure to meet you, Mr. Koch," said Joseph.

"Call me Simon," he smiled. "And who might this be?" Simon asked as he turned to look at Zach. Zach suddenly felt a cold breeze blow by him, sending a shiver through his body.

"This is Zach Miles, an American reporter here on business."

Simon extended his hand to Zach who shook it firmly as he looked into Simon's eyes. What he saw there frightened him. The man's eyes were like those of a shark—dark and lifeless—yet evil at the same time. Simon smiled at Zach as he finally loosened his flabby grip on him.

Simon pointed to two empty chairs. "Have a seat," he said. "Father, I think we'll seat you next to the ladies if you don't mind. Mr. Miles, you can sit next to me. Mr. Ventini will be here shortly. He's a little tied up at the moment."

"So tell me, Mr. Miles, have you recovered from the fire?"

"Yes, I'm okay," said Zach. "How did you know about the fire?"

Simon looked a bit flustered. "Mr. Ventini told me," he said. "So tell me, what brings you to Rome?"

Wait a minute! Zach thought. *This guy is moving along too fast. How did Mr. Ventini know about the fire? I was there when Joseph told him there was an emergency, but he never mentioned a fire.*

Simon waited patiently for Zach to respond.

"I'm sorry!" said Zach. "What was the question?"

Simon laughed. "Not fully recovered, I see! Tell us, Mr. Miles, why have you come to Rome?"

Zach was embarrassed for blanking out in the middle of Simon's conversation. "I came to interview Joseph—I mean Father Bastoni."

"I see," said Simon. "Interview for what?"

Zach really didn't want to have this conversation again—not tonight. Joseph sensed his wariness and saved the day by speaking up. "Zach is here to find out if there is a relationship between all of these recent disasters and the Return of Christ."

Simon nodded as Joseph spoke. When he was finished, he turned to Zach and said, "Return of whom?"

"Return of Jesus Christ!" interposed Joseph.

Simon laughed aloud while Zach sat there feeling foolish and looking pitiful. "Forgive me," said Simon, "but your employer spent money to have you travel the world in search of a myth?" Zach was getting tired of Simon in a big hurry.

"Do you believe Christ is a myth, Mr. Koch?" Joseph looked straight into his eyes.

"Please don't be offended, Father, but I am Jewish, and I've been taught that the legend of Christ's deity is a myth to say the least. Our deliverer has not been revealed to us yet." Simon was very frank.

"Mr. Ventini!" said one of the ladies sitting next to Joseph. Simon and Zach both turned around to see a tall, well-built, handsome man approaching the table. *Is this Mr. Ventini?* Zack asked himself. He was expecting an older man, but this man looked to be his mid-30's at best.

As Carlo Ventini crossed the floor, he looked over to the far left of the room. Zach's eyes followed his, and in the corner of the room at a much smaller table Zach could see two men—one white, the other black—sitting together. Carlo paused to look at the two men before turning towards Simon.

Arriving at the table, Carlo Ventini smiled brightly. "Good evening, everyone!" he said in a pleasant and commanding voice.

Zach thought this man would have had some kind of Italian accent, based simply on his last name, but if anything, he sounded like someone from the East Coast—maybe Maryland.

Carlo greeted each man and woman before sitting down on the other side of Zach. As he did so, he looked one more time to the table where Philip and Barthemaus sat. The look in Carlo's eyes as he stared their way was not one of fear or surprise, but one of loathsome hate for these two creatures of God.

******

As the night wore on, the discussion of the Return of Christ finally began to wind down. The last few comments came from Carlo himself. "I tend to agree with Simon on this issue. It has been 2,000 years since Christ was supposed to have ascended from this world with the promise of a speedy return. A broken promise, like all myths, is proof enough for me that Christ will not be returning."

Zach looked to Joseph for a reaction, but he was sorely disappointed in Joseph's unwillingness to argue his position. It seemed to Zach that Joseph's very profession was under attack. Why was he not trying to defend it?

Eventually the conversation got around to the topic of the disastrous winter that Europe had recently endured. Turning once again to Father Bastoni, Carlo asked him, "What are your people around Europe most concerned with—the return of Jesus Christ or feeding themselves this next year?"

That's a good question, Zach thought as he looked to Joseph. It was evident that this evening was not going as Joseph had expected. The enthusiastic nature of the priest was gone.

"I suppose most people are worried about feeding their families," Joseph replied.

"Yes, I think so too!" said Simon with a smile.

Carlo was obviously pleased with the direction that this evening's meal had gone. Lifting his glass of wine towards Joseph, Carlo said proudly, "If it's food they want, then its food they will get!" Joseph did not attempt to lift his glass, but instead he simply sat there motionless.

"Allow me to share my plans with you, Father. I think you will be pleased!" said Carlo. Over the course of the next hour Carlo laid out the details of his newly developed Agripod system, a method of growing all types of fruits, vegetables and, most importantly, grains all year round in a climate controlled, soil-free environment. "Our engineers and geneticists have worked closely together to develop a seed and climate combination that will produce bountiful crops year round."

"How many of these Agripods will be necessary to feed Europe?" Joseph asked suspiciously.

"Because we can grow plants continuously year round, we will require far fewer than you might imagine. Furthermore," Carlo went on, "we will build these structures to be multi-story to conserve space."

"We will not only be able to feed Europe," said Simon, "but eventually any part of the world we want."

Why does this bother me? Zach wondered. *An endless supply of food would stop all hunger in the world. We could survive any disaster and still be able to feed every nation. Maybe it is because with this new technology comes power and wealth. And possibly a new and dominant power could emerge from this. If people are hungry enough, they will do or pay anything.*

"Will this technology be shared with other countries?" Zach asked.

"Yes, of course!" said Carlo, "Under certain conditions."

"What conditions?" Joseph inquired.

Carlo rose from his chair, setting his empty wine glass on the table. "I'm sorry, ladies and gentlemen, but I'm afraid I must depart. I have another appointment that I must keep."

Simon nodded in agreement.

"Mr. Miles," said Carlo as he turned in Zach's direction, "A pleasure to meet you! And, Father, delightful once again. I will be in touch with you soon. I'd like to get your help on spreading the good news about what we have planned for Europe!"

What does he have planned for the world? Zach wondered.

Joseph nodded and stood as Carlo turned to leave.

Zach observed Carlo's gaze shift back over to the corner table. Looking in that direction Zach noted the table was now empty, but he couldn't remember seeing the two men leave.

******

It was a quiet drive back to Joseph's apartment. It seemed that Joseph was deep in thought, and Zach was just plain tired.

"What time is your flight tomorrow?" Joseph asked casually.

"5:30 p.m."

"Good! Then we can spend tomorrow finishing up our interview."

Joseph began to remove his collar even before they entered his apartment. Once inside he noticed the light flashing on his answering machine. Pushing the green button, Joseph played the messages on his recorder. The first one was Greek to Zach. Actually it was Italian, but to a man who speaks neither, what's the difference? Joseph made himself a small note and then forwarded the machine to the next message. Stephanie's voice rang through clear as a bell.

"I hope this is the right number," she said to the recording. "Zach, if you're there, Valerie told me about the fire. I'm glad you're okay. Call me when you can. Thanks."

Zach winced in memory of the promised phone call he still had not made to Stephanie.

"Sounds like a nice girl," Joseph observed as he forwarded the recorder to the last message.

"My son surely thinks so!" Zach grinned.

The next message was in English, as well, but the man speaking was obviously Italian. "Father Bastoni, this is detective Martin. I was given your number to contact Zach Miles. We would like to question him tomorrow—early if possible. Please call me at..." Joseph wrote down the number.

"We'll call him in the morning."

"Okay with me." Zach closed his eyes momentarily. It had been an exhausting evening for them both, and they were ready to call it a day.

"This couch makes into a bed," said Joseph. "I'll get you some sheets and blankets."

"Thanks, Joseph. I'm beat," said Zach.

The next day Joseph made Zach a great breakfast of fresh fruit, smoked salmon, and some terrific bread toasted on both sides. "You just can't get good bread in the States." Joseph's remark was affirmed by Zach with a nod as he gobbled down his food.

Breakfast was interrupted by a knock at Joseph's front door. "Expecting some company?" Zach asked.

"No!" said Joseph.

As the priest opened the door, Zach could see a man in a dark blue uniform with red stripes down the pant legs looking directly towards him.

"Come in, please, and have a seat," welcomed Joseph.

Pushing his stool away from the breakfast bar, Zach took one last bite. He walked into the living room to be introduced to detective Martin.

"Good morning, Mr. Miles. Sorry to bother you," said the detective.

"It's no bother. What can I do for you?" Zach sat down on the couch.

"Mr. Miles, do you have any enemies?" the man asked abruptly.

What an odd question. "No. Why do you ask?"

"Do you know of anyone who would like to do you harm or maybe see you dead?"

Zach was absolutely stunned by the question, and so was Joseph. "I don't know anyone in Rome or all of Italy for that matter," he said frankly.

"Mr. Miles, we have been investigating the hotel fire at the Castillo," continued Martin.

Zach leaned forward to more closely follow what the detective was trying to say.

"It seems that the fire was set intentionally."

Zach was amazed to hear this, but in the world we live in, anything is possible. "What does this have to do with me?"

"Mr. Miles, it appears that the fire was set intentionally under your room with towels soaked in some kind of solvent—maybe paint thinner."

Zach didn't know what to say.

"The really interesting thing is that in order to set the fire, someone had to crawl into the repair space between the first and second floors. According to the hotel manager, the only person with the key to open the fire door was the desk clerk, Ricco Spallini." Zach remembered the overly friendly Ricco. "And when we opened the locked fire door, we found the charred remains of Ricco and a hotel maid named Mary. We found a lighter still clutched in Ricco's charred hand. But what we can't figure out is how they ended up locked in the crawl space with the key still sticking out of the other side of the door."

"What do you remember about the two men who brought you out of the hotel?"

"Nothing!" he assured the detective. "I mean—it's all fuzzy."

"Try to remember, Mr. Miles. It may be the only clue we have."

"I don't remember how I got outside the hotel. All I can vaguely recall is a sense of warmth and peace and—" Zach paused.

"Continue, please"

"A smell," said Zach.

"A what?" the man asked.

"An unusual smell. Even though the hotel was full of smoke, I could still smell it."

"What was it like?" Martin asked.

"It can't be described."

"Was it familiar to you? Have you smelled it before?"

Zach paused again. *How can I explain this to him?* he wondered. "Yes," hesitantly he spoke. "I remember smelling it once. No," Zach corrected himself, "twice before."

"Tell me more," said Mr. Martin

"Both times when I noticed the smell," he said cautiously, "I was in danger. Or more precisely, the danger was over and I was safe." He explained the best he could about the two times in his life that someone had saved him from a certain death. He decided not to mention the near fatal wreck at the end of last week, but Zach now knew that this was more than a strange coincidence as well.

Joseph was fascinated by Zach's story.

"Well, Mr. Miles, for a man with no enemies, you surely have come close to dying a number of times. One last thing before I go," said the detective. "We have two witnesses that describe the two men that saved you as tall, strongly built, one white and the other black. It wouldn't happen to have been two men, one white and one black, who saved you those other two times, would it?"

Zach thought for a second. "No, it wasn't two men at all."

Joseph understood Zach's answer. He now also understood why Zach, while in the hospital, had asked him if one of the men was black. *The man that continues to save Zach from death is black,* Joseph decided.

******

Zach and Joseph enjoyed the rest of the day together as they wandered Rome. Zach had taken pages of notes from his interview with Joseph, and they would be valuable for putting the show together. He was going to be glad to get home, but he knew he had made a lasting friendship with Joseph, and he was going to miss this guy. Zach had few friends in his life. There just never seemed to be enough time for friendships with any real depth.

Heading towards the airport, he began to make plans with Joseph for the show. "So, you will be able to come over for the taping of the show on July 10, right?"

"Did I agree to that?" Joseph asked.

"No, not yet, but I am hoping. My station will pay for your trip."

"They'd have to!" Joseph laughed as he patted the worn dash of his old Fiat. "I'll tell you what. I'll do your show if you will tell me about the black man that continues to save your life."

Zach was caught a little off guard. "Okay, agreed! But you have to tell me about last night. Why didn't you defend yourself against Carlo's attacks on Christianity?"

Joseph didn't want to talk about last night. He didn't realize that Zach was paying such close attention. *I should have realized. After all, he's a reporter,* Joseph thought. "You first!" said Joseph.

"It's pretty simple really," Zach had never even spoken the truth about this to himself. "Every time I get into a dangerous situation, a large, stout, black man comes to my rescue."

"Who is this guy?"

"I really don't know, but he saved me once when I was nine, then again last month, last week, and two days ago."

Joseph didn't know what to think or what to say, so he said nothing at all. Noticing his struggle, Zach spoke up, "I feel the same way." Smiling weakly he said, "Now it's your turn."

"Okay, ask me the question again."

"Why didn't you defend Christ last night?"

"God's Word says that the Spirit draws men to Him. God doesn't need my defense. He can take care of Himself." Joseph figured this would satisfy Zach even if it didn't satisfy him. He knew that he had other reasons for not defending Christ, like his own lack of faith. It was fairly easy to become a priest. It was wholly different to become a disciple of Christ.

Zach could tell there was more to this than his explanation, but he respected Joseph's answer and did not ask for more.

Joseph agreed to come to Chicago and participate in Zach's show. *After all,* he thought, *when I get done, I can drive up to see Mom and my brother, Peter, if I have time.*

Joseph walked Zach into the airport. This time Zach had only one bag to carry, and it was a new one.

"Thanks for everything!" said Zach.

"It was my pleasure!" said Joseph.

"I guess I'll see you in six weeks or so," said Zach.

"Right!" agreed Joseph. Both men felt uncomfortable trying to say goodbye. In just a few short days they had developed a strong bond between them. This was similar to bonding experiences reported by survivors of traumatic events. It was not uncommon for people who spent mere minutes or hours together to feel very connected to each other as a result of sharing a common traumatic experience. Zach extended his hand to Joseph who took it into both of his hands.

"Stay safe, Zach."

"I'll try my best," he said.

Zach picked up his new leather bag and began heading towards the passport line. Joseph stood momentarily and waved goodbye as Zach walked away.

******

Comfortably seated in the airplane as it cruised at 35,000 feet, Zach felt calm and relaxed. He had Leo Thomas and now Joseph Bastoni for his interviews, and if Carl Perkins turns out not to be a dud, then maybe he would have a good show after all. Zach pulled the gray box out of his luggage and again began to look at the pictures of his departed family. Suddenly he remembered that he had not yet called Stephanie as he had promised to do. Picking up the phone tucked into his armrest, he dialed her number. "I'll bet she's out to lunch with Timothy," he hoped.

Chapter 10 - The Fires

The water temperature in the Gulf of Penas off the coast of Chile, all the way to the Coral Sea, had risen another three degrees in as many weeks. The ocean temperature throughout the southern Pacific was now an incredible 24 degrees above normal. This tremendous increase in water temperature resulted in eight months straight without a single measurable drop of rain from the western, northern, and southern portions of Australia.

In fact, even Sydney, the most southeastern part of the country, having been without any appreciable rainfall for many months, was as dry as an old bone. Dead fish from within the Coral Sea continued to wash up on the Queensland coast in record numbers as a direct result of the water temperature.

Ranchers and farmers throughout Australia prayed nightly for rain. Among those praying were Stan and Ruby Evans. The Evans family had been ranchers for the last 45 years, ever since Stan's parents settled in the town of Quilpie in the Queensland Territory.

His parents had been missionaries sent to Australia from the United States by their church. Stan's parents fell in love with Quilpie as soon as they came to this small town. They were well received by the townsfolk and decided to stay. Soon after they petitioned the church that sent them and asked for the funds to build a temple and to buy up surrounding land for ranching. Their petition was granted and the legacy began.

Stan's parents had now both passed on, but they left behind six sons and two daughters. The Evans family was spread out from Quilpie to Charleville. All of the children had elected to come back to Australia after completing their mission obligation to their church. Ranching had become the family's main business, and business had been very good for the Evans family, at least until now.

Stan was the eldest son of the family and, by default, the leader and business head. He had first met his wife, Ruby, while on a fishing trip to Lake Eyre nearly 30 years ago. It was love at first sight for both Stan and Ruby, but there was a problem. Missionaries had heavily influenced Ruby's family, as well, and she, too, was active in church, but it was not the same church. Ruby's family members were all Methodists, and they had been so much longer than Stan had been a part of this false religion which, of course, was his entire life. Stan and Ruby's relationship soon became as dysfunctional as Romeo and Juliet's had been. They were both considered pagans by each other's families, and the only time they could see each other was when they slipped away during the night. This went on for over a year until the inevitable happened. Ruby became pregnant.

One evening, late as usual, Stan crept down past an old bridge that spanned the Cooper Creek. This was where he and Ruby generally met. There were other places, but this had always been their primary meeting place. He waited for over an hour for Ruby, but she didn't show. Stan couldn't understand what could have happened to her. After all, it was Saturday night, and they always met on Saturday nights. After waiting another 20 minutes he decided to take a chance and sneak over to Ruby's house. Using the back roads he walked by the light of the large, yellow moon. Approaching Ruby's farm Stan hid himself behind an old eucalyptus tree.

Stan stared at the house, but he could see no activity other than a small light in the living room window. He began to get depressed. *I guess she can't get out,* he thought to himself. About that time he saw a shadow cross the living room floor. Just then the light went out. He decided to wait it out. "Maybe she had to wait for them to go to bed," he whispered to himself.

Twenty minutes passed when he suddenly heard quiet footsteps approaching. Stan's stomach began to growl and his hands began to perspire heavily. Turning his head, he flattened his body as close to the tree as possible. The footsteps were closer now. He listened intently as the steps continued. Snap! *What was that?* Stan held his breath as he listened carefully. All of a sudden the noise of the steps stopped.

"Who's there?" said a soft voice.

As Stan turned his head towards the voice, relief filled his body, and he stepped out from behind the tree. The yellow moonlight accented Ruby's natural beauty as she stood there in fear.

"It's me," he whispered.

Ruby stood frozen, and then suddenly she began to cry. Stan moved in and covered her in his arms.

"I'm sorry I scared you," he said gently. "When you didn't come to the bridge, I got worried and—"

Before he could even finish, Ruby whispered in his ear, "I'm pregnant."

Ruby worked his grip loose and backed up to look into his face. Stan could see shimmers of silver reflect off her short curly hair. "What did you say?" Stan asked.

"I'm pregnant!" As she began once again to cry aloud, Stan moved closer to hug her.

"It will be all right!" he said as he tried to console her. "I am here, and this is where I am going to stay."

******

The day finally came for Ruby to tell her parents about her current physical condition. Stan had wanted to be there with Ruby as she told them, but Ruby thought otherwise. Stan persisted but, in the end, Ruby's will was stronger than his courage. They both agreed to tell their parents separately but at the same time. They chose Saturday of the following week as the best time to drop the bomb.

Ruby spent the better part of the day planning what she was going to say while Stan spent the better part of the day just trying to get his father away from the rest of his siblings long enough to tell him. Finally his chance came when his father said he was heading out to fix the fence in the north pasture. Stan volunteered to help him before his father could draft another one of his brothers. His dad was a bit surprised by his desire to help. It seemed that lately Stan spent most of his time daydreaming instead of working.

Father and son drove along the bumpy, dirt road in the heat of the day. "So what's on your mind?" Mr. Evans asked calmly. Stan looked at his father in surprise and shame. Fear began to replace his desire to tell his dad about his problem. "Speak up, Son."

Stan cleared his throat and then cleared his throat again. "You know Ruby, don't you, Dad?" Mr. Evans began to slow the truck down as he turned off the road into a big green pasture. Stan searched for the right words to say, but could not find any that would work for him.

His dad stopped the truck and turned off the engine. Turning towards Stan, he asked, "Is she pregnant?"

His father's deductive reasoning stunned Stan. "Yes," he said as he hung his head in shame.

******

Just a few miles away Ruby and her mother were in the kitchen preparing the evening meal. "Are you feeling okay, Ruby?" her mother asked. Ruby looked towards her mom as she stirred the pot over the stove. "You've been quiet all day."

Tears began to stream down Ruby's face as she dropped the spoon on the counter. Ruby's mother walked over to where she stood and put her arms around her lovingly. "What is it?" she inquired.

Ruby backed away from her mother and, with a deep breath, she spoke as boldly as she could, "I'm pregnant!"

Her courage was commendable, but her timing was poor to say the least. At the very moment she spoke the words, her father pushed his way through the door into the kitchen. A horrible look of anger filled his face, and simultaneously a look of terror filled Ruby's. Tonight was going to a very long night for her. Ruby's father's indignation was fueled by the knowledge that the father of his soon-to-be grandchild was Stan Evans, one of many believers of a false religion.

******

It had been a difficult adjustment for Ruby to leave her family and church to enter Stan's, but it was thought to be the only logical solution. Besides, Ruby's father considered it the lesser of two evils. Better to have the shame of her in this false religion than for the community to become aware of her unwed pregnancy.

Ruby soon came to love Stan's family as they did her. The only area of her life that was not settled, nor would it ever be, was her involvement in Stan's church. At first it didn't seem too different from her own Methodist church, but over time she began to see significant differences that went against her Christian upbringing. The church referenced the King James Bible often, but it never really studied its contents. In fact, it was the church's belief that the Bible was an inaccurate account of God. In particular it was considered an inaccurate account of Jesus.

Throughout many years together Ruby would often ask Stan for clarification about the contradictions between the Bible and the book containing the guidelines governing Stan's church. Stan did his best to explain to her the revelation given to the church founder by a mysterious angel and what it meant for them today. After many years of dissatisfying answers to her questions, Ruby simply quit asking for clarification. No matter how hard she tried, Ruby could never accept the idea that when she died, she would become Stan's spiritual wife along with many others and that she and the other women would populate Stan's new planet with spirit children. *The Bible teaches that we will be as spirits in Heaven and not given unto marriage, at least in the usual sense of the word,* she told herself. *Besides, in 30 years of marriage I've had 10 children, and there's no way I'm having any more.*

Stan had his own doubts about his church. In fact, it had always bothered him that Jesus was considered to be the brother of Lucifer. It didn't make sense that an all-powerful God would have a Son as evil as the Devil. Furthermore, the Bible states in so many places that Christ was God's only Son. Over time Stan became accustomed to the many differences between the Bible and the church's teachings and, if it still bothered him, he never let it show.

******

It was 9:00 a.m., but the sky was as black as night. In fact, it had been more than three days since the sun's intense rays had been able to break through the dense black smoke. Fires had been raging through Australia for nearly two weeks, and there was no relief in sight.

It was at Darwin where the first lightning strike set a tree ablaze in the middle of an incredibly dry field, and the flames spread uncontrollably from there. Presently a storm was building in the Timor Sea, and with it came the hope that the northwestern part of Australia would finally see some rain. Unfortunately the only thing to come out of this storm so far was a spectacular display of lightning and thunder. Millions of misguided volts of electricity continued to strike the dry county as the storm moved southeast, thus igniting fires as it went slowly by. To date there were over 80 different fires, and nearly all of them were burning out of control.

At first it looked like the smokejumpers and fire crews would be able to contain these outbursts. After all, it took fuel to keep a fire going, and after eight months of draught, there wasn't much left in most places to burn. Unfortunately the winds had picked up considerably, packing gusts well above 45 miles per hour. These winds fanned the flames, enabling the fire to jump from fuel source to fuel source. Fifteen unlucky smokejumpers had already been trapped between two separate blazes and were burned to death. Planes and helicopters were used to try and suppress the fires with fire retardant chemicals, but the severe winds and dense smoke made this impossible. After one of the helicopters crashed into the heart of one of the largest of the fires, all further aerial efforts were halted. The focus was now on redirecting the flames away from the many towns directly in the paths of these infernos.

Ruby had been given specific instructions from Stan to take their only daughter and their two young sons down into their survival pod if the fires got any closer to their ranch. Stan, like many of his brothers and others from his church in Quilpie, had professionally installed survival pods buried some 25 feet under ground. Stan's was one of the larger pods since he had one of the largest families.

Ruby and Stan had always planned on 10 children. However, pneumonia took away two of their sons more than 15 years earlier and two more of their oldest sons were married and ranching up in Charleville. This still left six children with Stan and Ruby to occupy the 15'x30' underground dwelling. Stan believed in being prepared. In fact, that was one of the basic principles preached in his church. He prided himself on being able to survive nearly any catastrophe. His pod was full of life support items like food and water enough to survive an entire year if necessary. Stan also kept enough filters in his pod to ensure a clean air supply from the outside vents. If conditions were not radioactive, then his filters would last him even longer than his food supply.

The pod itself was powered by solar energy harnessed from the large, above-ground panels. There was enough available power stored in the huge batteries to run the climate control system and lighting in the pod without fear of this power supply ever running out, at least as long as the panels and batteries stayed intact.

It had been two days since Ruby had heard anything from Stan or the three sons he took with him. The men of the town of Quilpie were all dug in six miles below Cooper Creek. They were holding their ground trying to redirect the fire and thereby hopefully save their small town. Ruby hadn't been able to contact her two sons in Charleville either. Apparently the phone lines were all down. She knew her two older sons would be in the middle of the danger trying to save their own town and families. She had a lot to be worried about.

******

"The wind is shifting!" shouted one of the men who was dug in below Stan. "The fire is changing directions again."

Stan could sense it was time to go. He hoped Ruby could see the fire coming and get to the pod safely. He needed to get there too, but first he had to recover his sons from the fire brigade. "It's over. We've lost," said

Stan to the fire fighters around him. "Get home to your families and clear out right away!" The men dropped their shovels in disgust and disappointment. The exhausted men looked at each other with grave concern in each set of eyes. "Take care!" shouted Stan.

I've got to find my boys quickly, he told himself. The fire had begun to move around behind the fire line, and it wouldn't be long before anyone left in this location would be trapped for good.

Stan began to run the distance from line to line looking for his children. Panic began to replace concern. Finally he found two of his sons working hard to smother a fire that had moved behind them. "We have to go!" he said to his sons. "The fire is moving in behind us, and we will be trapped if we don't leave now. Where's your big brother?"

"The last time we saw him," said one of the boys, "was up about a mile, right next to the creek."

Stan's heart sank when he heard this. *A mile up...There isn't enough time to get there and back before this area would be a raging inferno,* Stan moaned. "You boys head back to the ranch and get your mother into the pod. I'll get your brother."

Stan left his boys and began to run as hard as he could towards the creek. Both of his sons knew that their father was risking his life to find their older brother, Christopher, and there was no way they were just going to head home and leave him behind to die. They both began to run in their father's direction, keeping a safe distance behind so as not to be seen by him.

Stan reached the next fire line in 10 minutes. All of the men there were grabbing their gear and heading back in the direction from which he had just come. Stan recognized one of the men heading his way. Stopping the man, he asked if he had seen his son.

"Yes," said the man. "Earlier—up by the creek."

The man grabbed Stan's arm as he turned to head towards the creek. "The fire there is out of control. You can't go up there!"

Stan pulled away from the man's grip and ran on with his sons close behind. The smoke was becoming dangerously thick, and Stan could feel the fire's heat. He knew it was close. As he reached the creek, he saw a small group of men wading across. He scanned the group intensely, hoping that his son was among them. From behind his two boys caught up to him. Stan was stunned to see them there. "I told you to go home!" he said angrily.

"We're not leaving you out here, Dad!"

Pride and love for his brave young children replaced his anger. He turned towards the sound of someone yelling. It was coming from the middle of the creek. It was Christopher, his lost son. Stan and the boys ran to the creek and helped the teenager out of the water. It was a happy family reunion, but it wouldn't last long.

"We have to get out of here!" warned Stan.

"Follow us, mister," said one of the men as he climbed out of the creek. "We are heading east around this fire."

"East!" cried Stan. "But the wind has changed direction. The fire will be worse that way."

"Mister, you go whichever way you want to. We're going east!"

Stan stood there as the men ran by.

"What should we do?" one of his sons asked. "We go south!" shouted Stan, "But first, I want everyone to take off your shirts and soak them in the creek." Stan and his three boys stood in the middle of Cooper Creek soaking their shirts. "Okay, now wrap them around your face like this." Stan demonstrated for his children by placing his soaking wet shirt over his nose and mouth as he tied the arms of the shirt behind his head. The children followed their father's example as he walked behind checking each knot. "Put your coats back on and let's go!" he said anxiously.

******

Ruby could see the fire coming her way as she looked through the kitchen window. The field was a wall of fast-moving orange flames. As she gazed into the horrible scene, things became even worse. Running through the field were numerous cattle kicking and bellowing. Some were on fire as they ran. This sickening scene was too much for Ruby. She turned away and began to cry. "Where are my boys and Stan?" she asked aloud through the tears.

"We have to get to the pod!" she said. Ruby gathered up her children and headed out the back door. The dense smoke and hot embers were overwhelming, and the wind gusts made it difficult to walk. Ruby and her children held hands tightly as they struggled to make the short distance to the survival pod.

******

Visibility was poor to say the least, and Stan couldn't make out the landmarks from where they were. There was too much smoke. To make matters worse, nightfall was nearly upon them. The shirts tied around the young men's faces had quickly become covered with ash and soot, and Stan's heart began to sink as he looked at his frightened children. The fire was no more than 100 yards away, approaching from the north as they ran south. Stan started to wonder if he had made a mistake by not going east with the other men from Cooper Creek.

"I know where we are!" exclaimed Christopher. "I used to ride out here to look for snakes."

"Are you sure?" Stan asked.

"Yes, Father, if we turn east from here, it is a straight line to our house. It's only a couple of miles further down."

Stan was encouraged by his son's insight. Looking over his shoulder at the fire, Stan urged them on. "Let's go quickly!"

******

Ruby and her crying children sat huddled together on one of the cots from within the pod.

"Where's Daddy?" little Carrie asked.

"He and your brothers should be here any minute." Ruby tried to mask her own fear and sorrow. She knew the fire must be very close to the house by this time.

Suddenly there was a noise down at the other end of the pod. Ruby stood in surprise. First down the ladder was Christopher, and then the other two boys followed. Eventually Stan made his entrance. Ruby ran to him and buried her head in his chest and cried uncontrollably as his daughter and youngest sons wrapped their arms around his waist.

This portion of the Evans family was lucky, although it would be days before they could leave their underground dwelling. It would be another week before Stan and Ruby would learn that both of their oldest sons and their families had burned to death over in Charleville trying to save their homes.

******

Thousands of miles away across the South Pacific fires raged out of control as well. In the town of Esperanza, Argentina, the city's dwellers prepared to evacuate as quickly as possible. The fires were not entirely a surprise to the people of the city. They had been experiencing a very harsh drought for the last couple of years, as was all of Argentina.

It was believed that the strange water temperatures of *La Nina* contributed to their lack of rain. There were also other more disconcerting reasons for this particular drought. South America relied heavily on its rainforest to provide the necessary atmosphere needed to generate rainfall and, in fact, there just was not enough forest left to help reduce the effects of the drought.

In addition, there were also the effects of the ozone hole centered over the lower part of Argentina with the eye directly over Punta Arenas, Chile. The size of this hole was constantly changing with each season, but from the Antarctic outward the ozone hole had grown to be four times as large as the continental United States. All of this added up to no rain.

Fires had been breaking out for months, and they had been successfully fought from the air until now. The change in wind direction from the southeast to the northwest had begun to push the smoke and fire towards the Cordillera of the Andes. The build up of smoke made it impossible for the fires to be snubbed out by air any longer and with the lack of rain came a lack of snow pack for the Andes. The *Eternal Snows* were no more. Nearly all of Argentina's grasslands were on fire, as was a good portion of Chile's, or they soon would be. Like Australia, the only hope for Argentina was for it to rain, and that wasn't going to happen anytime soon. The food supply in all of these dry countries was about to go up in flames—literally.

Chapter 11 - The Sand Storm

A storm was brewing in the Mediterranean Sea. It was the kind of storm that rarely came, but when it did, disaster came with it. The intense heat brought on by the horrendous drought throughout all of Northern Africa was having a terrible effect on weather patterns throughout the African continent and Asia Minor. The storm now building out in the middle of the Mediterranean Sea was pulling downward towards Egypt, and with it came an intense wind referred to as a *sirocco*. These were the sorts of winds that brought about sand storms large enough to bury an entire city the size of Cairo. Fortunately for Cairo, these winds were not heading in that direction.

Already the sand had risen hundreds of feet into the air as the hot wind blew from the sea across Egypt in a circular motion. The currents would carry the sand a great distance from the Red Sea and up past Jerusalem, burying everything in its path.

******

The fighting had become stalemate. It wasn't much of a fight in the first place. The entire region of Sederot had been disarmed on both sides. The PLO and the Israelis were very close to a peace settlement, and nobody wanted trouble at this point in the negotiations.

The new prime minister of Israel was a man typically unwilling to compromise for the sake of peace. This was not unusual for Israeli leaders. There was, however, an extremely high level of western political pressure for this new prime minister to find some solution to the violence.

The whole concept of peace had been foreign to the Palestinians and Israelis since the beginning of history, but history was about to change once and for all! It seemed at long last both sides were tired of fighting over the same small piece of land. The death toll from Biblical accounts until today had been incalculable. And all for nothing more than a small section of sand called *The West Bank*.

Although a peace agreement was imminent, there were still those who were vehemently opposed to any talk of peace. Among the opposition was a 16-year-old Palestinian girl, Jasmine Hamar. She was the daughter of an extremely violent man who had been an enemy of the Israelis for many years until his recent death.

Jasmine held every Jewish man, woman, and child responsible for her father's demise, and it was her intention to exact vengeance in her own small way. It didn't matter to Jasmine that her father had blown himself up trying to plant a homemade bomb in a shopping mall in downtown Sederot. It didn't matter to her that many innocent people had been killed along with her father. As far as she was concerned, the only good Jew was a dead Jew. In fact, her Muslim beliefs dictated that she oppose all other beliefs and, if necessary, kill the pagan non-Muslims.

Jasmine had never killed anyone herself, but she knew that her father had. There was a long family history of this kind of violence. It was all she had ever known, and now that there was serious talk of a lasting peace, Jasmine feared for her family's future.

It wasn't just the majority of the Palestinians that opposed the coming peace. In fact, there was considerably more opposition from the Israelis than had been expected. As a result, the Israeli government went to great lengths to ensure things did not get out of hand before a treaty could be signed. The military police had been alerted and dispatched to the violence-prone locations just in case trouble broke out. These included the Gaza and outlying towns such as Sederot. They had been instructed to use tear gas and rubber bullets whenever necessary. The last thing the PLO and Israeli leaders wanted right now was a bunch of dead and wounded civilians from the fighting in the streets.

The word was out that the military police were moving into Sederot before sunset. Elisha found all of this amusing. A native to Sederot, this 18-year-old had seen his fair share of fighting. And although no one in his immediate family had ever been involved or hurt during any of this violence, he still had a heart full of hate towards the PLO. Elisha Kaufman was from the tribe of Levi and, as far as he knew, the men in his family had always been men of peace—rabbis. Still, as a student of the Torah, Elisha knew that God had not intended the Jewish nation to share the land that had been given to Abraham with any other nation, especially not the Palestinians.

Elisha had made up his mind that he would do whatever he could to disrupt the peace process. "Besides," he thought, "the police are only using rubber bullets, and how bad can that hurt?"

******

Two days had gone by since Elisha had slipped away from his father's house. The first day had been full of excitement as he and many of the young men from his neighborhood taunted the PLO in that area. They had vandalized homes and businesses without any of them getting caught. The few skirmishes that they had gotten into had only resulted in rock throwing, name calling, and a couple of fist-fights. None of this, of course, would put much of a dent in the peace process.

Evening was falling on the second day, and the weather was starting to turn ugly, as was the violence. Elisha and the other boys had broken into the back of one of the local businesses. As they ransacked the building, one of the young men stumbled across an automatic weapon. The boy held his prize over his head as he yelled and danced in victory. The sight of this gun made Elisha nervous. It was one thing to go around pestering the neighborhood and chucking a few rocks at some old windows. But a gun was something altogether different.

"Let's go!" said one of the boys. All 12 young men ran out of the building with Elisha not far behind.

"Where are we going?" asked one of the boys. It was obvious where they were going. They were heading directly into a Palestinian neighborhood.

This is not good, Elisha thought.

About this time the wind really began to gust. Elisha could feel the sting of something hitting his face, but he was running so hard just to keep up with the group that he didn't have time to evaluate the pain's true source.

******

Only a small ring of orange and purple could be seen as the sun said its goodnight to Sederot. Jasmine and a dozen or so of the neighborhood teenagers were busy planning their retaliation for the recent vandalism of their district. None of the children had access to any serious weapons, so the first thing on their agenda was to invent some. Twenty-three wine bottles were lined up in a row as if on an assembly line. One of the larger boys was filling each bottle with gasoline as its original contents were emptied. Behind him a young boy was stuffing each filled bottle with a torn strip of cloth that obviously came from some mother's linen closet. Finally Jasmine picked up each rag-stuffed bottle and taped the neck tightly to keep the rag from falling out until impact.

******

Jasmine and the rest of the Palestinian gang moved through the streets quietly to avoid being caught. In the center of town military police had been stationed to deter any violence. There were patrols moving throughout the streets every 15 minutes or so to ensure peace in the area.

The large boy held up his hand, signaling for all the rest to stop. Jasmine moved up closer to see what was going on. Coming around the corner from two blocks up the street was a small band of young men, Elisha among them, and all of them completely unaware of the trap that was soon to be sprung.

The young PLO leader pointed to three of the gang members to move behind an old pickup truck. He then motioned to the rest to spread out among the cars and trees of the neighborhood. Jasmine followed the leader to a narrow strip between two houses. They both knelt in waiting as Elisha and the other boys approached.

This is a mistake, Elisha told himself. *I should just go home.*

Excitement welled up in Jasmine's stomach as she waited anxiously for the next move. The large boy beside Jasmine peered around the building momentarily; then, returning, he fished into his pocket until he came out with a small lighter. Cupping the flame in his hands to hide the sparks, he lit the wick of the bottle. Standing up slowly the boy stepped out into the dark street.

The surprise was complete. Neither Elisha nor his friends had any idea of what was coming. The leader yelled loudly and tossed the Molotov cocktail in the direction of two Jewish boys as they stood in fear. The bottle exploded on impact only a yard away from the two surprised children. Instantly both boys were covered in the fiery liquid. Their screams of pain could be heard throughout the neighborhood. Porch lights went on all around as other bottles of flaming gasoline came flying in from every direction.

The scene took on the appearance of a battlefield. Four of the young boys were rolling on the ground completely engulfed in flames and screaming in agony. The sight of the burning boys was more than Jasmine had bargained for. It seemed a lot easier to hate someone than it did to actually kill them. The odor of gas and burnt flesh pierced her nostrils until she finally became ill from the smell.

Elisha fell to the ground as three more bottles exploded in front of him. He felt pain as pieces of glass sprayed his face. Blood began to ooze from the numerous cuts in his forehead and cheeks. Adding insult to injury, the wind began to blow fiercely, pelting all the young adults with the stinging sand. The scene was chaos. Sirens could be heard quickly approaching from the distance. Elisha staggered to his feet just in time to see the young Israeli with a gun pointed directly at the Palestinian boy who had thrown the first gas bomb. The armed young man opened fire and cut the large boy to pieces in an instant. Elisha was sickened by what he had seen. None of this had turned out the way he had first believed it would.

Through the smoke and sand-filled air, Elisha could see bodies still burning. His heart mourned, as he could not see any movement in the bodies. Instead they lay still and lifeless in the street. He could see the young Israeli still firing his gun at other targets as they ran for cover.

Numerous emergency vehicles arrived quickly on the scene with sirens blaring and spotlights that lit up the battlefield. The children began to run in every direction as the soldiers came running in. The young man with the gun approached Elisha as they both attempted to run away, but three of the Israeli soldiers spotted the boy's weapon and opened fire on him before he reached Elisha. The young man was knocked backwards from the many rounds fired directly at him. He was dead before he hit the ground. *I thought they were supposed to use rubber bullets!* Elisha was terrified. A light shone on him, and he froze where he stood.

Jasmine was still hiding between the two houses when a soldier found her. "Hands over your head!" he said angrily. Jasmine could not believe the scene before her own eyes. What had she gotten herself into?

The sandstorm was intensifying so much that the soldiers were not able to pursue the other guilty individuals.

******

After being thoroughly searched, both Jasmine and Elisha were placed in the back of a military transport. They sat on benches on either side of the truck facing each other. Both of the angry and frightened youths looked at the rear doors as they closed behind them. The doors had no handles on the inside, but there were two small windows halfway up the doors allowing light to come in. The cab of the vehicle was separated from the passenger compartment by a steel reinforced wall.

Moving along, they had a bumpy ride in the back of the vehicle. Elisha found it curious that neither he nor Jasmine had been handcuffed. *Maybe they want us to kill each other,* he though sarcastically. *Or maybe they were in such a great hurry to get out of the path of the fiercely pelting sand they just forgot.*

Elisha was beginning to understand what his father had always preached to him. "We are Levites. It is our place to serve God and teach others. It is not our place to get involved in politics or violence," his father would say.

Why didn't I listen to him? Elisha's mind cried out.

Jasmine sat huddled up in the corner of the military vehicle. Her eyes burned with anger towards Elisha, but in her heart there was confusion over the events of the night. The sight of death up close had a severe impact on her. It all seemed so pointless! *What did we accomplish?* she wondered. *Is this the kind of stuff my father used to do?*

Outside the storm was ferocious! The wind and sand pelted the truck, blowing it off course continually. Elisha began to feel nauseated from all the motion, as did Jasmine. It was like being in the bottom of a fishing boat during a hurricane. Sand drifts moved across the road in front of the truck as it struggled to push ahead. The sand was already piling up on the sides of the streets, many feet deep in some places.

The vehicle continued on slowly for another half hour or so before coming to a steep hill. Here the sand on the road was piled up as high as the truck's front bumper. The driver locked the vehicle into four-wheel low gear and began to inch his way up the hill. About two-thirds of the way up, the truck's tires began to spin. The vehicle crawled forward for another hundred feet or so before it came to a complete halt. In a state of panic, the driver and his partner abandoned the truck and tried to walk through the storm towards their outpost. It would be months before the bodies of these two soldiers would be uncovered from beneath many feet of sand.

******

Five hours had gone by as the vehicle continued to sway and toss back and forth. It wasn't until the wind let up momentarily that Jasmine and Elisha realized that the truck was no longer moving.

"How long have we been stopped?" Elisha asked Jasmine before he had a chance to remember that she was his enemy.

Jasmine leered at Elisha without saying a word.

Another four hours passed while the truck continued to be pelted by the sand and wind. *The sun should have been up by now*, Elisha thought. He moved forward to the rear window and tried to peer out. All he could see was darkness. *I don't understand,* he thought to himself. *Even in a sand storm I ought to be able to tell the light from the dark. Why can't I see the sunlight?* The answer hit him even before he was through with the question. "Oh, my God!" he cried. "We're buried!"

This time Jasmine didn't ignore Elisha. "We're what?" she asked angrily.

"It's the sand," he said. "We're buried under the sand!"

Jasmine moved towards the rear window and looked out. She saw nothing but darkness as well. "Then why can we still breathe?" she asked.

Elisha looked up at a small vent in the roof which was being illuminated by a little rectangular dome light. "I guess that vent is giving us air."

"How long will that last?" she inquired.

"The wind is blowing pretty hard, so I don't think any sand has piled up on the vent yet."

"And when the wind slows down?" she asked rhetorically.

"Yes, that might be a problem."

Thirteen more hours passed before the winds finally subsided. The air in the back of the military vehicle was dangerously thin. One other problem was beginning to take its toll on Jasmine and Elisha. They had been in the truck for nearly 24 hours, and they both had a terrible need to evacuate their bladders.

Finally Jasmine spoke up. "I have to go to the bathroom!"

"Me too," said Elisha.

"I can't breathe very well either," she said.

"Me either!" Elisha returned.

Jasmine was growing annoyed with Elisha. "Well, what are we going to do?" Her anger was showing.

"First things first," said Elisha. "You go over by the door and relieve yourself and then I'll do the same."

Jasmine looked at Elisha suspiciously.

"I'll stand in that corner," he pointed forward.

What choice do I have? she thought. *Five more minutes and I'll wet myself.*

Elisha moved forward as Jasmine headed for the double doors. The anticipation of relief was nearly more than Elisha could stand, and the sound of running water was almost too much for him.

Finally, after Jasmine and Elisha had traded places and their immediate business was resolved satisfactorily, they turned their attention to survival and escape.

"Do you think the storm is over?" she asked.

"I don't know. Maybe."

"Then they should be coming for us, right?"

Elisha looked directly into Jasmine's beautiful brown eyes. They were full of fear. Looking at her, Elisha was just now aware of how young and pretty she was. "If they are even looking for us, it is unlikely that they'll find us. This vehicle must be nearly buried by now," Elisha was relatively sure of that.

"Then what will we do—just sit here and die of dehydration?"

Probably, Elisha thought to himself. It was certain that they would not be able to get the back doors open. They had no tools, and there were no handles. It was also a near certainty that no one was looking for them or at least, if they were, they would never find them in time. "Our only hope," he said thoughtfully, "is if we can get out through the vent in the roof."

Jasmine looked at the vent and then over to Elisha. *What was a guy like this doing here in the first place?* she wondered. There was no way he could have any experience fighting against the PLO. "Well, I may be able to fit through that vent if you can get me up there and if I can knock that cover off." Jasmine pointed up. "But you'll never fit through that hole."

Elisha was already aware of that fact, but better to save one of them if not both. Elisha looked at Jasmine. "Well, after sitting here for a few days without food or water, I'll probably be able to slide right through that little hole." Both Jasmine and Elisha laughed painfully.

"We're running out of air, so we have to do something soon," Elisha was voicing the thought already in Jasmine's mind.

"Can you lift me up there?" she asked as she looked up at the vent.

"I think so."

They were both becoming fatigued from lack of good air and from dehydration. Elisha interlaced his fingers and hoisted Jasmine up to the vent. Jasmine pushed against the metal cover with as much strength as she could muster, but it didn't budge a single inch.

"It won't move!"

"Try again!" Elisha strained to hold her up.

Jasmine changed her grip and pushed against the panel. It moved slightly this time with a squeak and then stopped. "I can't do it!"

"Yes, you can. You have to. Try again!" encouraged Elisha.

With tears in her eyes, Jasmine pushed until she screamed. Finally the vent made a loud popping noise and toppled off its bracket.

Sand poured down onto both Jasmine and Elisha. Elisha lost his footing and fell to the bottom of the truck with Jasmine landing directly on top of him. Through the small hole in the roof he could see the stars as their distant light twinkled. The fresh air came rushing into the vehicle as if it were being blown in. The air brought strength back to both of them.

"Okay!" he said with renewed vigor. "I'll lift you up again, and this time try to work your way out of the hole. Don't get stuck!"

"I'll try!" Her voice showed courage and determination. Elisha hoisted her up once again. This time he brought Jasmine's feet up to his shoulders to allow her to push off of him as she struggled to release herself from the tiny hole. Finally she was out of the truck and free.

Looking down through the roof, Jasmine stared at Elisha for a moment before she disappeared. *Well, at least one of us will live,* Elisha sighed.

Jasmine stood on the roof of the truck staring out through the night sky into the endless valley. The moon shone across the landscape giving it the appearance of a vast, turbulent sea. In every direction there were enormous mounds of sand piled up. It was an incredible and beautiful sight to behold. She jumped off the roof and onto a mound of sand lodged against the side of the vehicle, sinking nearly to her knees as she landed.

Working her way free, Jasmine began to walk slowly away from the truck. Not yet 50 yards away, Jasmine paused. She wanted to leave her enemy trapped in the vehicle. She knew he would die a horrible, lonely death. *This is what he deserves,* she told herself, trying to remember the hate she had grown up with—the hate her father gave his life for.

Jasmine took another step and, as she sank deeply into the sand again, she paused to consider the boy she had abandoned. "Why can't I do this?" she asked in a soft voice.

Inching her way back to the truck, Jasmine cleared the sand away from the passenger window and looked inside the cab. There in the ignition reflecting the moon's light were the keys to the military vehicle. *Hopefully,* Jasmine thought, *one of those keys will unlock the back doors.*

Jasmine cleared the sand away from the passenger door until she could finally get the door open enough to slide in and reach the keys. She was beginning to feel like a gopher as she burrowed her way to the back doors of the truck with keys in hand. "I hope that one of these work," she said aloud.

Another 15 minutes passed before Elisha heard a tiny sound outside the doors of the military vehicle. *What is that noise? It sounds like termites.*

The clatter grew louder until Elisha recognized the sound of metal scratching metal. Suddenly one of the doors began to move very slightly until it was opened a couple of inches.

"Push!" said the beautiful, welcome voice of Jasmine. Elisha moved quickly to the door and began to push with all his might. The door opened another six inches or so. He could not see anyone behind the door, but he knew Jasmine was there somewhere.

"Climb back on top of the truck, and I'll try to open this door," he instructed.

Jasmine climbed onto the roof of the truck, and with her feet she pushed against the door with all her strength. From the inside Elisha put his shoulder into it as well. The door began to move and then finally it stopped firmly against the sand.

"That's all we're going to get," he said.

"Try to climb out," she urged.

Elisha wasn't a very heavy young man, but he was broad and tall. "I'll try!" he said.

Jasmine held the door open with her legs until she thought she would die from exhaustion. Finally Elisha liberated himself from the truck and climbed up to meet Jasmine on the roof. The freedom was invigorating, as was the fresh air.

"Why did you come back?" he asked as he rested on the top of the prison that once held them.

"I never left," she said solemnly. "Besides, I think I've seen enough death to last me a while."

******

Jasmine and Elisha wandered over the sandy hills until they came down into a small valley. In the moonlight, these hills shimmered like glass. Everything as far as the eye could see was covered in sand. It was very difficult and tiresome to walk. Many times they found themselves wading through near waist-high sand heading towards the only recognizable sign they had been able to find. It was the sound of water—beautiful, wonderful, running water—something both of them needed desperately.

Eventually they reached the river, but it was hard to tell where the sand ended and the water began.

"Be careful!" said Elisha. "If we fall in here, we'll drown for sure."

"I'm thirsty!" she replied.

"I know, but let me go first"

Jasmine stood by and watched as Elisha bravely crawled out to the river's edge. Underneath his knees he could feel the sand eroding. "I think it will hold us long enough to crawl out here and have a drink, but we better hurry." Following his example, she wormed her way out to the river's edge. With her hand she scooped up the water to drink, while Elisha simply stuck his head down into the river. Prudence was a virtue he didn't possess, but after tasting a large mouthful of salty water, Elisha would be more cautious in the future.

"Yuck!" he cried out. "This water is all salt."

Jasmine was disappointed and still just as thirsty—maybe even more now that she had tasted the salt. The sand beneath Elisha and Jasmine started to give way. "Run!" shouted Elisha as he sprang back towards the more solid ground. Jasmine was there even before he was. "We need to move on," he said.

The wind was starting to pick up again, and it was a safe bet that more sand was on its way. "We need to find water!" Jasmine said desperately.

Just then there was a tremendous gust. "We need to find a shelter or we'll be buried alive!" Elisha corrected her as he protected his eyes from the blast of sand. The wind began to blow even harder, and Jasmine was quick to see his point.

The two of them wandered through the sandstorm for hours unaware that the sun was up because it was hidden by the sand-filled air. Fatigue had set in, and it wouldn't be long before neither of them would be able to go on. As the storm was intensifying, things were getting more and more desperate.

"I can't go any further!" Jasmine cried.

"We have to!" Elisha insisted.

"I can't!"

"Yes, you can! Just a little further and we'll find something. I am sure of it!" Elisha began to pray to God to save him and Jasmine from this certain death. Jasmine began to pray also.

Fifteen minutes later Jasmine could not continue on. There was no strength left in her body, and she fell to the ground thoroughly exhausted. As Elisha tried to lift her up, he realized it was no use. There was not enough strength left in him to carry her.

"Leave me" she said in a whisper.

"I won't leave you," he replied. She hadn't abandoned him, and he surely wasn't going to abandon her.

Elisha sat beside Jasmine holding her head and sheltering her face from the raging sand. "Lord!" Elisha cried out in desperation, "Forgive us both and allow us to enter Your kingdom."

All of a sudden the wind was still, at least where Jasmine and Elisha were huddled. There was a calm that seemed to have a physical presence. The exhausted young woman struggled to sit up. Looking out at the desert, it seemed the storm was still raging except for where they rested.

Suddenly a bright light engulfed them where they lay. A soothing voice began to speak. "Your hearts have been changed, and now you can be of service to the Almighty. Time is short, and soon Christ will return for His church. You have much work to do. Follow my light, and I will give you shelter."

Both young people trembled in fear as the light moved away from them. Again they were being bombarded by the sandstorm. Quickly they rose with renewed physical energy and ran forward into the light. As soon as they entered its protecting glow, the sandstorm could not reach them.

The young couple walked for a couple of hours, obediently following and trusting in the Heavenly light as it led them through the desert. Soon they came to the entrance of a small cave. They could hear running water from within the shelter.

The voice spoke again. "Take shelter here, and do not come out for 21 days."

"Lord!" said Elisha as he fell to his knees. "Twenty-one days? How will we survive?"

"Do not go to your knees for me. I am not the Almighty. You will survive by fasting and prayer," said the voice, "but if you become weak, the Lord will strengthen you. Have no fear, for God has chosen you both for His special purpose."

As the light moved above the cave and disappeared, the fierce winds began to blow again. Jasmine and Elisha rose quickly and made their way into the cave and toward the sound of running water.

******

Tomorrow the storm would be over, but the damage would last for years. Many cities were completely buried under the sand and along with them thousands of unfortunate people. All of the crops and livestock of that region were gone. This country had been known as the fifth largest producer of crops in the world, but now the question of the day was—how would they even be able to feed themselves?

Chapter 12 - The Interviews

It was now Thursday evening, and Zach would be home tomorrow. Stephanie and Timothy took advantage of his absence by spending every day together since he left for Rome. This particular evening had started off very pleasantly. Stephanie invited Timothy over for a home-cooked meal. The small table in the dining room of her apartment was tastefully decorated with spring flowers and two long tapers that were lit and flickering, adding ambiance.

Stephanie had taken the afternoon off just to prepare the meal. Her mother was Italian and had taught all her daughters how to cook when they were still very young. Tonight's dish was one of Stephanie's favorites. It was her mother's personal recipe for lasagna. She slid the garlic bread into the oven and turned the thermostat down to low. "There!" she said aloud. Her work was just about done.

While the lasagna was still cooking, Stephanie had dressed for the evening, wearing a peach-colored summer dress with a matching scarf tied around her neck. Initially she pulled her hair back into two small clips but later decided that it would look best falling naturally over her slender shoulders.

Moving to the living room, Stephanie sat in her glider and kicked off her sandals. Reaching over to the coffee table, she picked up her study Bible. *How many days has it been since I've read this?* she wondered.

Laying the book on her lap and closing her eyes, Stephanie began to speak softly, "Dear Lord, It's been a few days since we've spoken. As You already know, I've met a man, a really nice man, and I'm afraid I have been preoccupied. Please forgive me." Her prayer continued quietly for 10 minutes, and finally she closed by asking God to bless her relationship with Timothy. "…And please help him come to love You as I do," she asked. "Amen."

Stephanie turned in her Bible to 1 Corinthians. This was the section she had been working through. Today she read Chapter 15:51. *"Listen, I tell you a mystery,"* she read silently. *"We will not all sleep, but we will be changed in a flash, in a twinkling of an eye, at the last trumpet."*

What does this mean? Stephanie wondered as she read on. *"For the trumpet will sound, the dead will be raised imperishable, and we will be changed."* She pondered the mysterious verse. She knew it had something to do with the Rapture, or maybe it had something to do with the *Glorious Appearance of Christ*. She wasn't sure.

Just then her timer went off. "The bread's done," she said aloud. Setting her Bible back on the coffee table, Stephanie stood and headed for the kitchen.

******

Timothy showed up 15 minutes late but with a half dozen roses in his hand.

"How was your day?" she asked as they sat down to dinner.

"Okay, I guess," he commented, "kind of long, though. We had the building inspector out today."

"What does that mean?"

"Oh, I don't know," Timothy replied. "Just that this guy's kind of picky about everything and we had a lot of redo work."

It was obvious to Stephanie that he was a bit distracted, but she wasn't sure why. She dished him another plate of lasagna without asking if he'd like seconds.

"Thanks. It's really great!" Timothy's smile added emphasis.

"It's my mother's recipe," she said proudly.

"Really? Well, it's delicious!"

"Thanks!" she replied. *Okay, we're not making much progress here.*

All through dinner they made trivial little attempts at conversation. Eventually they found the subject of Zach and the hotel fire the most stimulating. Timothy shared his personal concern for his father's safety. "And this is the second time in just a month or so that he has come close to dying. I don't understand what's going on."

When dinner was over, they moved into the living room to enjoy their coffee. Timothy sat next to Stephanie on the small white sofa. "Well, my dad should be back tomorrow."

"Yes, he will. I guess he gets in about 5:00 p.m. Are you picking him up?" she asked.

"No, I think Mom is going to."

Stephanie wasn't surprised in the least to hear this. It had become very apparent to her that Zach and Valerie were still very much in love with each other.

Timothy sat his coffee down and looked at Stephanie fondly. "Thanks for dinner."

"My pleasure."

Timothy leaned in and kissed her gently on her soft pink lips. She kissed him back affectionately with her hands gently touching his arms. Timothy leaned in a little further until Stephanie was forced to lie back against the pillow on the arm of the sofa. Sensing the intensity of his kiss, she now understood why he had seemed so preoccupied. *He wants to take our relationship to the next level.* Stephanie began to inch her way back up along the arm of the couch as the kiss continued. *What should I do?* she wondered. Admittedly she wanted an adult relationship with him too, but she knew this wasn't the way. *I had an affair. It was wrong, and I have been forgiven for it.* Stephanie vowed to herself that she would have God's blessing on this relationship and that they would remain pure until marriage.

Stephanie put a hand gently on his chest and, with just a slight amount of pressure, she began to push him back. Timothy was surprised but very quick to respond. He had been thinking about this part of their relationship for a while now, but he had little experience and a lot of insecurities.

Stephanie sat up and reached out for Timothy's hand, but he did not offer it to her. The look on his face was one of embarrassment and frustration. "Maybe I'd better go," he said flatly.

She really loved him very much and understood what he was feeling. She felt the same way. "I don't want you to leave," Stephanie said softly. Timothy was thoroughly confused, and his face revealed it. "Let me try to explain this to you, okay?" Stephanie knew the day would come when she would have to explain her past relationship with Carl, but she had hoped it would be much later, perhaps after they were married.

"A while back before I started working for the news station," she said nervously, "I used to work for an evangelist. Somewhere along the line I got confused and thought I was in love with him." She wanted to look up and make eye contact with Timothy, though she was afraid of what she would see in his eyes.

"Did you sleep with him?" The disapproving look on his face was the very one that she feared she'd see.

"Yes," she said as she looked down again.

"Just once?" he asked.

"No," Stephanie whispered.

"Why'd you stop?" he asked, unable to hide his disgust.

Tears began to well up in Stephanie's eyes. *I'm going to lose him,* she felt sure. "Does it really matter?" she asked in defeat.

"It does to me!" he said.

Stephanie looked down at her feet as the tears began to stream down her face. "He was married," she cried.

"You must have known that before you had the affair, right?"

She nodded silently.

"So why did you stop? Let me guess. His wife caught you?" He got no response from Stephanie. "You mean that's it? His wife caught you?"

"I thought I was in love. I didn't consider the sin I was living in," she began to sob. "I asked God to forgive me and to help me live life the way I should, and that's why I want us to wait before we take the next step." She began to break down. "Don't you think I want to be with you as much as you want to be with me? I love you, Timothy, but I want God's blessing over us, and I can't live in sin anymore."

Stephanie sat silently waiting for him to reply. She wondered if she had lost him forever. Timothy didn't know what to think or what to say.

He felt jealous and betrayed even though he didn't even know Stephanie when all this had happened. He felt angry that once again God came between him and his own desires. He also felt angry with himself for allowing her to sit there crying without him putting his arms around her to comfort her, but he just couldn't bring himself to do what his heart told him. "I guess I'd better go," he said as he rose from the sofa.

Stephanie looked up at him with a pathetic, sorrowful look. "Please don't go, Timothy!" she begged. He took a handkerchief out of his pocket and dried her eyes.

"I have to go. I need time to figure this out."

Stephanie knew Timothy was a cave dweller and that was how he figured out his own emotions. She knew he had to go.

He let himself out the front door as she sat quietly on the couch. As soon as the door closed, Stephanie broke down and began to bawl. She knelt down and prayed earnestly. "Father!" she sobbed. "I know that I am reaping what I have sown, but Lord, please, please don't let me lose Timothy because of my past sins."

******

Valerie was at the Chicago airport an hour earlier than necessary. She was so anxious to see Zach that she just couldn't wait. As it turned out his plane was a little early, so she didn't have to wait very long after all. Valerie greeted Zach as soon as he stepped up the ramp by throwing her arms around his neck and kissing him. *What a pleasant surprise!* he thought. Zach felt the same way as Valerie. He couldn't wait to get back to Chicago to see her. The two of them walked out of the airport hand in hand.

******

A week had gone by since Stephanie had last heard from Timothy. She was beginning to show the signs of stress. When confronted by Scott about the day's interview with Izuho Saeki, the Japanese man who narrowly survived the 200-foot tidal wave, Stephanie was impatient and abrupt with him. "I have what I need for the interview, and I don't need your help."

Caught totally off guard, Scott walked away dejected. Zach overheard the conversation and moved towards Stephanie after Scott drifted away. As he reached out and put his hand on her shoulder, she began to cry. "I don't know what happened with you and Timothy, but I know that you two are meant for each other. He'll come around," Zach said encouragingly.

"Do you really think so?" Stephanie asked optimistically.

"Yes, I'm sure of it." Zach smiled, but the fact was, he wasn't sure about it, and frankly, he was worried. He and Valerie had hoped Timothy would marry her, but now something was wrong, and he didn't know what it was. *It's time to find out,* he told himself.

Zach knew Stephanie would be tied up all day with Izuho, so he took advantage of the opportunity to step out of the office. He wanted to locate his son and find out what was going on. He would have to walk a fine line with Timothy when approaching him about this. His boy was a very private and self-sufficient person like his father.

Zach dialed Timothy's cellular phone. "Hey, Timothy," he said cautiously.

"Dad," said Timothy, "is everything all right? Is Mom okay?"

"Yeah, everything is fine. I just wanted to see what you were doing for lunch."

Timothy knew that his father had a different motive in mind. He had never called and asked him to lunch before, but it didn't matter to Timothy. The fact was he missed his dad, and his problem with Stephanie, although personal, required some guidance. "Sure, Dad, let's have lunch. I'm in Rosemont today, so let's eat at Ditka's old place."

"Okay," said Zach relieved. "I'll see you at noon."

******

Stephanie picked up Izuho from O'Hare and brought him back to the station for the interview. She took him directly into Zach's office for an introduction. "How do you do, Mr. Saeki?" Zach greeted him with a handshake. "It is nice to meet you. I understand you are a lucky young man."

Izuho bowed slightly toward Zach and smiled in agreement. "Very lucky!" he said with some difficulty. Zach smiled at Stephanie. She was going to have a long day just trying to understand Izuho.

Next Stephanie took the young Asian man down to the camera room where she had taken the time to have the room set up with everything she would need for the interview. She had footage of the recent disaster in Okinawa, snacks for Izuho to eat, and a cameraman to tape the interview. She poured Izuho a cup of coffee and then poured one for herself. Taking a long sip, she tried to focus her mind on the task at hand. Stephanie was nervous because she had never done an interview before, and she was distraught over Timothy. She wanted these interviews to go well to impress Zach and Scott, but somehow that seemed less important to her today. "Okay, Mr. Saeki, I'd like to start by viewing the footage of the tsunami, and then I'd like to get your perspective on what happened." Her guest nodded compliantly as she started the tape.

Instructions had been given to the cameraman to focus on Izuho's reaction as he watched the tidal wave footage. The only drawback was that a close-up of him was also a close-up of Stephanie because of where they were both sitting. Since she had never viewed the tape, the look of horror was even greater on her face than on Izuho's. She was not prepared for the massive devastation and loss of life that she was seeing. The footage included numerous drowned adults and children, all of them bloated by the sun and salt water, many of them partially eaten by birds and fish. Stephanie began to feel ill. She leaned over and turned the VCR off. "I think that's enough," she said softly.

Stephanie looked into the face of the handsome, bright-eyed, young man. She was so taken back by the video that she hadn't even noticed that Izuho was crying. "Are you all right, Mr. Saeki?" she gently asked.

"Yes, I am just sad. And, please, call me Izuho."

"Tell me what was going through your mind as you watched this footage, Izuho," she urged him compassionately.

"I was thinking about Mr. Tomoya Nishizaka and my family."

"Who is Mr. Nishi—?" Stephanie could not repeat the name correctly.

"Tomo was a very successful man in Okinawa. He took care of the people that worked for him, and he saved many lives before the giant wave came."

"How did he save lives?"

Izuho told Stephanie the story of what happened that horrific day. He explained to her how Tomo had selected him to fly one of the jets full of people. He also told her about the three members of his family that died that day—his mother and two sisters. His father had already been dead for many years. Now all Izuho had left was an older brother who worked for a Japanese automotive company in Tennessee. Stephanie felt sorry for the young man.

"How does it make you feel to know that you were within minutes of dying? If Mr. Nishi—" she tried to pronounce his name again. Giving up, she changed the name to Tomo. "—if Tomo hadn't selected you from the crowd, you would have died. Do you think this was just luck?"

The young man smiled brightly at the last part of the question and then saddened as he prepared to answer the first part. "I think about what it must have been like for the people left behind," he said sadly. "Their deaths must have been painful and frightening. I think about how close I came, and I guess I don't understand why I was so lucky."

It was an odd interview, full of sadness, but also full of amusement as they tried to communicate. Izuho continued to share his thoughts on being saved by Tomo's grace only minutes before the disaster.

Finally Stephanie got to her last question. Looking directly at Izuho, she asked the young man if he had considered that maybe God had saved him from this disaster.

"Which god?" he asked in all seriousness.

Stephanie rephrased her question quickly, so as not to lose the moment. "Do you believe a god saved you from death?"

"I don't know. After the tidal wave, I prayed every day to Buddha to help me understand, but I still don't know. I tried praying to statue gods, but still nothing," Izuho continued. "So if a god saved me, then he does not want me to know who he is."

Stephanie wasn't exactly sure how to end the interview, so she thought she'd try one more question. "Izuho, I assume you've heard about Jesus Christ."

Izuho nodded cautiously.

"Have you ever heard the term Rapture, or Return of Christ?"

Izuho looked at Stephanie as she tried to explain the Rapture. It was obvious that he was lost on this topic.

"Okay then, never mind," she said foolishly.

******

Zach entered the restaurant five minutes before Timothy. He stared at the walls, fascinated by all the memorabilia. Each one was covered with Chicago Bear jerseys and signed pictures of players like Jim McMann, William *The Refrigerator* Perry, and even a signed picture of Mike Ditka, the previous owner of the restaurant. He ordered a Pepsi and continued to study the walls as he waited for his son. He didn't have long to wait.

As Timothy walked in, Zach stood and waved so his son could see where he was seated. A smile from his son indicated that he had seen him.

Both men ate lunch while making small talk about their jobs, the weather, the Bears, and whatever they could come up with until Zach finally got up the nerve to ask his son what was going on with him and Stephanie.

Timothy looked at Zach as if to size up what he thought his dad might already know. "What did Stephanie say to you?"

"Nothing at all," he said, "but it is obvious by her unhappiness and you not coming around that there is a problem."

Deciding that his dad was telling the truth, Timothy spoke up, "I don't know, Dad. It just sort of fell apart the other night." He sat silently for a moment reflecting on the events of that evening nearly a week ago.

"I'm listening."

"Stephanie had a boyfriend."

"So?" said Zach without any compassion for Timothy.

"It was a preacher, and he was married!" This surprised Zach. He had underestimated Stephanie.

Timothy felt a little guilty sharing Stephanie's past with his father, but he didn't have anyone else to help him figure out his own feelings. Zach chewed on this information for a couple of minutes before he responded. "So she was doing all of this while you guys were dating?"

This statement surprised Timothy. "What? No, of course not! I mean, no, this was before she came to work at your station."

"So should she have cleared this with you beforehand?"

Timothy could see where his father was coming from and realized how unfair his jealousy was. "You're right, Dad, but I can't get it out of my mind. I can't believe she could do something like this."

"Haven't you ever made a mistake, Timothy?" Zach asked. "Did you ever do something you believe to be so bad that you'd never share it with anyone?" He went on before his son could even respond. "Life is full of choices, and even with good guidance we can still sometimes choose poorly."

Now Zach was talking about himself. He was talking about the divorce. He was talking about not being there for Timothy the way he should have been.

Timothy spoke up. "She wants us to wait until we are married before—" he paused and restated himself. "Before—you know."

Zach knew.

"She said that she wanted God's blessing on our relationship and that we should remain pure. Can you believe that?" Timothy asked incredulously.

"What's really bothering you, Son?" Zach asked. He knew there was more. There had to be an underlying issue that was being skipped.

"If we have issues over God this early in our relationship, then what will our lives together be like? Will it be like—?" Timothy caught himself a little too late.

"Will it be like your mother and me?" Now he hit the nail on the head. "Timothy, my life is not your life. My regrets don't have to be your regrets. My issues with God aren't, and shouldn't be, your issues too.

Don't do to yourself and Stephanie what I have done to you and your mother," Zach said flatly as he tried to hold his emotions together.

"Son, you think about this and then decide if it's right to hold Stephanie accountable for an affair that happened before she met you. Can you blame her for wanting to wait until she is married to have a physical relationship with you? Isn't that the way it is supposed to be? Will you lose her just because she wants God to bless your lives?"

Zach stood and dropped a $10 bill on the table. "I have to get back to work. If you need something, you call me. I want to be there for you."

"Thanks, Dad, I will." Timothy's heart was overflowing with love for his father.

******

As Zach drove back into the city, he felt compelled to stop by and visit Pastor Thomas. He parked his car in the empty parking lot. *It looks like no one is here,* he told himself. Zach decided to get out and walk around the building anyway. Even before he got to the side entrance, he could hear Leo singing an unfamiliar gospel song. Rounding the corner he found Pastor Thomas knee-deep in a hole with a shovel in his hands singing as he scooped. "Hello, Leo," Zach smiled.

"Hello, Zach. I've been waiting for you," Leo's grin matched the welcome in his voice.

"For me?" said Zach. "What for?"

"You said you'd come see me when you got back from Rome and we'd get ready for your program or show—whatever you call it."

Leo climbed out of the hole he was digging. As he did, Zach nearly laughed at the sight of the skinny old man standing there in knee-high rubber boots. Leo extended a hand towards Zach. "Good to see you, Son. How was your trip?"

"It was unusual to say the least."

"How was this Bastoni guy?" Leo inquired.

"He's a good man." A recommendation from Zach regarding a religious man was remarkable to Leo. He knew how guarded Zach was about people that followed after God.

"I can't wait to meet him," said Leo.

"In about a month he will be here for the show, and then it will finally be over."

Leo nodded. He could sense that this was a real stretch for Zach since none of it was in his comfort zone, but then again, that is the way of the Lord—to put us in places where we never dreamed of so He can grow our character. "Let's have a seat," the old man chimed as he pointed to a small wooden bench. "Tell me what you learned while you were in Rome."

"I learned lots of interesting things while I was there, I can tell you that."

"But first," the pastor interrupted, "tell me about the fire."

This caught Zach's breath momentarily. "How did you know?"

Leo looked into his concerned eyes. "Valerie called me and asked me to pray that God would protect you from further harm."

Valerie had never even said a word to him about this. *I guess she was afraid I'd probably get mad. How foolish I am,* he thought. "What do you want to know?"

"Everything you know!" said Leo with a smile.

Zach told him the entire story, including the part about his pictures being saved and about Joseph taking care of him.

"Coming face to face with death twice and having someone save you is odd, but having someone save you three times—twice within a couple of weeks—now that's just downright weird."

"Actually it's been three times in as many weeks."

"What do you mean, son?" Leo asked. "Did somebody else try to kill you?"

He told Leo about the yellow truck incident and about how there was nobody inside the little white car.

"Boy! You surely have got angels looking after you," said the good reverend with a shake of his head.

"Maybe so, but why? Why are people trying to kill me?"

"I don't know," observed Leo, "but as long as God has His angels around you, can't nobody hurt you!"

What happens if He takes them away? Zach wondered.

"What else did you discover while you were there?" Leo asked.

"Well, it seems that all of Europe has been seriously hurt by this awful winter. They are running out of food, and they have a man who is their agricultural minister named Carlo Ventini trying to solve the problem with some fancy new technology."

Leo found this bit of information almost as interesting as Zach's fire story. "How's he going to do it?" Leo's question was just like a child asking his father how Santa Claus gets down the chimney.

Surprised by his interest, he explained. "Pods—big, tall Agripods that can grow plants all year around without soil."

"Pods," Leo mused. "No threat from bad weather or drought, and no need for pesticides either, I imagine."

Zach wasn't sure about all that, but he was sure that these Agripods were going to be a big hit. "Maybe I'll do a story on them sometime later this year," he said aloud.

"What else did you find out? Did you learn anything about the Return of Jesus?"

"As a matter of fact, I did learn a few things."

"Such as?"

"I learned that there are a variety of opinions about whether or not there is such a thing as a Rapture. It seems that some don't believe in this Return of Christ stuff at all. Others say we have a lot of things to finish before Christ can come back."

"What things?"

"Treaties and temples and a bunch of stuff like that. You'll have to ask Joseph—I mean, Father Bastoni—for more detail."

"I'll be sure to do that!" Leo had a mischievous grin.

Zach spent a few more minutes explaining to Leo what the plan for the show would be. "We'll do it on Sunday, July 10, about 2:00 p.m."

"Can you come by and pick me up?" Leo asked.

Zach realized that he had never seen a car in the church parking lot whenever he came by. *Did Leo even own a car? Or maybe he couldn't afford one.*

"Sure, I'll come around 1:00."

"Fine by me," Leo smiled.

They shook hands goodbye. "Stay away from trouble, won't you," said Leo. Zach smiled weakly as he and Pastor Thomas walked back towards his car.

******

It was 24 hours later before Timothy called Stephanie. "Can we have lunch together today so we can talk?" he asked.

"Are you going to tell me that you want to break up?" she cautiously replied.

"No!" Timothy said. He missed Stephanie. He missed her fire and her gentleness. *What a fool I've been,* he thought.

"Okay then," said Stephanie with a little more confidence in her voice.

They met in the small café just below her office building. As Stephanie walked into the restaurant, anxiety began to fill her empty stomach. What was Timothy going to say to her? Worse yet, what was he going to ask her? Stephanie wanted—hoped—to avoid the details of her affair with Carl. *It's in my past and that's where it belongs,* she thought.

Timothy was already sitting at a table when she walked in. He met her with a timid smile. "It's good to see you."

"You too," she said softly.

"Are you hungry?"

"I'm not sure," she said. *That was a silly answer.* "I'm kind of hungry," she said again.

Stephanie sat down at the table and adjusted her seat towards Timothy. "I'm glad you called. I didn't think you would."

"I'm sorry!" He reached over and took her long, thin hand into his own powerful one. "There is no excuse for my behavior. I was being selfish and judgmental."

Stephanie was surprised by his confession. "No one is to blame," she said. "So where does that leave us now?" A hopeful, small smile crept across her face.

Timothy reached over, kissed her cheek, and confided, "I love you."

"I love you too!" Tears began to well up in her eyes.

Timothy turned Stephanie's hand over, palm up, and with the other hand, he reached into his pants pocket and brought out a small silver box and placed it in her open palm.

Stephanie held her breath as she stared at the shiny little box. She looked up at him surprised. "What is this?"

Timothy cleared his throat and took a deep breath. "I don't ever want to be without you again. I know we still have a lot to learn about each other, but the one thing I already know is that I want to spend the rest of my life with you. So if you're willing, I would like you to marry me."

When Stephanie agreed to meet for lunch, she never imagined this would happen. After all, she and Timothy had only been dating for a couple of months. She was certain, however, that she loved him greatly. She leaned into Timothy and kissed him lovingly. "I'd be honored to be your wife!" She exclaimed with the joy of a child, "When should we get married?"

"I thought we could go out to dinner tomorrow night and talk about it."

"I can't!" said Stephanie bluntly.

Timothy looked at her with a face full of confusion. *She can't what—have dinner with me, or worse yet, she can't marry me?*

Stephanie could see that Timothy was confused. "I have to be in Kansas tomorrow. Remember my interview in Leavenworth?"

Timothy nodded, disappointed but relieved.

"How about you come with me?" Stephanie smiled.

"I don't want to get in the way of your work. I'll just wait until you come back," he said.

"Let's get one thing straight right now. My priority is always going to be to our marriage. In fact, when we have children, I'd like to be home to raise them."

Stephanie had a lot of good qualities and, if Timothy looked very hard, he might just find out that Stephanie was an awful lot like his own mother when it came to an old-fashioned, uncompromising set of values.

Regardless of the affair that she entangled herself in, she was at heart a virtuous woman.

"Okay! I'll go with you, but maybe I should stay at the hotel while you are interviewing this guy."

Stephanie knew that she was going to get a lot of attention in this all-male military prison and none of it would be pleasant. "Yeah, maybe that would be the best thing to do. I'll have my travel department make a plane and hotel reservation for you." The last part of the statement cleared up the issue of hotel rooms. He would have his own and she would have hers.

Timothy figured he could wait for the honeymoon. *Just a few more months, that's all.*

******

Stephanie broke the news to Zach just after lunch.

With a big hug and a warm smile, Zach spoke, "I will be pleased to have you for a daughter-in-law."

With this, she beamed. Life was good! But there were so many things to do all of a sudden. Stephanie's head was twirling with the thought of the plans that would need to be made. *But first I have to get through these interviews.*

Timothy called Zach 15 minutes after Stephanie had left his office. Zach pretended not to know what was going on between the two lovebirds. "What's up, Timothy?" He asked casually.

"Dad, I've asked Stephanie to marry me."

"Well, what did she say?" as if he didn't already know.

"She said she would be honored!" he repeated excitedly.

"Congratulations, Son!"

"Dad, I wanted to thank you for helping me figure this out," he said awkwardly.

"I'm glad I could help," Zach said solemnly, wishing he had always been there to help. He had instead hidden himself away in his work and away from his regrets.

******

Stephanie and Timothy checked in to the Holiday Inn at the edge of town. "Should we try and get something to eat or just call it a night?" he asked.

Stephanie looked at her watch. It was after 10:00 p.m. already. She gazed up at Timothy with a weary look on her face.

"Tomorrow morning for breakfast then." Timothy smiled as he pulled her into his arms.

Stephanie nestled herself into his strong chest. "Breakfast sounds good to me."

He lifted her chin and kissed her softly. "Goodnight, sweetheart."

The next day Timothy drove Stephanie to the prison's main entrance. "Are you sure you don't want me to go in with you?"

"No," she said. "I'll be fine, but be back in one hour, okay?"

What Stephanie didn't know was that Timothy had no intention of leaving the parking lot until she returned safely.

Stephanie walked up the steps to the front lobby. Her stomach was turned upside down. *I wish I hadn't eaten breakfast,* she admitted to herself. Stephanie stepped up to the counter where an extremely heavy black man sat behind a desk. He stared at her in pleasant surprise.

"Can I help you?" asked the guard with a baritone voice.

"Yes, my name is Stephanie Miller, and I have an interview with one of your prisoners, Calvin Fraser."

The officer pointed to a heavy metal door. "Go through there," he said casually.

As Stephanie walked to the door, her fear level was beginning to rise. *How did I get myself into this mess?*

She pushed the heavy door open and stepped into a small room. Inside was a glass partition with a set of wooden chairs on either side. Stephanie sat down in one of the chairs and waited for whatever was to come next. All the while she felt like someone was watching her. A large, gray door on the opposite side of the glass finally opened and in stepped a fairly short, well-built black man accompanied by a security guard. The man walked towards Stephanie and sat down in the opposing chair.

"Calvin Fraser?" Stephanie inquired.

"Yes. Are you Stephanie Miller?"

"Yes, I am. It's nice to meet you, Mr. Fraser. Well, shall we get started?" she asked rhetorically.

Calvin, somewhat amused by her formality, nodded and folded his hands on his lap.

"Mr. Fraser, you are—were— a captain in the Air Force, correct?"

"That's right," he said passively.

Stephanie could already tell that Calvin was a sad and depressed person. *But who wouldn't be?* she thought. *If I had to stay locked up in this place all the time, I'd be depressed too.*

"What exactly did you do in the Air Force?"

"I was a fighter pilot flying F-15 jets."

Stephanie was impressed. This guy obviously had some things going for him. *Our government doesn't let just anyone fly those $30 million planes, now do they?*

"I understand that you were on Mount Denali when it erupted." Stephanie looked at Calvin to see his reaction.

"That's not exactly true." His face had little expression. "I was on the mountain before it erupted, but not during the eruption."

This guy sounds like he's been spending too much time around lawyers or something, she thought. "Were you alone on the mountain?"

"No, I was with a friend." Annoyance was building up in his voice. "Why are you asking me these questions? Don't you already know this stuff?"

"I'm sorry, Mr. Fraser, but I wanted to hear it from you so I can repeat it accurately."

"How long have you been a reporter?"

Stephanie looked at Mr. Fraser with embarrassment. "Days," she said lightly.

"Call me Calvin."

"Okay, Calvin. Do you mind if I set this video recorder up and tape the rest of the interview?"

"It depends." he said. "Why do you want to tape this interview?"

"Calvin, I am sure you are aware of the many disasters that have attacked our planet lately."

Calvin nodded.

"Well, I have been asked to find out if these terrible things are a sign of the end of the world—the Return of Christ."

Calvin looked at Stephanie suspiciously. "Are you serious?"

"I know that it seems odd, but I am really serious about this. There is a growing belief that Jesus is coming back soon and these disasters are signs forewarning us of that truth." She continued, "I understand that you may have had a supernatural experience of your own while you were on Mount Denali."

Calvin stared deeply into Stephanie's light blue eyes. She knew he was deciding whether or not he wanted to confide in her. "I had something weird happen to me on the mountain, but I can't prove it. That's why I'm here right now."

"What do you mean?"

"My friend died on that mountain, but I didn't. The military thought it was suspicious that I could be alive while my partner was dead. I told them that a voice had warned me to get off the mountain. I said I tried to ignore the voice, but it was persistent. I told them that I asked the voice to let me get Mark, but the voice said that he had a different path than I did."

Stephanie sat back videotaping while listening to this man explain his strange experience. She stared at Calvin trying to determine if he was lying or maybe just plain crazy. *He looks sincere to me. He really believes that he heard voices.* Another thought occurred to her. *He did leave the mountain and as a result was saved. Maybe he is telling the truth. Maybe he did hear some kind of voice.*

"What did the voice sound like?" Stephanie really wanted to know.

"It was an ordinary voice, I guess," Calvin remembered. "But something was different. It didn't talk to me, so much as it kind of talked through me. It's really hard to explain."

"Did you feel anything else while the voice was talking to you?"

Calvin paused briefly. *Why is she asking me this? Has she heard the voice before?* he wondered. "I felt something. I don't know exactly what it was, but it felt safe, kind of peaceful."

Stephanie made herself a little note and then looked back at Calvin. "Why do you suppose this voice warned you and, I guess in reality, saved your life?"

Calvin shrugged his shoulders. "That's a question that I've been asking myself over and over again. If it was so important to save me, then why am I sitting here in this place?" He looked around the room.

"Do you believe in God?" Stephanie asked boldly.

Calvin looked into her lovely face and said, "I don't really know. I used to think that a man had to make his own way through life as best he could. I worked hard to break away from the life that society had planned for me, but now I'm not sure. Maybe there is a God. Probably so, but what does He want from me?"

"Calvin," said Stephanie softly, "once before, thousands of years ago, God allowed a young man to suffer in prison for 12 years before He lifted him up. God made him a great ruler."

Calvin understood from Sunday school as a youth that she was talking about Joseph from the Old Testament.

Stephanie studied Calvin. His face was so sad. "Why exactly are you in prison?"

"The prosecution charged me with manslaughter because I left Mark Hendricks, my partner, on the mountain and climbed down to safety. They also charged me with grand theft auto for taking his Jeep when I left. Finally they convicted me of grand theft in the first degree and reckless abandonment in the second degree."

"How many years will you be in here?"

"Maybe seven," Calvin answered bitterly. "It depends on my behavior they say."

"One last question and then I'll leave you alone." *Poor choice of words,* she thought. "Have you ever heard of the Rapture?"

"Yes," Calvin nodded. "My parents took me to church every week when I was a young boy, and the pastor spent a lot of time talking about the Return of Christ."

"Do you believe He will?" she asked simply.

"I don't know!" he said bluntly. "But if He does, He won't be taking me with Him."

A somber Stephanie met Timothy in the parking lot. "Well, how was it?"

Stephanie was a little distant as she reflected on what she had seen and heard. "It was—" Stephanie paused for a moment to think of the right words, "—it was not what I expected. I mean the prison was, but Calvin wasn't."

"Who is Calvin?" Timothy asked.

Chapter 13 - The Plague

Another two weeks had gone by, and Zach and Stephanie were preparing to leave for L.A. in the morning. Just a few more weeks before the show, and there was still much to do. Stephanie had read all the information on Mount Chimborazo's volcanic eruption, as well as the pertinent information about Tommy and Tina Glover.

It was difficult for Stephanie to focus on the remaining tasks. She so wanted to spend her time planning her wedding. She and Timothy had spent nearly every night together talking about their future—how many kids they would have, where they might live, and where they might honeymoon. It was amazing that two people who had known each other for such a short time could be so much in love.

******

"But you've only known him for a few months!" argued Stephanie's mother.

"How long did you know Dad before you knew that you wanted to spend your life with him?"

"You've got a good point. But go slow and be careful! Don't get ahead of God."

Stephanie had attributed her love for Christ to be the result of watching her mother live the life of a true Christian. She was so proud to be her daughter. "Right after the show we will come out to visit you, and then you can see for yourself what a good man Timothy is, okay, Mom?"

******

Zach had spent the majority of the last week organizing his questions for the panel interview. He even went so far as to read portions of the Bible in preparation for the event. He tried to read Revelation, but it was a lost cause for him. *This stuff is cryptic,* he told himself. He tried to read the book of Daniel but found it too difficult as well. Finally he found himself reading the book of Mathew. This at least was easier to follow. The signs as described by Jesus were pretty straightforward. *But these could be interpreted in so many ways, and what about this nation against nation stuff and kings defeating kings? What does it all mean?* he wondered.

Zach made himself a note to ask this question during the interview. He hated to admit it to himself, but the time he spent in reading the Bible began to affect his mind. He found himself thinking about the many things he had read. Zach found himself wanting to read even more. *I'll be glad when this interview is over,* he finally told himself. *At least then I can have my old life back.*

******

Zach and Valerie spent the evening together at Valerie's house. She had prepared a light supper for the both of them. "So how long does it take to get to L.A.?"

"If we could fly direct, it would take about four hours or so," he said, "but Stephanie and I have to change planes in Ontario and take a little commuter to Los Angeles."

It was obvious that both Valerie and Zach were a little apprehensive about this trip, especially after the fire in Rome. Valerie slid across the sofa closer to Zach. She picked up his hand and held it in her own. "You need to be careful. I have a bad feeling about this trip."

"You had a bad feeling about the last trip," he reminded her.

"Yes, I did and you almost died, didn't you?" she responded with a concerned look.

"Good point!" Zach laughed.

He lifted Valerie's hand and held it gently. "I don't know what is going on, but I think maybe somebody is trying to kill me," he said with a grimace on his face.

Valerie stared at him closely thinking he might be teasing her. "What?"

"It's true! I tried to deny it myself, but it's true." Zach finally leveled with her. "There have been four attempts on my life, and all four times someone has come to my rescue, but I don't know if that will last. And I don't understand why anyone would want to kill me in the first place."

Valerie sat and listened as Zach explained each event to her. She was stunned!

"Why didn't you tell me?" she asked angrily.

"I wasn't sure, I guess, and I didn't want to worry you."

******

The sun was just starting its slow rise towards the west as the squadron flew low, just barely 100 feet above the surface of the ocean. As they moved away from Cuba, they regrouped and headed north at full speed. The squadron would make the Florida Keys in a few hours and then the majority of their targets within another eight hours or so.

******

John Carter stood in the middle of his field staring at the billions of hearty grain stalks as they stretched up towards the rising sun. Three hundred acres of the most fertile land he had ever owned. *Two more months, then harvest,* thought John. This was going to be the crop he had always hoped for. No more disappointments, no more costly failures. He would soon be able to pay off the bank and live a debt-free life like he and his wife, Carol, had always planned. They had moved from Ohio to Nebraska over four years ago and, except for the birth of their daughter, they had not had a bit of good luck. The money was all but gone, and if this crop didn't come in, they would lose their dream—their farm.

******

Back at their old two-story farmhouse, Carol was cooking a big country breakfast for her family. The sun shone through her kitchen window giving the room a warm, comforting glow. Carol's three-year-old daughter, Pamela, was already dressed and out in the yard playing on the jungle gym that her father had lovingly made for her. John Jr. was still upstairs sleeping when his mother called him down to breakfast. John Sr. stepped in from the back porch and slipped off his work boots. If nothing else, he had learned not to step into Carol's house with dirty shoes.

"Well!" she said. "Is it still there?"

John smiled at his playful and beautiful wife. "It's still there." He moved in to give her a big hug.

Carol laughed as she pulled away from his powerful grip. "Quit it! I'm cooking! Now go and get your lazy son out of bed."

John stole a kiss as he left the room and headed up the back staircase to his son's bedroom. "Wake up, Lazy Bones!" he said loudly. John Jr. grunted and rolled over. He was on summer vacation and had no desire to get out of bed.

"How would you like to go fishing this morning after breakfast?"

With that, his nine-year-old son rose out of bed with all the energy of a well-rested, young boy. "All right, let's go!"

"Hold on! First pick up this room and then come downstairs for breakfast."

John Jr. whined compliantly as his father walked out of the room and back down the stairs. John sat down at the kitchen table as Carol slid a large plate of fried potatoes, fried ham, and fried eggs in front of him.

"There are biscuits on the table too. Would you like some jam?"

"Of course!" mumbled John through a mouthful of eggs and potatoes.

"What kind, apple butter or strawberry?"

"Strawberry."

John Jr. hopped down the stairs and into the kitchen. "Well, good morning, Lazy Head!" said his mother with a smile.

John Sr. took a sip of coffee and asked, "Where's Pamela?"

"Where else?" laughed Carol.

John smiled brightly. He was glad he had built the jungle gym and playhouse for his little princess.

"Has she eaten?"

"Of course!" said Carol proudly.

******

John and his son sat on the edge of the small lake listening to the birds sing their songs as the pair fished for whatever was hungry enough to take their bait. Trout fishing was a northern specialty, but John was just as glad to catch a big catfish. He loved the way Carol could fry it up with potatoes and corn bread.

"Dad?" John Jr. said.

"Yeah, Son?"

"Are we going to be rich after this next harvest?"

John laughed and slapped his son on the thigh. "I don't know about rich, but for once we won't owe anybody anything."

"Dad?" said the boy.

"Yes, Son."

"Can I have a new motorcycle after we pay off the bank?"

John began to laugh again. "If we have the money, you can have the bike," he promised with a grin.

The young boy's grin could match his father's except, of course, for the four missing teeth.

The fishing trip was a success, and both father and son had enough fish between them to feed the family at least twice. John loaded up the truck and headed it in the direction of his farm only a few miles down the dirt road.

******

Carol had finished all of her chores and decided to take a bath, but first she stepped out on the porch to check on Pamela. Her daughter was kneeling in the doorway of her little playhouse talking to two of her small dolls. Carol watched Pamela play make believe for a few minutes. It was a blessing to have such a wonderful daughter, and the scene filled Carol's heart with joy.

******

Sixteen hours earlier the low flying squadron had flown over Key West and had split into two separate, but still huge, groups. One group headed west towards the Rocky Mountains via the Gulf of Mexico while the other squadron went straight up north fanning east and west as they went.

******

"Dad?"

"Yeah, Son."

"What's that?" John Jr. asked as he pointed in the direction of a massive dark cloud.

John Sr. nearly drove the truck off the road as he stared at the fast-moving swarm. He slammed on the truck brakes and stopped just short of hitting a big, old pine tree. John climbed out of the truck and stared in disbelief as the deadly cloud approached. "My God!" he exclaimed. "Oh, my God!"

"What is it?" his son cried out in fear.

"Locusts!" said John. "It's locusts!"

John got back into the truck and tried to start the motor, but it would not start. He began to yell at the truck and pound the steering wheel as he continued to turn the ignition key, but the truck refused to start. The locusts moved in like a thunderstorm and covered every inch of ground within the viewing range of John and his son.

The insects quickly covered the truck so completely that they blocked out the sun and turned the cab into total darkness. John Jr. began to cry aloud as his father turned the ignition key one last time. The battery was nearly dead. John hit his wiper button and the blades made one slow sweep, clearing a path just long enough to reveal a most incredible scene. The entire area was a thick cloud of grasshoppers. The schistocera gregaria were roughly two inches long, each with dark bodies, long wings, and very short little horns sticking up out of their hideous heads. It was like being inside of a hive. John couldn't tell the landmarks anymore. He couldn't even make out the trees for the billions of locust that were swarming over everything.

    Back on the farm Carol was relaxing in a hot tub of foamy water. Her eyes were closed as she listened to the CD player's mellow tune. She could feel the heat of the sun filtering through the open blinds as she soaked in the hot water. Suddenly she felt a cold chill creep across the room as the sun's rays were blotted out of the sky. Opening her eyes, Carol leaned forward and tried to look out of the window. *What is going on?* she wondered. *Why is it so dark in here?*

    Climbing out of the bathtub to see where the beautiful sunshine had gone, Carol walked towards the glass with water and bath bubbles dripping off her body onto the hardwood floor as she went. Just before she got to the window, a swarm of locusts pelted the glass, terrifying her.

    Screaming in surprise and stumbling backwards, Carol slipped on the wet floor and fell against the iron tub, hitting her head solidly against the edge. She lay there bleeding and unconscious on the bathroom floor as the grasshoppers continued to devour everything within view.

******

The locusts had made it inland as far north as Nebraska and as far west as Colorado. The destruction as these deadly squadrons moved on was complete. Not only had they eaten everything in sight, but they also caused major issues with transportation.

    There were numerous multiple car pile-ups as a direct result of billions of grasshoppers landing on the highways in many of the states. The roads were literally covered in grasshopper guts, just as slippery as ice, and with a visibility of virtually zero, there were wrecks everywhere. Highway 80 outside Denver had the worst wreck of all. More than 90 cars and semi trucks had been surprised as the locusts assaulted the highway in an instant without warning. Before long the road was nothing but a pile of twisted metal and mangled bodies as fire and smoke bellowed from the five-mile stretch of carnage.

Automobiles were not the only victims of these grasshoppers. In fact, there had been three separate train derailments as a result of the locust-covered tracks becoming too slippery even for the hundreds of tons of fast-moving steel. One of the trains was an Amtrak loaded with college students heading east for summer vacation. When they finished counting the young, mutilated bodies, this train wreck would go down in history as the worst in North America.

Yet still far worse than the car and train wrecks were the multiple jetliner crashes. The locust swarm had flown so low that radar didn't pick them up until it was too late to warn any of the hundreds of passenger planes away from the infested locations.

The first plane to fod out due to its engines filling up with thousands of grasshoppers was a United Airlines Boeing 737 with 107 people aboard. The plane lost power at roughly 6,000 feet and smashed into the ground 12 seconds later. Soon after a Boeing 747 took off from Washington Dulles Airport on its way to Frankfurt. The plane ascended to 2,000 feet before losing power. The pilots saw the swarm and then tried desperately to bank the plane to the west for an emergency landing. The windshield of the 747 was completely blocked with the corpses of the thousands of locusts. The plane rolled over and crashed before any of the passengers had a clue as to what was going on. Before the day was over, three more commercial jetliners would crash. The total loss of life was not yet known, but needless to say, it would be another record.

Farmers from every town in each state east of the Rocky Mountains were trying all they could to kill the locusts before they had time to eat all their early crops. Many lit small fires in hopes of scaring the grasshoppers away, even if it meant burning up a portion of their land. Others tried to use pesticides dropped from small crop-dusting planes, but in nearly every case the small planes crashed shortly after take-off as grasshoppers clogged the intakes of each plane. Some tried explosives hoping the vibrations would send the locusts away. One creative farmer even tried loud music. He remembered how it had worked in Panama, so out of desperation he set large speakers at the edge of his fields and began to blare out rock-and-roll music. His results were mixed, but he was convinced that it helped.

Scientists from many states were called into an emergency session to discuss the problem and how best to resolve it. The mystery of why grasshoppers change from a solitary species to a much more aggressive gregarious species is not fully understood. It has to do with the female of the species laying her eggs too close to another female, eventually creating too many grasshoppers at a single point in time. This causes the grasshoppers to become agitated, resulting in a metamorphosis whereby the grasshopper develops shorter legs and horns and longer pairs of wings for long-range flight. The United States had not experienced a major locust outbreak since the early 1930's, and then it was in the Pacific Northwest. Previously in the 1870's locusts had infested parts of the Rockies and many southwestern areas of the U.S.

"There is no logical reason for this," said one young scientist. "We could never have predicted it. And even if we had, we certainly would not have expected a swarm to be so big. The largest swarm ever recorded," he continued, "was thousands of years ago near the Red Sea. It was estimated that over 2,000 square miles were affected by that plague."

"So you are saying that this is a plague of Biblical proportions?" asked another scientist.

"I didn't say that," said the young man, "but if you want to put it that way, I won't argue."

The locusts continued to move slowly north and west from town to town and farm to farm. In another two days the majority of the swarm would be in Canada, moving from Alberta to Saskatchewan and on to Toronto.

******

Back on John Carter's farm the locusts devoured everything and moved on. John and his son were finally able to walk home after nearly 16 hours of being trapped in his truck. What John saw as he walked along with his son was more than he could take in. The land and trees in every direction were completely destroyed. Not a leaf or blade of grass was left behind. There were dead grasshoppers everywhere; apparently, they had gorged themselves so much that they simply exploded. There were also carcasses of livestock eaten down to the bones. John could not imagine a nuclear explosion doing more damage than this.

As he approached his own farm, tears filled his eyes. It was impossible, but the field that he had stood in a day or so ago was completely gone. The knee-high stalks of grain, literally billions of them, were now nothing but stubble.

John began to walk faster as he approached his farmhouse. There was no activity, no animals, and no people. Something was very wrong. John began to run towards the house with John Jr. not far behind. He entered his home through the front door calling out Carol's name as he went. He checked the empty kitchen and then headed up the stairs. Pamela's room was also empty. Next he checked his bedroom. Carol and Pamela were nowhere in sight. Finally he went into the bathroom, but before he took a step, he noticed there was something wet and slippery covering the floor. Stepping in carefully John found Carol lying on the floor in a large pool of blood. "Dear God!" He cried as he knelt over his wife's body. John touched her face. It was cold, as was her hand when he picked it up. Tears burned his eyes as he began to sob.

"Dad!" John Jr. cried out.

Again with panic in his voice his son yelled, "Dad, come quick! It's Pamela!"

"Pamela!" John cried. "Oh, God, no! Not Pamela too!"

John gently placed Carol's lifeless hand over her breast and covered her with a nearby towel. His heart was heavy with sorrow over the loss of his beloved wife, and now the thought of losing his daughter, as well, was overwhelming. He ran down the stairs, nearly falling as he went out the back door. By this time John Jr. was screaming at the top of his lungs. John rounded the corner, and there stood his son staring at something lying in front of the jungle gym.

"Dear God, no!" cried John as he ran toward his son.

As he neared the scene his eyes made contact with the pile of partially eaten flesh that his son was standing next to. Bones could be seen sticking up through the pile. The sight was horrible and unrecognizable, all except for the small plastic doll lying next to the mass of tissue.

Agony filled John's heart as he approached the dead body. He could hardly see through his tear-filled eyes to recognize what he was looking at. Just as he started to kneel down beside the corpse, he heard a soft, little voice coming from behind him. His heart leapt as he heard his daughter calling out to him saying, "Daddy! Daddy!"

John turned around quickly to see his small daughter running towards him from her dollhouse. John fell on his knees and cried uncontrollably as Pamela collapsed in his arms. She was completely unhurt, although seriously traumatized by the events of the day.

"I was afraid to leave my dollhouse," she explained. "I saw the big bugs eat Samson, so I closed my door and stayed inside with my dollies."

"You did good, Sweetheart," cried John as he hugged his little girl.

The Carter family would get over the loss of their dog, Samson, but they would never get over the loss of Carol, nor would the hundreds of other families who lost loved ones during the plague of locusts. The United States would have its own problems trying to feed its 260 million people this next year, as would Canada.

Chapter 14 - The Final Interview

Stephanie stared out of the plane's window into the evening sky. She was already lonely even though Zach sat only inches away. The many weeks of preparation had taken a toll on him, and he was fast asleep, hunched over uncomfortably in his seat. Stephanie hated to leave Timothy behind, but this was the one trip she did not want him to be a part of. She wasn't planning to spend any time around Carl, but she knew that she would undoubtedly see him, at least in the Los Angeles airport. She didn't want Timothy by her side when she confronted Pastor Perkins for the first time since she fled London over six months earlier.

Stephanie tried to curtail her anxiety over seeing Carl by focusing on her interview with Tina and Tommy Glover. *I wonder what they are like,* she thought to herself, *and why neither of them has married...speaking of marriage, as soon as I get home we are going to set a date, and I hope it is soon!*

The sun was just setting in the west as she gazed out the porthole. They had wanted to take the morning flight to Ontario, California, and then catch a commuter to L.A. Due, however, to the many cancellations as a result of the recent and unpleasant locust epidemic, this was the best any airline could do.

Zach began to stir in his sleep. This caught Stephanie's attention as she watched her soon-to-be father-in-law struggle his way through a nightmare, one of many he had endured over the last week. Sweat began to emerge from his forehead and then suddenly he lunged forward and opened his eyes. Slowly he became aware of his present location. He also became aware of the fact that Stephanie was watching him.

Zach was grateful when the flight attendant stepped up and asked him if he wanted something to drink. "Orange juice, please," he said with a weak smile on his face.

Stephanie could sense his embarrassment. "How long until we get to Ontario?" she asked, with the answer already in her head.

"Less than two hours by my watch," he replied.

"Zach," Stephanie was cautious. "I have something I think you need to know."

She had been dreading this conversation, but she knew it would be unfair for Zach to be caught off guard by Carl. *Besides,* she told herself, *if anyone is going to tell him, it ought to be me.*

"Carl Perkins is not exactly—," she paused. "What I mean is that he and I—"

Zach raised his hand to spare Stephanie the pain of revealing her shameful past to a man she had come to love very much. "It's all right," he said gently. "I already know."

"Timothy?" she asked.

"Don't be angry with him. He was just a little confused at the time."

Stephanie was relieved that she wouldn't have to explain herself, although she now found it difficult to make eye contact with Zach.

He sensed her shame and softly put her at ease. "We all make mistakes. I've made more than my fair share."

Stephanie took his hand into her own. "Thank you for not judging me."

Stephanie and Zach ate the dinner provided by the airline—chicken breast and wild rice. It looked good, but the taste just wasn't there. "So what's your plan?" Zach asked.

Stephanie took the opportunity to think about something other than the food in front of her. "I'm going to stay at the Sheraton near the airport and drive to Long Beach for the interview tomorrow. How about you?" she asked.

"Mr. Perkins has asked me to stay at his house for a couple of nights. I've never stayed in a mansion before, so I thought I'd give it a try. I'll meet you back at the airport by noon, two days from now."

Zach sat back with his eyes closed. So many things had happened to him since Easter when he was almost killed. He had learned many things that he had never considered until now. *This assignment really hasn't been all that bad,* he thought, *and now I have a good relationship with my son. Heck, I even found him a wife. I've made a couple of good friends in Joseph and Leo and, most importantly, Valerie and I are really getting along great.*

He didn't want to admit it, but he knew that he had also reconciled many of his differences with God. Oh, sure, he still had anger in his heart, but it was hard not to be grateful for the loving protection God had given him recently even if he still did not understand why. *Just a couple more weeks,* he continued to think, *and all of this will be over. What will I do then?* He knew somehow that his life had changed forever as a result of this assignment. *Maybe,* he mused optimistically, *Valerie and I can fix our problems and get remarried. Yes! I'm sure we can!* he thought with a smile.

The flight landed on time, and Stephanie and Zach found themselves wandering down a wide corridor heading towards the shuttle gate for the 20-minute flight to L.A. Zach veered off to the left. "I need to step in here for a minute," he said as he pointed to the restroom.

"I'll meet you at the gate," Stephanie said with a smile.

As Zach stepped up to the sink to wash his hands, in walked a tall, gray-headed man wearing a pilot's outfit. "Good evening!" Zach said politely. "Going to L.A.?"

"You bet!" said the man brightly, "just as soon as I take care of a little business."

Both men laughed as Zach walked out of the restroom and on towards Stephanie and his departure gate.

The pilot, Captain Stark, stepped into the stall furthest away from the entrance, the one designated for the handicapped. Carefully he sat down on the edge of the toilet seat and bending over the pilot reached for his luggage. Digging around for a moment, he soon came out with a full pint bottle of Scotch. Slowly and quietly he turned the lid of the fat little bottle. Captain Stark took a long, greedy gulp of the liquor and, with a sigh, sat back on the toilet lid. Soon the bottle of Scotch was an inch from being emptied. Just then there was a slight rumble on the locked door. Stark reached for his bag to put away his poison, forgetting to put the cap back on, when suddenly the door swung open and in walked a frightful-looking man with a hideous grin covering his evil and ugly face. His red eyes flickered as he walked toward the pilot.

"Who? What? Who are you?" Captain Stark asked in fear.

The demon held up his clawed hand as if to say "hush." The pilot began to stand on his frightened and intoxicated legs. The demon reached out his disfigured hand and grabbed the captain by the throat.

Captain Stark was a tall, powerful man even under the influence of alcohol, but he was no match for this evil creature. Slowly his body became rigid as the demon increased his grip on the drunken man's neck. Captain Stark didn't want to look into the fiery eyes of the creature, but he felt compelled. His gaze was met by an evil stare from the demon. "Like your booze, huh?" Suddenly the pilot began to shake as the demon entered into his very soul.

Zach and Stephanie sat with eight other passengers waiting to load the plane when Captain Stark walked by Zach wheeling his luggage behind him. Zach smiled and nodded, but the captain acted as if he didn't even recognize him. That wasn't entirely true since part of him did recognize Zach, but that part was not in control any more.

Stephanie and Zach were the last two to board the small commuter plane. Their seats were in the very back. The plane was designed to seat two passengers on one side and one on the other. The 10 rows altogether could seat 30 people, but not on this flight. Today, there were only 10 passengers, 1 flight attendant, a co-pilot, and 1 demon possessed Captain Stark.

Zach looked over his shoulder as he walked down the narrow passageway to his seat. He could see the pilots making their preflight checks. As he began to turn back towards Stephanie, his eyes caught the gaze of the pilot. The captain smiled as if trying to reassure him that all was well. Zach sat down next to Stephanie without saying a word. He had been in enough situations recently to know when something was not quite right. He began to perspire across his forehead.

"Everything okay, Zach?"

"I guess so," he said cautiously.

"What's wrong?"

"I don't know, but something about that pilot seems strangely familiar to me."

"Familiar in a good way or a bad way?" she asked as the door to the plane slammed shut causing them both to jump in their seats.

The seats directly in front of them were empty. The next nearest passenger was two rows up and in the single seat on the other side. The flight attendant shut the cockpit door and locked it, as dictated by FAA regulations. This helps to prevent hijacking apparently, but unfortunately it does nothing to prevent a crazy pilot from killing his co-pilot.

As soon as the door was locked, Captain Stark called his partner's attention to a small gauge at the base of his instrument panel. As the co-pilot leaned in to look at the gauge, the possessed captain grabbed the back of the unsuspecting co-pilot's neck and smashed his head into the console with enough force to break out many of the gauges. Alarms began to blare until the pilot switched off each broken instrument. The co-pilot's forehead was concave, as if it had been hit with a sledgehammer, and blood poured from the man's wound as well as from his ears and mouth.

The plane taxied out onto the runway, narrowly missing a large jet that was coming in from some distant place. The tower radioed the small plane in an attempt to stop its progress. "Flight 211, this is the tower. You do not have clearance to depart. Do you copy, Flight 211?"

Captain Stark switched off the radio and ripped the microphone from the console. The air traffic controller stood in amazement yelling, "We've got a runaway!" All the other traffic controllers instantly started redirecting traffic away from the delinquent jet.

The plane lifted off the ground with a roar from its engines as its wings tossed from side-to-side erratically. Instantly passengers began to scream as the plane rose to 500 feet in just a few seconds. A minute later the jet stalled and dove towards the ground as if the engines had gone out. In fact, they had been turned off.

Stephanie screamed and wrapped her arms around Zach. What happened next was hard to explain. The plane crashed into the airport runway at terminal velocity, nose first. In an instant the plane shattered into many smaller pieces. Flames were everywhere as the jet fuel exploded on the runway. The air was thick with black smoke. It was apparent by the now-silenced screams of the terrified passengers that they had all perished in the crash.

A terrified Stephanie was somehow still clinging to Zach, and it was obvious that the rear section of the plane where they were seated had somehow stayed intact. Zach could not see anything except smoke and flames all around him. He wasn't entirely sure he hadn't died and gone to Hell; by the look of the fire and smoke around him it could have been Hell. A soft warm glow began to illuminate both Zach and the frightened Stephanie. Suddenly Zach knew that he, and hopefully Stephanie, would not die in this crash.

"What is it?' Stephanie cried. "What's going on?"

Zach held her tightly and prayed, "God, please save her from harm." Then all of a sudden, Zach felt himself being pelted by a soft cool liquid. "It's foam!" he exclaimed.

Soon firemen were working their way down through the burnt-out pieces of partially intact plane. "I've got two more dead over here," said one of the firemen.

"I've got one over here too," said another.

Finally a young stocky fireman got to where Zach and Stephanie sat still belted in their unburned seats. "I've got two over here," he said before realizing that they were still alive. "Holy smokes!" he said. "They're alive!"

The other firemen looked in the direction of the young man. "Are you joking?" one of the men asked wearily.

Zach looked up at his rescuer gratefully.

"Mister, you're alive!" said the young rescue worker.

Seeing this the other firemen ran to where the man was standing. "Well, I'll be!" said one man in amazement.

"Praise God!" said another elderly fireman as he lifted a hand toward Heaven.

Carefully the men extracted the two from their seats and out of what was left of the small commuter plane.

******

After many hours in the hospital emergency room, during which the FBI asked Zach and Stephanie numerous questions, they were finally released since they had not a single injury. Although both were very shaken by the experience, they felt the need to push on. Zach got them a taxi to the airport rental car lot where he proceeded to rent a vehicle for the drive to Los Angeles.

Stephanie sat in the passenger side silently as Zach drove them through the California darkness towards the Sheraton Hotel. "What happened back there?" she asked seemingly still in shock.

"The plane crashed," said Zach, trying to lighten the conversation. He was getting somewhat accustomed to near-death experiences. His humor was lost on her, however, as she continued her search for understanding.

"Why are we alive? Why didn't we die like those other poor people, and what happened anyway?" She continued, "It sounds like the FBI think the pilot was crazy."

"I don't know," said Zach. "Someone has been trying to kill me ever since I was nine years old, but for some reason God chooses to save me." There! He finally said it without any doubt in his voice. "God is protecting me. For what, I don't know. But I think it has something to do with this show we are working on," he said plainly.

"Why did He save me?" she asked.

"I'm not sure," Zach replied, "but I asked Him to, so maybe that's why, or maybe He has a plan for you too." There! He said it again. God had a plan for his life. Soon he would know what it was.

"I want to call Timothy," she said. Zach felt compassion for his soon-to-be daughter-in-law.

"We'll be at the hotel in an hour. That will make it 5:00 a.m. at home. You can call when we get there."

Stephanie nodded and closed her eyes. *What had Clorisa said months ago? "God has a plan for your life." I guess He does. But what is it, and why me?* she wondered.

It was 2:00 a.m. when Zach and Stephanie checked into the Sheraton Hotel. "It's too late to call Reverend Perkins. I guess I'll call him first thing this morning. He probably thinks we were killed in that plane crash." The thought made Zach shudder.

Stephanie threw her bags on the floor and picked up the phone as soon as she entered her room. Timothy answered the phone with a suspicious and sleepy, "Hello?"

At the sound of Timothy's voice, she began to cry.

"Stephanie, is that you? Is everything all right? Is my dad okay?"

She sobbed, "We're okay, but we were in a plane crash."

Stephanie began to calm down, and eventually she told the entire story to Timothy as he listened silently. "God saved us, Timothy. He really did! There was a warm glow," she went on. "I had a sense of peace while the plane was burning all around me."

The two of them talked for another 30 minutes before Stephanie finally said, "I probably ought to try and get some sleep. I have an interview today. But I just had to hear your voice."

Timothy didn't want to say goodbye, but he knew she was right. "Please take care of yourself and my dad too. I love you!"

"I love you too!" she said. "Good night."

In the next room over Zach made a similar call to Valerie. He, too, felt better after hearing her voice, and once she calmed down they had a pleasant conversation.

"Valerie," he said, "maybe it is time we start to think about getting back together."

Valerie's heart nearly jumped out of her chest. It was what she had been praying for, for too many years to count. "We'll talk about it when you get home," she replied. For some reason, however, Valerie felt in her heart that she and Zach would never be husband and wife again. Maybe she just didn't want to get her hopes up after such a long wait.

******

Uncharacteristically Carl Perkins answered the phone himself this morning, a task usually performed by one of his live-in servants. But today Carl was a little anxious. He knew that something had happened to the man he was supposed to meet at the airport, but he didn't know what. Carl really wanted to do this television show. The timing could not have been better. He was starting a new tour in one week, and recently he had published his latest book called *The Aftermath*. He was amazed at how frightened people were about all the disasters in the world even though he saw these disasters as mere coincidences. He was equally amazed that even after so many false End of Time predictions by the so-called experts, some of which were in his own previous millennial book titled *The Countdown*, people bought these ridiculous books. Fear was his friend. He knew that so long as people were afraid of what they didn't understand, he would have an opportunity to take advantage of them.

"Hello," said Carl as he picked up the phone.

"Mr. Perkins, this is Zach Miles."

"This is Reverend Perkins, but you may call me Carl if you'd like. How do you do, Mr. Miles?"

"I am sorry for the inconvenience, but we had an accident yesterday and, as a result, we did not reach Los Angeles until early this morning."

"I hope everyone is okay?" Carl asked sympathetically.

"Yes, we are fine. But I need to give my co-worker our rental car, so if it's not a problem, could you possibly pick me up at the Sheraton by the airport?"

"Why, of course!" said Carl. "I'll be there in an hour."

Zach hung up the phone. *This guy seems nice enough to me,* he thought.

******

Stephanie struggled against the late morning traffic as she steered the rental car towards Long Beach for her interview. She had been in and out of southern California many times over the years as she worked with Carl, but she had never lived there, so her personal experiences of driving through the heart of Los Angeles were limited. She had pretty good directions, but nothing, not even living in Chicago, could have prepared her for the morning rush of traffic fighting its way through L.A. Stephanie finally arrived in the city of her destination a little before noon.

I'm hungry, she thought as she drove across the intersection and onto the beachfront road. To her left was an In-N-Out Burger restaurant. She had always heard people from California brag about this place and its great cheeseburgers with grilled onions. They would rudely say that her White Castles could never compare to this food. "Maybe it's finally time to try this place out," she said aloud. Stephanie pulled through the drive-up window and ordered a cheeseburger with fries and a chocolate shake.

As she drove along the California coastline she was amazed at how marvelous the Pacific Ocean really was. She had seen it before many times, but every time was like the first time for her. Stephanie slurped the last of the chocolate shake and looked down at the empty box of food. The cheeseburger and fries had been entirely devoured. *I guess they're right! This food is much better than White Castles'.*

******

Stephanie pulled her rental car into the driveway of the small, two-story beach house. *What a lovely view they have,* she thought as she closed the car door and headed up the front steps of the house.

Tommy met her at the door before she could even knock. "Stephanie Miller?" he asked.

"Yes, and you must be Tommy Glover." She extended her hand to Tommy who shook it lightly.

"Come in, please," he said as he stepped aside to allow her to pass.

The house was decorated in a Maine fashion with old Victorian furnishings and a mixture of earthy coastal items thrown in to make it feel rustic, which it certainly did. There were pieces of driftwood on the coffee table and real oil lamps over the mantle. There was even an old ship wheel still attached to the helmsman's control stand. Brass and wood were mingled all around. The lace curtains softened the sun's rays as they entered through the large bay windows. Colorful wing-backed chairs and an old Victorian sofa were the final touch, sending out a statement that the owners were both educated and tasteful but somewhat earthy.

"Please have a seat," he offered.

Stephanie chose one of the two wing-backed chairs and sat down. About this time Tina came strolling into the living room. Stephanie's reporter instincts looked her over as well as the light in the room would permit. *She looks fairly young, perhaps younger than me,* she thought. She was kind of earthy looking yet attractive, but for some reason she tried to hide it behind her plain attire and short haircut.

"How do you do?" said Tina passively.

"I'm fine. Nice to meet you, Miss Glover," she said. She could tell Tina was not comfortable with the interview.

Tommy reentered the room with a fine silver tray of teacups and an adorable little teapot full of steamy liquid. "Would you like some tea?" he asked.

"Oh, yes, please!" she said thankfully.

"None for me," Tina blurted abruptly.

Tommy gave her a little scowl and then asked Stephanie if she would prefer lemon or milk in her tea.

"Lemon, please," she said without taking her eyes off Tina.

Tommy handed Stephanie the tea. She, in turn, said, "Thank you," as she admired the little china cup. "Well, let me try to explain why I am here and what I'd like to accomplish."

Tina and Tommy both sat on the sofa and stared attentively at Stephanie. She felt a little nervous. *These two are somehow intimidating,* she surmised. *Maybe it is because they both seem so intelligent but odd and definitely antisocial.*

Stephanie began in her usual way. "I have been asked by my station manager to interview some survivors of the many recent disasters that have plagued our world."

"Why?" Tina asked before Stephanie could get out another word.

"I'm getting to that!" Stephanie said sternly.

She was beginning to see how Tina worked. *She respects strength and authority. If I show any weakness, she'll eat me alive.*

"It is believed by many that these disasters could be a sign from God that the end of the world as we know it is near. In other words, that His Son is soon to return."

Tommy and Tina both stared at Stephanie. Then Tina piped in, "Are you serious?"

"I know that this seems odd, maybe even absurd to the both of you. But believe me, there are millions of people who believe the Rapture of the Church is close at hand and that these disasters are evidence of that certainty."

"Do you believe it?" Tommy asked.

"Mr. Glover, in the past two weeks I have interviewed a man that was on Mount Denali before the eruption." This got Tina's full attention. Stephanie went on. "He was talked off the mountain by an invisible voice just before it exploded."

Tina leered at her suspiciously.

Stephanie was aware of her skepticism but continued on. "I also interviewed a man who was saved from a 200-foot tidal wave just minutes before it completely destroyed Okinawa. This, added to the recent locust plague, numerous earthquakes, devastating weather patterns, and your very own volcanic eruption, makes it look like God is up to something. Don't you agree that there have been many unexplainable natural disasters in the recent past?" Stephanie paused. "Then there is the promise from God, as stated in the Bible, that He will come back for His church before His final wrath is poured out." Stephanie threw this out intentionally. She knew that Tommy and Tina were scientists and it was unlikely that they were followers of Christ, but that was the truth as she knew it.

******

Zach sat in the hotel lobby waiting for Carl. He watched each person as they walked into and out of the hotel. He suspected that he could pick Carl out of the crowd even though he had never seen him in person. Finally through the sliding doors walked a tall, sophisticated man of around 40 years of age. He was dressed in an expensive olive green suit and was wearing a pair of sunglasses that looked like they must have come from somewhere in Europe. *This is Carl,* Zach thought as he stood to greet the man.

Carl stared at Zach for a second before walking over to him. "You must be Zach Miles," he said.

"You are correct," returned Zach, "and you must be Carl Perkins."

"I must!" said Carl with a laugh. "My car is just outside. Do you have any bags?"

"Just one and I've already checked out."

The two men stepped out into the parking lot. Zach followed Carl as he walked directly up to a black 580 SEL Mercedes. Somehow Zach knew this guy would be driving a Mercedes. They made small talk as they drove from Los Angeles to Belair. Zach noticed the cars starting to improve in quality and cost as they approached this exclusive community. Shortly after he began to see an occasional mansion until finally Carl drove into an area where every house was a mansion.

Who lives in that place? He wondered as he looked at the most spectacular house he had ever seen.

"That used to be owned by Lucille Ball," said Carl, as if he had read Zach's mind.

Two blocks later Carl turned into a driveway while simultaneously pushing a button on the dash of his foreign car. The wrought iron gates began to swing open as the car approached. Carl drove through a park-like setting full of palm trees, fruit trees, and monstrous manicured hedges. As they approached the house Carl looped the car around a large pond with a fountain in the middle. Finally the car approached the huge, spectacular mansion. In all his days Zach had never seen a house like this. The face of the mansion had massive pillars, four on each side of the front entrance. Rounding the side of the house Carl pulled his car into the first bay of the six-car garage. Zach noticed two smaller homes at the back of the property. Both were bigger than the house he and Valerie had lived in for years.

"Who lives back there?" he inquired.

"Our help," said Carl flatly.

Carl took Zach around the large pool, through the courtyard, and finally into the house through the rear entrance. Zach stood in a large parlor that was fabulously decorated with statues and busts of unrecognizable faces. There were marvelous paintings on the walls and expensive furniture hardly covering the huge jade floor. He looked up at the roof and held his breath in awe of the exquisite painting of two angels staring down at him. One was a large black angel with massive wings outstretched to eight feet. The other was a handsome white angel with his wings pulled in and pointing up six feet over his head.

"Wow!" said Zach aloud before he could catch himself. "I think I know that one." He pointed to the large black angel.

Carl laughed, "Yeah, he's a friend of mine too." *I doubt it!* Zach thought.

One of Carl's servants took Zach's leather bag and led him upstairs through the long, winding staircase leading to his bedroom. When Zach reached the top of the stairs, he stopped in the center of a huge foyer to look at all the pictures on the walls. He was not a connoisseur of art, but he suspected that these paintings were quite expensive.

Looking down the hall as the servant marched along, Zach was amazed at how many bedroom doors he saw. He began to count all of the doors as he followed behind his luggage. The man finally stopped at the eighth door down from the foyer. "Door number eight," said Zach under his breath. *I'd better remember that number or else I may get lost up here.*

He entered the room behind the servant and stood in the entry area. To his left was a huge living room and over to the right was another door that he was certain led into his bedroom.

"Would you like me to unpack your bag?" the man with a heavy Spanish accent asked.

"No, thank you," said Zach. "I'll take care of it myself."

"Is there anything else I can do for you?" the man inquired.

"No, this is great! Thanks!"

******

Stephanie listened intently as she recorded her conversation with Tommy and Tina. She was fascinated with their description of the eruption of Mount Chimborazo. Tina's voice lowered as she described the last time she and Tommy saw Marcus Walker alive. "He just had to see it," she said quietly as tears filled her eyes. Tommy patted his sister's hand gently. Stephanie was moved by this show of affection between brother and sister. She never had a brother of her own, although she had always desired one.

"Did either of you feel something warning you or pulling you away from the danger?" Stephanie ventured.

What an odd question, Tina thought.

Tommy understood Stephanie's question. In fact, he had felt the need to leave even before the volcano erupted, but he had kept this feeling hidden from Marcus and Tina. He was not sure where the inspiration was coming from. He did not hear a voice, yet he felt something warning him away from the mountain.

Tina shook her head and said boldly, "We felt nothing! And we were surprised that the volcano even exploded."

Tommy decided to keep his mouth shut. It was illogical to think that he had received a warning from some spiritual realm.

"What about you, Tommy? Did you feel impressed to flee to a safer place?"

Tommy didn't make eye contact with Stephanie. He simply answered the question, "No."

Stephanie suspected that he was not telling the whole truth, but she decided not to press him. She was so intrigued with Tommy and Tina that she just had to ask some personal questions to better understand these two. How did the both of them become volcanologists? Why had neither of them married? What was it in their lives that made them so close to each other yet so distant from the rest of the world? *This will be tricky with Tina,* she thought. *I'd better work my way into it.*

"Have you two always lived together?" she blurted out.

By the look on Tina's face it was obvious that Stephanie hadn't eased her way in like she had hoped. "What does that have to do with this interview?" Tina asked sternly.

"I think it is important to know the both of you so that I can represent you fairly to our audience," she said carefully.

There, that ought to hold her off for a little while, she erroneously thought.

"Why does the audience need to know our personal lives?" Tina was very suspicious.

But before Stephanie could react, Tommy spoke up. Apparently he had decided that Stephanie could be trusted enough to share a little of their personal history with. "Tina and I were orphaned at a young age."

Tina looked at Tommy in a disapproving way, yet he continued. "Our father left our mother when we were very young, and a few years later, our mother was killed in a car crash. The authorities said they could not find our father and, since we didn't have any other relatives, we ended up in a state home for children."

"Why were you never adopted?" Stephanie asked.

"Tina and I are twins, and the state of California tries to keep twins together. And since most people only want to adopt one child at a time, we were never picked."

Stephanie had a much better understanding of these two now. They were each other's support group. They did not trust anyone, nor would they likely ever leave each other for a husband or wife. What a tragedy!

"One final question," said Stephanie, "and then I'll leave you alone."

Tina was prepared. *She'd better not ask us another personal question.* Her temper was running short.

Stephanie spoke up, "Do either of you as scientists see these disasters as out of the ordinary? I mean more than just natural happenings?"

That's a good question, Tommy thought. *After all, these disasters are a bit unusual. They are happening too close together and in some very strange places.*

"Maybe," Tina surprised both Tommy and Stephanie with her answer.

"What do you mean?" asked Stephanie.

"I don't think it has anything to do with your prophecy," she clarified, "but it is strange that there are so many disasters and such big ones. This is unusual as well."

Spoken like a true scientist, Stephanie thought.

Tommy nodded affirmation. "Yes, and in strange places that we just wouldn't expect these sorts of things."

Stephanie thanked both of them for their time and began to pack up her gear for the trip back to the hotel.

"Ms. Miller," said Tommy.

"Yes," she said softly.

"Do you really believe that Christ is coming back soon? In fact, do you really believe in God at all?"

"Mr. Glover," she replied, "If I ever had any doubts, they were all erased yesterday."

Both Tina and Tommy listened in fascination as Stephanie told them about the plane crash and how she and Zach had survived. "The sense of peace—that all would be well—was overwhelming," she said, the emotion in her voice obvious. And with that she left them standing on their front porch as she got into her car and drove off.

******

Zach headed back downstairs after storing his clothing in the nearest closet. At the base of the stairs a housemaid greeted him and asked if he would like a snack before dinner.

"We are having a special dinner tonight with guests, but if you would like something now, I'd be glad to make it for you."

"I'm fine really, but maybe a little iced tea if you don't mind?" Zach knew that the young woman felt the need to do something for him, and tea would suffice.

He strolled into one of the many living rooms and stared out of the large window into the park. *What an amazing thing that people actually live like this,* he thought. He spotted a door at the end of the living room and followed it into the library. The walls were covered with thousands of books in every direction. He moved closer to read some of the titles. *Adolescent Physiology* was the first title that caught his attention. In fact, there were numerous books on physiology, as well as financial management.

"You must be Mr. Miles?" said a soft, friendly voice from behind him.

He turned to see an attractive woman of about 40 years of age smiling at him. He extended his hand. "Call me Zach, please. I hope you don't mind me wandering around like this, but this place is spectacular."

"Hi, Zach. My name is Clorisa. I'm Carl's wife, and you are welcome to wander all you want," she said genuinely.

I like this lady already, Zach thought. Just then the maid came in with a tall glass on a silver tray. There was a large slice of lemon peering over the edge of the glass. Zach took it and thanked the young lady with a smile. She walked out of the library quickly as if she had been trained not to loiter which, of course, she had.

"How many servants do you have?" he asked curiously.

"Far too many!" Clorisa answered with fatigue in her voice. She could remember when she took care of her home all by herself, but unfortunately she could no longer recall the last time she even cooked a meal.

"If you'd like to take a swim, hit some golf balls on our driving range, or if you'd like to ride one of our horses, please help yourself. Apparently Carl is a little busy right at the moment, and we are having some guests for dinner, so you have a few hours to relax."

"Thank you!" said Zach. "But I think I'll just take a walk around outside for a while if you don't mind."

"How about I show you around a little bit?"

"That will be fine," Zach smiled.

Clorisa and Zach walked silently for a while until they reached the stables. Clorisa climbed onto the wooden fence rail and whistled softly. Soon a large, buckskin quarter horse came walking over to where she stood.

"Hi, Sweetheart." Clorisa scratched the horse's forelock. "This is just about the only thing that I am grateful for around this place."

This statement astounded Zach considerably. *How could anyone have so much yet be so dissatisfied?*

Clorisa looked at Zach. "Are you surprised to hear me say that?"

"Well, it seems to me that you have a lot to be grateful for." Clorisa was a hard one for Zach to read.

"Don't misunderstand me," she said. "I am a truly blessed person, and I thank the good Lord for it, but I don't want or need all of this to be happy. Conversely, it seems to me that I was much happier before we—I mean Carl—made all this money. You see, Zach," she went on, "before all of this I had dreams and goals, and I enjoyed working towards them. But now there is nothing left for me to dream about. I don't need anything, and I don't do anything."

Zach listened carefully without commenting. *She's not looking for a response from me,* he thought. *She is just apologizing for having too much. She feels guilty.*

Clorisa climbed down from the fence and led Zach out towards the small forest behind the stables. "I understand that you work with Stephanie?" she said.

Oh, boy! Here we go, he thought. He forgot that Clorisa was the wife who had been cheated on. "Yes, I do," he said cautiously.

"How is she?" Clorisa asked with genuine kindness in her voice.

"Alive! And grateful, I suspect," he said. Clorisa looked at Zach for clarification. He took the time to explain the plane crash as she listened.

"It seems that God is protecting you and Stephanie," she observed.

"I'm now convinced of that," he said flatly.

"You don't seem overly grateful," she said.

"Oh, I am. But I don't understand *why* He keeps protecting me." Clorisa knew there was a story in there somewhere, but she decided to focus on something else that she had noticed in Zach's tone.

"Are you a Christian?" she inquired.

"How does a person know if they are a Christian?" he retorted.

Clorisa smiled. His comment confirmed what she had suspected about him. Zach was in that terrible place between serving and rejecting Christ. "That's a good question!" she said with a smile. "People often confess they are Christians without any understanding of what a true Christian really is."

Clorisa had Zach's full attention at this point. He really wanted to understand this issue. "Simply put," she said, "whom do you live for?

What is your main focus in life? Who do you crave to spend time with daily? What do you really love—the world or God?"

"You see," Clorisa continued, "a true Christian is not one who steers away from sin but still lives his life as he pleases. A true Christian is not one who lives in sin and then cries out to God daily. A true Christian is not even the one who goes to church and reads the Bible."

Zach listened closely. *Okay, then what is a true Christian if there is such a thing?*

"A true Christian is a person that carries Jesus in their heart wherever they go. Their desire is to serve God, not the world. This person has given over their own life in favor of what God wants them to be. You see, Zach," she went on, "we all struggle with sin. That is Satan's plan for us. We all struggle to lead our own life; that is our nature. But when the Spirit of God enters your heart, there is no room for anything of this world in your life. I'm sure pious men go to Hell, just as I'm sure sinners go to Heaven. God knows our heart, and the heart is what matters, not our works."

Clorisa and Zach walked out of the forest and stood just in front of the driving range. "So tell me about Stephanie," she requested. "Are things going well for her?"

"She's doing fine!" he said. "In fact, she is going to be my daughter-in-law very soon."

Clorisa smiled radiantly. "How wonderful! Stephanie is very precious to me, and I love her very much."

Zach was confused. *Did this lady know that Stephanie had had an affair with her husband?*

Clorisa saw the confusion on Zach's face. "So she told you, I see."

He nodded affirmation.

"Zach, you really don't know Carl yet, but by this evening your understanding will be much clearer. Stephanie is young, and she was overwhelmed by her surroundings and by Carl's charismatic personality. I have forgiven her, and so has God."

He was amazed by Clorisa's pure heart. *This is what a Christian is supposed to be like,* he told himself.

Zach dressed for dinner in the best clothes he had brought with him. *I hope this is not too formal.*

Carl had been gone all afternoon, so Zach had not had an opportunity to discuss his upcoming show. He had hoped to get this completed before the day was over, but that no longer looked like a possibility.

Heading downstairs and into the nearby living area he was greeted once again by the pretty, young maid who this time held a platter of fine hors d'oeuvres up to him. "Would you like one?" she asked.

Zach couldn't resist. *Besides, it might hurt her feelings if I don't,* he justified to himself. "Thank you," he said as he picked out a large crab-stuffed mushroom.

Carl entered the room with a glass of wine in his hand. "May I offer you a drink?"

"No, thank you," replied Zach. "I'm fine."

"I'm sorry that I've been so busy, but such is the life of a minister. We have an hour or so before our dinner guests arrive, so if you'd like, we can go into my study and talk about your program."

"I'd appreciate that very much."

Carl's study was nearly as large as Zach's entire apartment. The walls were covered with pictures of Carl alongside many of our presidents and foreign dignitaries. There were no family pictures on the walls, nor were there any pictures of Jesus or even a cross anywhere in sight. The study was broken into three separate sections, four counting the bathroom. The first compartment was more of a living room with large comfortable chairs and antique tables. The second was a private office like one might expect for a bank president. The third was a small gym room complete with a sauna at the far end.

Carl chose one of the chairs in the living area and sat down in it. "Tell me your strategy." Carl sat his glass of wine on the expensive, antique table.

Strategy! Zach thought. *What a strange choice of words, but I guess it is appropriate.* He explained the show's purpose and his approach as best he could. Carl nodded as he followed along.

"It sounds like you've done a lot of work to prepare for this," Carl admired, "but tell me, who is this Leonard Thomas you've referred to?"

"He was my family minister as I grew up in Chicago. He's a friend of mine," Zach added.

"I guess it will be all right to have a layperson's perspective on the Rapture," said Carl snidely. Zach knew from many of Carl's other mannerisms that he was an arrogant man, but this statement about the faithful Pastor Thomas confirmed that Carl saw himself as head and shoulders above all others in his line of work.

Carl and Zach spoke briefly about the finer details of the program, and Carl agreed to be in Chicago the Saturday before the program.

"Now tell me about some of the questions that you intend to discuss."

"The major point of this interview is focused on the many world disasters that we have been experiencing and whether they prove or disprove the theory that Jesus is coming back," explained Zach.

"Only God knows that," said Carl with a smile on his rosy face. The wine was starting to enter Carl's bloodstream along with the cocaine that had taken him the better part of the day to find.

"So I've been told," said Zach.

"But God does give us clues," continued Carl, "and if you know the Bible well enough, you can figure out approximately when Christ is coming back." Carl had convinced Zach that he knew his Bible well.

What Zach was not sure of was whether or not Carl believed what he read. "Do you think Jesus is returning soon?" Zach asked.

"Yes, I do!" said Carl, too quickly and with a slight slur in his voice. "God has given me visions and warnings to share with the people. In fact, I have written about some of them in my new book called *The Aftermath*. I will share this with the people during your show." Carl sat the empty glass of wine on the corner of the table and stood weakly. "Well, I'd better get ready for dinner," he said.

Zach knew that was his cue to leave. "Thanks for your time. And now I think I'd like to call my wife before your guests arrive. He headed up to his room while Carl headed into the bathroom of his study for one more blast of cocaine.

******

The dinner guests entered the house in small groups. There were 12 of them altogether, rich men and politicians. A wife or some young, attractive woman accompanied each man. Zach sat down at the large table next to Clorisa as the servants were busy filling the glasses with wine and cold water.

The only person who appeared to be missing was the good reverend himself. Clorisa took the opportunity to introduce Zach to each guest. He quickly realized that this was more of a board meeting than a formal dinner since every member in attendance was apparently a business owner or investor in some large food chain. Some were owners of large farming conglomerations, while still others owned distribution and warehouse channels for moving and storing food. Zach was not exactly sure what the role of each politician was. He assumed they must be lobbyists of these large food-related companies and, as such, a part of the legal bribery system of the United States. In some way every guest in the room was an extension of a large food supply chain.

Zach sat back and listened to the conversations going on around the room. The main topic was the disastrous effects of the recent locust outbreak east of the Rocky Mountains. Others discussed the global effects of many disasters depleting the world's food reserves. "We will be able to sell even the worst of our crops this year at a considerable profit," said one of the men joyfully.

Zach was aware of California's tremendous contribution to supplying our nation's food requirements, and it now appeared as if these men held all the cards necessary to determine who would eat and who would starve.

Carl entered the dining hall carrying another glass of wine. To Zach's surprise, following alongside Reverend Perkins was Carlo Ventini. When they entered the room, all of the men at the table stood to greet Carlo and Carl cordially. Carlo shook hands warmly with each man until he finally reached Zach. "Mr. Miles, how good to see you again," he smiled wearily.

"Likewise," said Zach with just as much enthusiasm. Carlo made him very nervous, but he never understood why.

"Still looking for Christ to show up?" he laughed. Every person at the table looked towards Zach and laughed along with Carlo.

Clorisa watched all of this with fascination. *How does Zach know this man?* she wondered.

Carl, the unlikely hero, came to Zach's rescue. "Mr. Miles is doing a very interesting story on the possibility of the recent world disasters being connected with Christ's imminent appearance and, of course, I share his interest."

Out of respect for Carl the guests nodded politely, all except Carlo who seemed to sneer at Zach as he sat down at the table.

Throughout the night Zach watched as the rich and powerful men drank and extolled themselves as if they had planned all of these disasters personally. Occasionally someone would ask Zach a question.

"So, Mr. Miles, you live in the Midwest, right? Was the locust attack really as bad as they say?" one man asked optimistically.

"I am afraid so!" Zach responded.

"What a pity," said another without any emotion in his voice.

"Have you heard from Father Bastoni recently?" Carlo Ventini piped in.

"No, but he will be in Chicago next Friday."

"So then you actually convinced him to do your little show?" Carlo asked condescendingly.

"As a matter of fact, he was glad to do the show," Zach said.

Carlo turned towards him and looked him dead in the eye. "Really! Well, who else have you recruited?"

Zach looked at Carl. Carlo turned quickly in the same direction. "You too?" he asked in an obviously annoyed tone.

Carl was gulping down another glass of wine when Carlo confronted him. "Sure, why not?" he said. "Besides, it will be great publicity for my new book." *Oops! Did I say that?* he thought.

"Is there anyone else on this show that I know?" Carlo was inquisitive.

"No," Zach said flatly. *As if it is any of your business who I have on my show,* Zach thought angrily.

Clorisa could sense Zach's anger rising. "Zach, if you are done eating, maybe you'd like to stretch your legs?"

Zach pushed his chair away from the table. "Sounds good to me!" he said without taking his eyes off Carlo.

"Yes, fresh air is good for the soul!" Carlo winked at Zach.

That guy is a real jerk! Zach told himself as he followed Clorisa through the massive kitchen.

Zach and Clorisa spent the rest of the evening sitting by the pool talking. Zach found her to be a charming person. It was a wonder how she could ever have married a man like Carl Perkins.

"How many children do you have?" Clorisa inquired.

"Just one," said Zach with a smile for his son.

"How about you and Carl?"

Clorisa's face saddened, "None."

"Why not? You surely can afford them."

Clorisa sighed softly, "Yes, well it turns out that Carl is sterile."

"Why didn't you adopt?" he asked cautiously.

"Carl said that if it was God's Will for us to have children, He wouldn't have made him incapable."

Clorisa changed the subject. "How long have you been married?"

"I'm not," he said, "but I hope to fix that soon!"

Clorisa needed a little clarification. "I don't understand."

"My wife and I have been divorced for 14 years, but it's not your typical divorce." Clorisa listened while Zach shared his personal life with her. He trusted her completely.

"So you are going to ask her to marry you again?" she asked.

"Yes, I need her in my life, Clorisa," said Zach.

"That's good! I don't believe in divorce."

That explains why she is still married to the good Reverend Perkins, he thought.

"Why did your marriage fail the first time?" she asked.

"It was my fault. My wife is a Christian, and we just didn't see eye to eye on lots of things."

Clorisa nodded. "And now, Zach, do you see more clearly?"

"I'm starting to," he admitted with a smile.

"God wants that none should perish," she said boldly. "Whatever has made you angry at God is not His fault. You must get this out of your life, and then you will be free."

Zach knew she was right. He had no real right to be angry at God, but he would need to settle that on his own. "Well, I think I'll call it a night," he said.

"It has been a real pleasure!" Clorisa extended her small hand towards him. "You are a good man," she said as she shook his hand.

"Coming from you, that means a lot," he said shyly.

******

Carl drove Zach to the airport the next morning. He wasn't in his best form, having drunk at least two bottles of wine by himself the night before. "I hope you don't have the wrong impression of me," he apologized in his own fashion. "I am not doing your show just to advertise my new book. I want the world to know the truth of Jesus' soon return so they may prepare to meet Him." His voice lacked conviction.

Zach had Carl figured out. He seemed to be able to live in multiple worlds simultaneously, and as long as no one tested his genuineness, he'd continue to fool most people. It was too late to exclude him from the show, and besides, Scott really wanted to meet him. Zach did not want to give Carl the satisfaction of easing his conscience. He simply said, "I guess we'll see you on Saturday, July 9, then."

Carl got the message. He had lost Zach as a potential disciple. He was always leery of reporters, but for some reason he had forgotten his standard protocol around Zach. The damage was done. Zach knew who Carl really was. *Oh, well—you win a few and you lose a few,* the cavalier Reverend Perkins mused.

As they drove into the airport terminal, Carl told Zach he would like to take a minute to say hello to Stephanie.

Zach wanted to spare Stephanie the humiliation of Carl's visit, so he quickly said, "Stephanie took an earlier flight back home this morning." Of course, he lied—not something Zach often did—but he loved Stephanie, and he didn't like Carl, so it seemed appropriate.

Carl was obviously disappointed. "Oh, well! I guess I'll see her Saturday."

Undoubtedly! Zach thought. *There's no way around that, but she'll have Timothy with her then and that'll keep Mr. Carl Perkins at bay.*

Stephanie and Zach met at the terminal gate for their flight to Chicago. They were extremely glad to see each other. Stephanie gave Zach a big hug and began to cry.

"I know!" said Zach. "Let's go home."

Needless to say, both Zach and Stephanie suffered severe anxiety until the plane landed safely at Chicago's O'Hare Airport. As Stephanie was walking up the long ramp she could see Timothy peering in like a small child waiting for his mother. She nearly ran to him as she exited the tunnel. He hugged her until she thought he might break her ribs. She kissed him softly but firmly on the lips. Zach patted his son on the shoulder as he walked by him on his way to Valerie. Zach dropped his bag and wrapped his arms around Valerie's waist. He lifted her off the ground briefly. She giggled like a child. "I love you!' she whispered in his ear.

As Zach let Valerie down gently, he looked into her beautiful brown eyes. "And I love you!"

Timothy and Stephanie stood back briefly watching this beautiful scene. Life was good for the Miles family.

Chapter 15 - The Show

The time had gone by quickly. Scott was back from his tropical vacation and now sat listening intently as Zach and Stephanie shared the final details of the upcoming show. He was pleased with the way things had come together. "And tell me about Carl Perkins," he said excitedly. "Is he everything that he appears to be?"

Zach looked at Stephanie and then back to Scott. "And then some," he said lightly.

"Great! When will he be here?"

"Joseph—I mean, Father Bastoni—is coming in this afternoon, and the Reverend Perkins will be here tomorrow," said Zach.

"Have you made reservations for dinner yet?" Scott asked Stephanie.

"Yes, dinner will be at 6:00 p.m. at Lowry's."

Stephanie was dreading the dinner, but it had to happen sooner or later.

"Everything is set then," said Scott as he stood to leave. "I told you this show wouldn't kill you!" he said as he walked out of his own office. His humor was lost on both Stephanie and Zach.

******

Zach had a couple of hours before he had to pick up Joseph. He felt compelled to go and see Leo. He told himself that he really just wanted to make sure Pastor Thomas was ready for the show, but that wasn't the only reason for the visit. In fact, it wasn't even the main reason.

Zach opened the door to the side of the church and walked down the dark hall towards Leo's small office. As he approached he could hear Leo singing a Christian song along with the radio. He couldn't help but smile. Leo just seemed to exude joy. He had grown very fond of this man.

Zach knocked on the door just below the small nameplate. Leo opened the door and grinned broadly. "Well, where have you been? I expected to see you as soon as you got back from California. I'm glad to see you, Son."

Zach felt a little guilty. He had intended on coming around sooner, but lately he spent every extra moment with Valerie. He just couldn't seem to get enough time with her, and he hated to leave even for a short visit to the People's Church.

They spent 20 minutes or so talking about the recent events. Leo didn't seem to be a bit surprised by Zach's opinion of Carl Perkins, but he did think it suspicious that Carlo Ventini was in L.A., especially at Carl's house.

"It seems that Carlo is working with the major food growers of California. Maybe he is trying to get them to invest in his Agripod system."

Leo nodded. "You're probably right. It's probably just part of his business."

Zach shared in great detail all that Clorisa had spoken to him.

"She sounds like a lovely person," Leo commented.

Finally Zach shared the events of the plane wreck, including how he had prayed for God to protect Stephanie. Leo sat back in his chair and closed his eyes for nearly a minute. Zach was not sure if the old man had fallen asleep or if he was praying.

"Zach," he said, "do you realize that you actually put your faith in God when you asked Him to save Stephanie?"

He had not really thought of his prayer to God as a confession of faith but more as a logical argument: If You are going to save me, then why not Stephanie also?

Leo looked intently at him, "Are you ready to accept Christ as your savior?"

Zach thought carefully about what Leo had asked him. "I don't know!" he said. "I'm not sure what is happening to me. I know that God exists, and I'm not mad at Him anymore." Leo listened closely. "But," he continued. "I don't really know who Jesus is or what it means to follow Him."

He needs more time, Leo thought. *But does he have more time?* "Okay," said Leo, "Let's talk about it some more tomorrow."

Zach sat still for a few minutes before he finally said to Leo, "I want to marry Valerie again."

Leo smiled. "Well, it's about time!"

Zach nodded in agreement. "Yes, and I'd like you to marry us."

"What's your plan, Son?" Leo inquired.

"First I have to get Valerie to say yes," he said, though he was pretty sure she would. "I thought we could do it next week once this show is behind me."

"Son, things are starting to look up for you!" Leo said. *Now if we can just lead you to Christ,* he thought silently.

Zach invited Leo to attend their dinner Saturday night. He enthusiastically accepted.

"You'll pick me up, right?"

"I'll be here by 5:00 p.m."

"Good enough. I'll be ready."

******

Back at the airport once again Zach was feeling pretty tired of this place, but he was looking forward to seeing Joseph. He had to wait an additional 90 minutes because Joseph's plane was delayed. He spent this time sitting and watching the thousands of people hustling through the airport.

We are a multicolored species, he thought as he observed people from seemingly every part of the world walking or running from the ticket counter towards the terminal.

Finally a weary Joseph exited the secured area wheeling his luggage behind him as he headed for Zach.

"Good to see you," said Zach.

"You too!" smiled Joseph.

"Did you have a good flight?"

"It was long!" he sighed.

Zach led Joseph out of the airport and to his car. "I thought we'd go back to my apartment where you can clean up. Then I'd like you to meet my family."

Joseph was delighted. "Sounds good to me! I've been waiting to meet the Miles family."

Joseph was impressed at how plain and empty Zach's apartment was. *How lonely,* he thought.

"It's not much," Zach admitted. "When Valerie and I got divorced, I left most of my stuff over there. Through the years I just kind of grew accustomed to living out of both places. Please, come in and make yourself at home."

Joseph made himself comfortable in the bachelor's apartment. He, too, was used to living in a home that was lacking a woman's touch. Just the same, home was home.

With Joseph unpacked and showered, they were on their way to Valerie's. Timothy's car was already there when Zach pulled up. Joseph liked the look of the small house. It reminded him of his own childhood home in Wisconsin.

Valerie met Joseph and Zach at the door. She was dressed attractively in a summer dress with her hair pulled back neatly. Zach kissed Valerie on the cheek and then turned to introduce Joseph. "This is Father Bastoni."

"Call me Joseph, please!" the young priest smiled.

Valerie leaned in and hugged Joseph. "Thank you for taking care of my husband," she whispered.

Joseph whispered back to Valerie, "My pleasure!"

Next Zach introduced Stephanie as his future daughter-in-law and finally his son, Timothy.

"You two look good together," Joseph said in a friendly way.

Timothy shook his hand firmly. "Nice to meet you, Father—I mean, Joseph."

Zach seated Joseph in his favorite chair and followed Valerie into the kitchen to help her with dinner. "What can I do?"

"You can chop the lettuce for me," she said as she pointed to the salad ingredients sitting on the cutting board.

Zach picked up a large knife and began to slice the lettuce into moderate sized pieces. "I visited Pastor Thomas today," he said carefully. He wanted to broach the issue of marriage with Valerie, but he found himself suddenly very nervous.

"Really! How's he doing?" She knew Zach was up to something, and she had a good idea of what it was. However, she thought it best to listen patiently.

"Oh, he's fine. I'm picking him up for dinner tomorrow."

"What dinner would that be?" she asked.

"Stephanie and I are going to meet with all the guest speakers for Sunday's show. I would like you and Timothy to be there too."

Valerie looked down into the pot of noodles. As she stirred she smiled at how nervous Zach was about his imminent show. "I'd be glad to go. Will you pick me up too?"

"Sure!" he said happily. "There's something else." Zach lowered the knife.

Valerie stopped stirring the noodles but did not take her eyes off the large pot.

"I asked Leo if he would consider marrying us—that is, if you'd consider marrying me," Zach whispered.

Valerie turned slowly towards him. She was so lovely. Her beauty melted Zach's confidence. *How could I have ever let her go in the first place?* he wondered.

"Does it still bother you that I am a Christian? Because that will never change!" she said boldly. "And I will still be going to church on Sundays and Wednesdays."

"No!" said Zach with a sense of freedom in his voice. "It does not bother me, and if you want, I will go to church with you."

Valerie's heart broke and she began to cry audibly. In fact, she cried so loudly the sound brought Timothy in from the living room.

Zach stepped up to Valerie and wrapped his arms around her tenderly. "Is that a yes?" he whispered.

Timothy stared at his parents in momentary disbelief. *Is what I think really happening?*

Valerie looked into Zach's worried face. "This is the answer to my prayers," she said. "All I've ever wanted is to be your wife."

Timothy eased his way out of the kitchen without being noticed and headed directly into the bathroom to dry the tears from his face.

Stephanie met Timothy as he came out of the bathroom. "Is everything all right?"

Timothy could barely hold back the tears of joy as he reached for Stephanie's hand. "He asked her to marry him, and she said yes!"

Stephanie kissed Timothy and said, "Now there are two happy girls in this family."

Joseph was completely fascinated during dinner by the love he felt among the members of this family. He often wondered what life would be like if he had not chosen to become a priest. Maybe he would have a nice family of his own by now. The thought brought on some depression for Joseph. Over the last year he had struggled continually with trying to find a purpose in his life. He had always thought that the nobility of being a priest would fill his life, but recently he felt empty and alone. Something was missing, but he didn't know what.

******

Saturday was a pleasant day for Joseph and Zach. The two of them took advantage of their time together by driving down to the lake. They walked and talked for over an hour. It seemed that this time Zach was the one listening as Joseph shared from his heart. "I've tried to do what God wants from me. I've made many sacrifices, and I've tried to be a good person," he said plainly. "I follow all the Catholic requirements for mass and prayer time, but lately it seems like a waste of time." Joseph stopped and turned towards Zach. "Are you surprised to hear me say this?"

"Yes, but when I think about it, you're only human, right?"

Joseph nodded in agreement.

"You know," said Zach, "I met a lady the other day in Los Angeles who told me that God is not impressed by what we do. She said that God knows our hearts. He knows if we are living for Him or not and if we are carrying Jesus inside of us."

Joseph was perplexed. *Could this be the same guy he met only six weeks ago in Rome? Out of the mouths of babes!* he thought.

Zach had delivered him a message from God—one that Joseph already knew, but one that he did not know how to apply to his own life. He was caught up in the formality of serving God, but he didn't know how to establish a personal relationship with Christ. It was a hopeless and terrible feeling for him.

After changing for dinner, Zach and Joseph drove by the People's Church to pick up Leo. They met him in the parking lot. He was dressed in a pair of gray, baggy slacks and a short-sleeved, white shirt.

Leo climbed into the back seat and, leaning forward, he extended a hand to Joseph. "Leo Thomas. And you must be Father Bastoni."

"Glad to meet you. Please call me Joseph."

"Okay, Son. You got it!"

Joseph laughed at this. He liked Leo already.

"Next stop my house to pick up Valerie." said Zach with a smile.

"Well, what's the good news?" Leo asked. "Did you ask her?"

Zach grinned. "She said yes!"

Joseph smiled and Leo slapped Zach on the back smartly. "Way to go, Son. Now you're cookin'!"

******

Stephanie and Timothy sat in the restaurant waiting for the rest of the group to show up. Stephanie was extremely nervous.

"You're awful quiet tonight," Timothy observed.

Stephanie had wanted to tell him all week that Carl was the man she had an affair with, but there never seemed a good time to bring up the subject. Now, however, she had no choice. Stephanie breathed a silent sigh and spoke with a quiver in her voice. "It was Carl," she said cryptically.

At first Timothy didn't understand what she meant. "Who is Carl?"

"Carl Perkins, the evangelist," she said more plainly.

Timothy stared into her uncertain eyes.

"He was the one," she said in a whisper.

Timothy nodded and reached a hand out to Stephanie. "It's okay," he said softly.

Valerie entered the restaurant ahead of Zach with Leo and Joseph close behind.

"Hi, Mom!" said Timothy with a warm smile.

Zach sat next to Stephanie. He leaned in towards her and said, "Hang in there! This will all be over soon."

She smiled and patted his hand.

Valerie sat on Zach's other side with Leo next to her and Joseph next to him. "I understand that congratulations are in order for you, Valerie!" said Leo with a broad smile.

Valerie whispered into Leo's ear. "Fourteen years of prayer has finally paid off," she laughed cheerfully.

The group dined on bread and water as they waited for Carl and Scott to show up.

Joseph and Leo were busy getting to know each other while Zach listened carefully to Timothy as he shared the wedding plans that he and Stephanie were making. "August seems like a good time to us." he said enthusiastically. "How about you, Dad? When are you and Mom going to tie the knot?"

Valerie looked directly at Zach in anticipation. They hadn't had this conversation yet, and she hoped that Zach would say, "Soon!"

Zach looked at her for confirmation as he spoke, "I'd like to do it next week—maybe Saturday." Valerie's smile gave him the confirmation he was looking for.

Carl and Scott showed up 30 minutes late, and to Zach and Stephanie's surprise, Clorisa was with them.

All the members at the table rose to greet the late arrivers. Clorisa headed straight to Stephanie and held out her hands. "I'm so glad to see you," she said in a loving way. "This must be your fiancée," she said as she turned towards Timothy.

But Timothy was not paying attention. He was watching Carl as he went around the room shaking hands. Soon Carl made it around to Stephanie. He reached in to hug and kiss her, but before he could narrow his approach, Stephanie extended a hand towards him.

"Hello, Carl," she said lightly.

Both Clorisa and Timothy watched this closely, and so did Zach, although he remained inconspicuous as he did so.

"I understand that you are getting married. Is this the lucky man?" Carl said as he turned and looked at Timothy. Carl extended his hand like a politician running for office. Timothy knew that a man never turned down a handshake even when he didn't like the other person, which he definitely didn't. Timothy shook his hand with extra force, nearly enough to crush Carl's unexercised grip.

Scott sat next to Carl the entire evening. He was like a child who had just found a new toy. He listened to everything Carl said and mindlessly agreed with each comment. A couple of times when Leo and Joseph were talking, Carl would interrupt their conversation to interject some of his own wisdom. By this point Scott was sure that Carl was the wisest man on the planet, although Leo considered him an arrogant nuisance.

Joseph was enjoying the night considerably. He found Leo refreshing and entertaining. It seemed to Joseph as if the man didn't have a care in the world, yet he knew Leo had a more intense side. Tonight, however, Leo had decided to keep himself in check. Joseph found himself wishing he had the old man's passion for life. *Maybe it comes with age,* he postulated.

Scott raised his glass in a toast to the success of tomorrow's show. He nearly spilled the contents as he brought his glass up to his mouth. He had been trying to keep pace with Carl as the two of them exclusively drank the bottle of wine on the table.

"So, Stephanie," mumbled Scott, "tell us about tomorrow. How's it going to work?"

Stephanie suspected Scott might try to put her on the spot tonight, so she was prepared.

Just as she was about to respond, Carl lifted his glass of wine towards her and winked. "Tell us, Steph. How's it all going to work?" Carl laughed.

Timothy's face grew red as he observed Perkins taunting Stephanie. *And what is this Steph stuff?* he wondered.

Stephanie reached under the table, groping until she found Timothy's hand. She spoke boldly as she informed everyone at the table how they would proceed with tomorrow's interviews. When she finished, Clorisa gave Stephanie an approving smile and a wink of her own.

Finally the dinner was over. Stephanie and Timothy drove away from the restaurant. Stephanie sat in the passenger seat waiting for Timothy to say something. He had gotten quiet during the last half of the evening, and she knew why.

Timothy had allowed his own imagination to get the best of him, and now he felt jealous and hurt. "He's a creep!" he said all of a sudden.

Stephanie had to laugh. The stress of the evening was beginning to fade, and she was with the man she loved. Things could only get better. "I love you!" she said through her laughter.

Timothy began to laugh as well. "And he's ugly too!" he said. At this last comment Stephanie nearly choked on her laughter until her sides hurt.

******

The big day had finally come. It was Sunday and in just five hours Zach would finish what he had started months earlier. He was excited about the show, but he was also a little sad it would soon all be over. It was kind of like preparing for Christmas. Everything was full of mystery and excitement, but by Christmas night it was all over. *These last many weeks have changed me forever,* he thought. *I have my wife back, my son is getting married, and somehow I've changed for the better.* Zach knew that all of this was the result of God's work in his life. "Thank you, Lord!" he whispered as he finished knotting his tie.

Zach walked into the living room. There sat Joseph dressed in his priestly vestments. Zach smiled at the nervous priest. "Are you ready?"

he asked.

"Yeah, let's go."

As the two of them pulled up to Valerie's house, Joseph observed her sitting on the porch. "You are a lucky man," he said with personal regret in his voice.

"How right you are! And it only took me 14 years to figure it out."

Somehow this last comment gave Joseph a little hope.

Valerie greeted them with a kiss for Zach and a smile for Joseph.

Ten minutes later the three of them entered the front entrance of Leo's church for Sunday morning service. Zach hadn't been through these particular doors since his mother died years ago. The memory of that sad day flooded his mind, but this time it wasn't accompanied by anger. Zach had finally reconciled his differences with God.

My mom was a real Christian, the kind Clorisa spoke about, and I know that she is in Heaven with my dad and brothers. He said a short silent prayer, thanking God for this new revelation.

Leo greeted all three of them at the entrance to the sanctuary. "Come in and sit down in the front so you can hear the music better."

Zach and Joseph met many friendly people as they made their way to the front. There were also numerous stares at Joseph because of the way he was dressed, but in this church everyone was welcome. Leo wouldn't have it any other way. The choir rose and began to sing. The music was wonderful, although Zach figured he could hear it from the back of the sanctuary just fine. In fact, he could probably hear it from the parking lot without too much effort.

Joseph was a bit more solemn during the worship portion of the service, but he soon loosened up as Leo began to unfurl his morning sermon. He spoke from the text of Matthew 19:14. "'Let the little children come to Me.' We are the children," said Leo loudly. This was followed by hundreds of amen's from the crowd. "We are God's children," he continued, "and He loves us all! He longs to gather all of us to Him," said Leo as he wrapped his arms around his own chest. "But," Leo said slowly, "you must receive Christ. You must go to Him and ask Him into your life. He will not enter uninvited, and if He doesn't enter at all, then there will not be a place for you in Heaven."

Joseph listened carefully to Leo's message of a relationship with Christ. The idea of a personal relationship was not foreign to Joseph, but he had always felt that it was unnecessary. As long as we follow the rules, we are saved. This was what he had convinced himself over the years, but even today Joseph struggled with the emptiness of his life.

Leo's message was powerful and motivational to Zach. He felt a tug on his heart, a desire to proclaim Jesus as his savior, but he didn't understand why he felt this way or even what to do about it. At the end of the service Leo asked that all unsaved people come forward to receive Christ into their lives. He looked directly at Zach as he made his request. Zach knew that he had planned his message around his visit, and he really wanted to go forward, but something held him back.

Valerie put her hand on Zach's forearm. "I'll go with you if you want," she said encouragingly.

Zach hesitated. "I'm not ready yet. I need more time."

Both Leo and Valerie understood Zach. They knew that he was close and when his time was right, he would confess Christ as his savior, but now wasn't the time.

"Its okay,' said Valerie. "When the moment is right, you'll know it."

******

Zach drove the small group including Leo directly from the church to the studio. The mood in the car was one of excitement as everyone was anticipating the day's events. That is, everyone except Zach. He had been quiet the entire drive.

Valerie reached over and ran her hand along Zach's neck. She smiled at him lovingly. "You okay?" she asked.

Zach smiled weakly. "I'm fine," he replied.

But he wasn't fine at all. He was still thinking about the morning's sermon. He was thinking about what it meant to accept Christ into his life and about the many years he had run away from God with a heart so full of anger that it nearly destroyed his life. *Enough is enough!* he thought.

It's time to decide once and for all what I stand for.

Zach pulled into the studio parking lot and parked next to Timothy's truck. "Okay, we're here!"

The day had finally come. Let the show begin!

Zach led the group into the back entrance of the studio with Joseph right next to him and Valerie and Leo a few steps behind. As Leo turned to watch the security door close, his attention was momentarily distracted by the sight of a large black man standing in the entrance of the parking lot. Leo stared at the person, and it appeared as if the large man was looking directly at him. Finally from the elevator Valerie called to Leo. He turned in her direction and then backwards towards the parking lot, but this time the man was gone.

Exiting the elevator on the 17th floor, Zach led the group through the front office and into the main studio where he did all his interviews for television. Stephanie met them cheerfully as they entered. "Hello, everyone. There are sandwiches and drinks over on that table," she said pointing to the long table in the corner. The studio was small, but it did have enough room for an audience of eight or so.

Joseph stepped over to the table and greeted Timothy who was standing there looking at all of the food. "How are you this afternoon, Timothy?" he inquired.

Timothy liked Joseph. He saw him as a gentle and kind person. "I'm fine, Joseph. Are you ready for the program?"

Joseph nodded yes, but all of a sudden he wasn't sure if he was ready. In fact, Joseph wasn't sure if he even believed any longer those things he had always been taught.

"We are ready as soon as Carl and Scott show up," Stephanie said as she gave Zach a brief summary on the status of all the preparations. This was going to be a live interview, so she was a little concerned that they might be late.

"Stephanie, in case I haven't told you before," said Zach, "I want to thank you for all your work in preparing for this show. I couldn't have done it without your help."

Stephanie beamed with pride as she kissed Zach's cheek. "It's the least I can do for my father-in-law!"

She smiled at Valerie and Leo and then walked over to where Timothy and Joseph stood. This gave Zach an opportunity to talk to Leo and Valerie in private. "Will the two of you come to my office for a few minutes?"

Valerie could sense something important in Zach's voice.

They followed Zach down the long hall and into his small office. "Good morning, Mr. Miles." said one of the station employees as he passed by, but Zach was so focused that he didn't hear the greeting. Valerie smiled at the person as she went along.

Entering Zach's humble office, Leo and Valerie took in the pictures on the walls. Leo knew personally every family member on the wall, but Valerie had known only his mother and then not for very long.

Zach turned and closed the door after they were all safely inside the little room. "What is it, Zach?" Valerie asked. "What's wrong?"

"Nothing," said Zach with a little embarrassment in the tone of his voice. He looked at Leo and then towards Valerie. "I want to accept Jesus into my heart. I mean—" he continued, "I want to follow after Him, and I want to go to Heaven when I die."

The smile on Leo's face could have lit up the room, and tears of joy streamed down Valerie's face.

"Well, then, let's get to it!"

Zach was not sure what would come next, and he was a bit nervous.

"Accepting Christ into your life is as easy as breathing as long as you truly believe and if you truly want to be changed and follow Him," said Leo calmly but sternly.

Zach nodded attentively.

"Then all you have to do is to pray and ask God to forgive your sins and to fill you with His Holy Spirit," said the kind pastor.

Zach, Valerie, and Leo formed a small circle by holding hands. "Repeat after me," Leo said, "and pray this from your heart, Son. Dear Jesus, I believe You are the only Son of God."

Zach repeated slowly.

"I believe that You are the only way to Heaven. Lord, please forgive my many sins and fill me with Your Holy Spirit. Lord, guide me and lead me all the rest of my life."

Leo was silent for a minute or so as he prayed a personal prayer over Zach. Finally he lifted his head and squeezed Zach's hand firmly. "And now you are a saved child of God!" He smiled at Zach with tears in the corners of his eyes.

Valerie began to weep as she threw her arms around Zach's neck and hugged him tightly. "Praise God!" she whispered.

Zach took a personal inventory. He still had all the same body parts, and his mind was still the same. *What is it about me that has been changed by the sinner's prayer?* he wondered. *I feel like the same person, but I feel good, lighter, and somehow free. Free from guilt,* he thought.

"Now!" said Leo. "You need to start reading your Bible and attending a church somewhere. God's babies need food." Leo gave Zach a bear hug and a slap on the back.

Zach held Valerie's hand as they walked back into the main studio.

******

Carl made his usual grand entrance dressed in his finest suit and with all his gold jewelry on. With him he carried a faded old Bible and a copy of his new book. The faded Bible, Carl believed, made him look even more pious, and the book, of course, was the main reason he was here today.

Scott bounced around the studio like a hyperactive child who had forgotten to take his Ritalin. "Okay," he said, "places everyone."

The set was tastefully decorated with a long, mahogany table in front of four neatly placed chairs. Joseph sat down next to Zach with Carl in the middle and Leo on the end.

"No, no! That won't work!" said Scott.

"I want Carl next to you, Zach, and, Joseph, you sit in the middle." This way, Scott thought, the camera would be on Carl each time it was on Zach.

"Live in three, two, one," Scott pointed to Zach.

"Good afternoon, ladies and gentlemen," said Zach politely. "I am Zach Miles, and this is another edition of the Miles Report."

The show began with footage of the many recent disasters: volcanoes, earthquakes, fires, floods, snowstorms, and even the recent locust plague. Next came the footage of Stephanie's interviews with Izuho, followed by Tommy and Tina Glover, and ending with the mysterious story of Calvin Fraser being talked off an exploding mountain by an unknown source.

Stephanie had done a marvelous job putting together all of the disaster scenes and weaving in her interviews with the survivors. The evidence that something unusual was happening in the world was now laid out on the table, and it was overwhelming.

Zach turned back to the camera. He had an astonished look on his face after seeing the footage for the first time. "Our discussion today is whether or not these disasters are a sign from God that the end of the world is near or, shall we say, that the Return of Christ is soon to come."

"Reverend Carl Perkins, let me begin with you. What is your impression of all these disasters?"

Carl turned to the camera and smiled beneficently. "Dear children," he said. "My dear children, the Lord, our God, is punishing us for our sins! We need to repent and come to Him!"

Zach listened to Carl. As he spoke, it was obvious that the man had charisma, and if he hadn't known the reverend, he might have believed him to be genuine.

"I have outlined in my recent book, *The Aftermath*," said Carl as he lifted his book up to the camera, "how we must repent or we will face His wrath."

Zach cut Carl off before he could get rolling. There was an obvious look of disapproval from both Carl and Scott as he did this. Turning to Joseph he continued, "Father Bastoni, do you believe these disasters are a sign from God?"

Joseph thought about the question and his answer for a long time as Zach sat patiently by. "I don't know," said Joseph.

At this Carl smirked and Scott grew cold. *I can't believe I paid to fly him all the way from Rome just to hear him say he didn't know,* Scott thought with indignation.

"I mean," Joseph said, "if you are asking me if this is the end of the world, then the answer is no!" He continued. "Let me explain." Carl exhaled a sigh of boredom as Joseph began to explain his personal position on the book of Revelation. He spoke eloquently citing specific areas in the Bible to support his take on the fulfillment of Biblical prophecy.

While Joseph was speaking, Zach looked out to Valerie and Timothy as they sat side by side. He loved them both very much. He had made their lives miserable over the years. *But now,* he thought, *I will make up for lost time.* As he was looking at Timothy, he realized how much his son was just like him—lost in the complexity of this world and full of disappointment over what life had dealt him. Zach was glad that Stephanie had come into his son's life, but he was concerned that Timothy still held many things against God. Zach decided that as soon as the show was over, he was going to tell his son about his decision to become a Christian. *Maybe,* he thought, *Timothy will be able to make peace with God when he realizes his father has.*

******

Over the course of 30 minutes Zach had given each panel member an opportunity to answer his specific questions on the recent disasters. Now it was time to move to the final question. Turning to the camera once again Zach began to speak. "There is a belief among many in the world that Jesus Christ is coming back soon to take away the Christians before the wrath of God is poured out on the world. Pastor Leo Thomas, could you please share with us your thoughts on this issue?"

Leo sat forward in his chair. "It's simple, really. Jesus promised us, before He went to Heaven, that He would come back for us. He even gave us signs to look for," he added.

"Such as?" asked Zach.

Leo smiled at how professional Zach was being. "Luke 21:10 described great earthquakes, wars, and rumors of war," he said. "Then there is 1 Thessalonians 4:17 where the Apostle Paul describes for us the Rapture and how we will be caught up in the air. Again in Revelation 3:10-11, Jesus is talking to the Church of Philadelphia which is a metaphor for the saints from all of his churches regardless of denomination."

"So then, Leo—I mean, Pastor Thomas—you believe that the Lord is returning to Rapture, or to save His church, and all these disasters are a sign from God?"

Leo beamed. "Yes, I do, Zach, and you're going to be there for it!"

Zach returned Leo's smile, then turned to Carl. "Do you believe that Jesus is coming to Rapture His church?"

Once again Carl turned on the charm. "As I have said in my new book, as well as in many of my other books," Carl said boastfully, "God has not appointed us to wrath."

"Can you be more specific on what you mean by God's wrath?" Zach inquired.

The chore seemed laborious to Carl, but he obliged Zach's request. "In 2 Peter 2:4-7 Peter describes the kind of God we serve. He describes how God protects the righteous man or woman." Carl smiled at the camera and then out to his own wife, Clorisa, who had just walked into the studio. Carl finally sat his book down as he continued to expound. "And in 1 Thessalonians 5:9 that wonderful man of God, Paul the Apostle, tells us that God has not appointed us to suffer those things that are foretold. This, of course, is also found in Revelation 3:10 like our good brother, Pastor Thomas, has already said."

"So then," said Zach, "you believe that God is going to protect us from the tribulation mentioned in the Bible?"

"He will protect those who repent," said Carl sternly, theatrically.

"Do you believe that Christ will Rapture us before the Seven Year Tribulation begins?" Zach asked directly.

"I don't see why not," Carl replied. "Read my book and find out."

"Pastor Thomas, do you believe that there will be a Rapture before the Tribulation begins?"

"I'm not sure that we are not already living in the first half of the tribulation and, in any case, it really doesn't matter. God will deliver us in

His own good time. This will hopefully be before His wrath is poured out. If that is before or after the seventh seal is opened, it doesn't make any difference." Leo continued, "Christians have died in the past, and they continue to die every day in God's service. But when it is God Himself that begins to destroy the world, then—" Leo shook his head sadly, "—many will die. However, the children of God will be saved forever."

Zach turned to Joseph who was listening in fascination as Leo spoke with such great faith.

"What is your position on this issue?" Zach asked. He already knew what Joseph would say, but it was worth hearing twice.

"I have been taught," said Joseph. He paused and reconsidered what he was about to say. "1 Corinthians 15:51 says that Christ will come back at the last trumpet." He added, "In Revelation 10:7 the last trumpet references the completion of God's plan. This is at the very least during the tribulation after the temple is desecrated."

"What temple?" Zach asked for the benefit of the television audience as well as for himself.

"It's the Jewish temple that is supposed to be rebuilt over the original sight of the Holy of Holies. But this is presently the site of The Mosque of Omar, commonly referred to as The Dome of the Rock," said Joseph.

"Is there any chance that the believed location is incorrect?" Zach inquired.

"I suppose," Joseph said, "but it still does not resolve the fact that 2 Thessalonians 2:3 states that the day of the Lord will not come until the rebellion has occurred."

"What is the rebellion?" Zach asked with considerable interest.

"The revealing of the Antichrist and the desecration of God's temple," said Joseph softly.

"And you believe that we Christians will be here to see all of this?" Carl asked disapprovingly.

Joseph shrugged his shoulders. "Maybe."

"What about Revelation 7:14 where Saint John refers to those who came out of the great Tribulation?" Carl sneered.

"Is the book of Revelation chronological?" Joseph asked.

"Yes!" said Carl sternly.

Zach was amazed at Carl's passion over this issue. It had to be ego-driven, because Zach knew it wasn't for a love of God.

"And what about Jude 1:14-15? Will we not come back to judge the ungodly?" said Carl. "Will we not be transformed in the twinkling of an eye as spoken of in 1 Corinthians? What about our bodies being transformed as spoken of in Philippians 3:21?"

Carl amused Leo. *Boy howdy! He can really wing out those verses,* Leo thought with a smile.

Joseph was not as amused as Leo. In fact, he was getting very tired of Carl.

"Mr. Perkins!" said Joseph. "This is not a personal issue. I am only stating my belief which comes from what I have read and been taught."

"Well, it surely doesn't make you right, now does it?" Carl asked.

Joseph was about to tear into Carl when Zach saved him from lowering his standards. "We have just enough time to allow each of our guests to give us a one minute summary of today's topic. Pastor Thomas, will you go first, please?"

"God loves you very much and He has prepared a place for you in Heaven, but you must ask Him into your heart first in order to have your name added to His great Book of Life."

"Thank you, Pastor Thomas," said Zach. "And now Reverend Perkins, do you have any words of wisdom for us?"

Carl lifted his book one more time. "People, time is short! Buy my book today and learn what is necessary to inherit the Kingdom of Heaven, and may God bless all of you."

"Father Bastoni," said Zach, "we have about 30 seconds left. Do you have anything to add?"

Joseph was not the kind of man who could think quickly under this kind of pressure, so he struggled for something intelligent to say. "Study your Bibles. The answers are all in there somewhere," he said with a very weak smile.

Scott stepped up. "Commercial in two, one, and cut." Scott began to clap his hands loudly and proceeded over to where Carl was sitting. "Great job!" he said as he extended his hand to Carl as if he were the only person in the room.

Stephanie came running out from behind one of the cameras where she had been standing during the show. Her smile told the story as she headed straight over to where Zach sat.

Zach looked up to Stephanie with eyes full of pride. "Your interviews were excellent!" he told her.

"So were yours," she giggled in delight.

Zach turned and shook Joseph's hand. "Thank you for doing this show for us."

Joseph said solemnly, "I only wish I could have done a better job."

"You were great!" Zach's sincerity showed.

Zach thanked Carl for his support and proceeded over to where Leo had ventured.

Leo put his arm around Zach's shoulder. "We've only got one thing left to do," he said with a serious tone that made Zach think he'd left something very important undone.

"What's that?" Zach asked with concern in his voice.

Leo laughed. "Get you and Valerie here married up."

Zach laughed and exhaled a sigh of relief.

Valerie reached out and held Zach's hand. He gave her hand a little squeeze as he searched the room for his son. Timothy was standing next to Stephanie and Joseph. "I'll be back in a minute," Zach said to Valerie and Leo.

He headed over to where Timothy stood. "Great job, Dad!" said his son with pride in his voice.

"Thank you, Timothy." Zach cleared his throat. "Son," he said a little nervously, "can I talk to you for a minute?"

"Sure, Dad, what is it?" Timothy asked anxiously.

Zach led Timothy over to a vacant corner of the small room. Valerie and Leo, as well as Stephanie and Joseph, observed passively while Scott was busy entertaining Carl and Clorisa.

"What's up, Dad?" Timothy inquired.

Zach felt uncomfortable as he tried to tell his son about accepting

Jesus into his life. "Son, I've made a lot of mistakes in my life."

"It's okay," said Timothy.

"No, let me finish," Zach insisted. "I was not as good of a father as I wanted to be, and I want you to know that I am sorry. I love you very much!"

Timothy began to swallow hard as tears filled his eyes.

"You see, I was angry at God for taking away all of my family, and as a result, I neglected my real family—you and your mom. I'm so sorry that I have let you both down."

Tears began to run down Timothy's cheeks as Zach spoke. Valerie watched this as her heart melted with the love and joy she now felt. However, Stephanie watched all of this in total confusion. *What was Zach saying to Timothy that could cause him to cry?* she wondered.

Zach continued. "I want you to know," he said, "I am no longer mad at God. In fact, I have asked Christ into my heart, and I plan on following Him for the rest of my life."

Timothy was stunned by this new revelation. "I've wasted so much of my life for nothing," Zach added, "and from here on I plan on making up for lost time. I just thought that you ought to know that, especially before you and Stephanie get married."

Timothy wiped the tears from his face with the back of his hand. He wasn't sure what to say so he said nothing at all. Zach reached in and gave his son a huge hug. He held Timothy as if it were his last time to hug his son. It had been so long since the two of them shared this kind of intimacy. Over the years it just became too uncomfortable for either of them to show affection even though they both needed this hug greatly.

"People, can I have your attention?" Scott asked. "It's time to celebrate! I want everyone to follow me to my house where I've planned a party for us."

This is a nice surprise, Zach thought, but all he really wanted was to go home with Valerie, sit in his favorite chair, eat chocolate chip cookies, and drink cold milk.

All of the crew members followed Scott into the elevator. Clorisa stood next to Zach and whispered into his ear, "I'm proud of you!"

Does she know that I was just saved? he wondered. *No, how could she?* Zach turned and smiled at Clorisa. "Thank you for everything!"

They all had done their part. The show was a success, and now it was time to celebrate. The group proceeded out into the parking lot with Zach trailing behind to reset the alarm system. At the corner of the building hiding in the shadows stood Philip, tall and strong. Zach moved out from under the doorway and headed towards his car where Valerie, Joseph, and Leo stood.

Suddenly in the parking lot sped an out-of-control black Camaro. Zach could hear the sound of the car accelerating as it headed straight towards him. He looked at the car and saw the driver had a hideous grin and a look of determination on his face.

Zach was frozen where he stood. He had seen this face before, once when his father was killed and again in the many nightmares he had suffered after nearly being stabbed to death.

"Watch out!" Valerie yelled at the top of her voice.

Timothy ran from his truck towards his father and into the path of the speeding car. Quickly he was within a few steps of his father. The car's engine roared as it approached where Zach stood paralyzed by a memory from his past. Timothy struggled to get to his father, but there just wasn't enough time. He turned to see the Camaro a mere 10 feet away from him when suddenly Philip rushed in and snatched Timothy from the car's path as it sped past them both and directly towards Zach.

Zach's body disappeared from sight as it slid under the Camaro. The unrelenting car continued at full speed until it crashed head-on into the wall of the office building. The driver was launched through the windshield and straight into the concrete wall. His face and head were smashed beyond recognition.

Timothy lay on the ground in Philip's powerful arms. He pushed his way up to look where his father had been standing. What he saw broke his heart. Zach was laying flat on his back in a pool of blood.

Timothy bolted off the ground as Philip loosened his grip. Valerie met her son as they raced towards the spot where Zach lay crumpled.

Leo ran towards Zach and then stopped directly in front of Philip.

"It's you!" he said. "You were the one who saved Zach at my church years ago."

Philip nodded lightly.

"You've been protecting him all along. But why not now?" Leo asked with tears running down his black face.

"You will understand later, Leonard," said Philip. "Now go to them. They need you."

Valerie and Timothy were kneeling next to Zach as he struggled to catch his breath. Joseph stood by holding Stephanie as she cried uncontrollably. Scott was on his cell phone calling for an ambulance. Clorisa knelt and began to intercede in prayer as Carl stood by watching.

Zach looked up to Valerie as Leo moved in by her side. "I'm sorry it took me so long to ask you to marry me. I love you," he said.

"I love you, Zach," Valerie whimpered.

"Timothy," Zach whispered, "Take care of your mother and remember what I told you. I love you, Son."

Zach coughed as blood trickled out of his mouth. He looked at Valerie, smiled weakly, and then closed his eyes forever. Valerie lifted his head onto her lap and began to rock him slowly as she cried aloud. Leo put his arms around Valerie's shoulders and began to cry as well.

Timothy held his father's hand and whispered, "I won't forget, Dad. I promise."

Leo turned to look for Philip, but he was nowhere in sight.

Chapter 16 - The Funeral

Timothy and Stephanie had spent the last two nights with Valerie. The mood in the house was one of terrible sorrow. There was a knock on the front door, another delivery of flowers. The city of Chicago had come to life after Zach's death. The reviews from his show would have made him very proud, and the love the people were now showing would have made him cry.

Valerie sat in Zach's favorite chair with the phone up to her ear. It was Clorisa again. She had called once already as soon as she and Carl had gotten back to Belair. "I am so encouraged by your faith," said Valerie, "and I thank you for your kindness." She hung up the phone and stood to her feet. It was time to get ready for the funeral.

******

Joseph was in a somber mood. He had grown to love Zach in the short time they had together. *Why was someone always trying to kill him?* he sat and pondered. *Zach was just an ordinary man.*

Joseph had been in Zach's apartment for the last couple of days. He wanted to stay for the funeral, but Valerie didn't want him to have to pay for a hotel, and there just wasn't enough room at her house for him with Timothy and Stephanie both staying there.

As he sat on the sofa he picked up the small, gray box off the coffee table. This box of pictures meant so much to Zach. Joseph began to look at all the photos. He knew from conversations with Zach that every family member in this box was dead except for Zach, but that was no longer true.

Joseph stared at all the happy family memories and suddenly began to cry. "What is this life all about?" he asked aloud. "God, if You are really up there, why has this happened?" He felt so empty. Joseph stood, took off his collar, and then removed his jacket. "I can't do this anymore," he cried.

******

Valerie had asked Leo for a graveside service for Zach. She didn't want the traditional church service with the open casket viewing, and she didn't want a public funeral. The guest list was short—only the immediate family and a few people from the station were invited. Valerie had prayed for sunshine for the funeral, but it seemed that God had not heard this prayer, because it was a gray and drizzly day. She made arrangements for a wake to be held back at her house after the funeral. The caterers would come in and set everything up while they were out.

Timothy pulled his mother's car into the cemetery parking lot and got out, opening the door for his mother and Stephanie. Timothy had been very quiet over the last three days. He had made a promise to his dying father that he would remember what Zach had told him about forgiving God and receiving Christ into his life, but now Timothy found himself struggling again with God. This time he was angry his father had died. *What good does it do me to accept Christ?* he wondered. *God, is this how You reward faithfulness and obedience?* Timothy knew that he couldn't keep his promise to his father and be angry with God at the same time. He was a man of his word, and it hurt him to wrestle with this issue.

Leo met Valerie at the front office to the cemetery. He reached out to her, and she gripped his leathery old hands in hers and smiled at him. "We'll get through this," he said lovingly.

Leo looked at Timothy. "How are you, Son?" he asked softly.

"I'm okay," Timothy lied.

Leo knew that he wasn't okay at all. He knew that in time Timothy would heal, but time can move very slowly when we are in pain.

The rest of the guests began to show up over the next few minutes, and each of them came forward to give their condolences to Valerie and Timothy. The last one to show up was Joseph himself. Valerie was surprised to see him wearing an ordinary suit and not his traditional vestments. Joseph looked at Valerie solemnly and moved over to where Timothy was standing. It seemed that Timothy was his comfort zone. He had grown to like the young man very much.

The family and guests moved to the grave site for the funeral service. Instead of chairs, they all stood loosely around Zach's casket. Valerie stood next to Leo while Stephanie and Joseph stood next to Timothy. Scott and the rest of the office workers mingled in between each other. Leo opened his Bible to 2 Timothy 4:7. "'And I have fought the good fight,'" he read. "'I have finished the race. I have kept the faith.'"

As Leo spoke, Stephanie interlaced her fingers with Timothy's.

Three rows in back of Leo and the group of mourning people, kneeling behind a large old headstone, were two hideous creatures grinning and snarling as Leo spoke. To their right next to a large, old, oak tree, stood Philip and Barthemaus.

******

While Zach's funeral was going on, hundreds of miles away Calvin Fraser sat in his cell listening as one of the other inmates directly across from him read aloud from the book of Genesis Chapter 1. "'In the beginning, God created the Heavens and the earth...'" Calvin listened as he looked through his bars.

"God," he said softly, "Why am I here? What have I done wrong?" Calvin leaned back against the wall and closed his eyes as the inmate continued to read.

******

Izuho sat in his car outside a Buddhist temple in downtown Tokyo. He had been searching for truth ever since his life had been spared during the tidal wave. He so wanted to praise whoever it was that had graciously saved him, but no matter how hard he looked, he could not find the god responsible.

"I can't go back in there again!" he cried aloud. "The god I'm looking for just isn't in there." So Izuho sat in his car all alone thinking about what Stephanie had asked him about Jesus Christ. "Who are you, Jesus?" he asked in a whisper.

******

Stan and Ruby Evans' world had been destroyed. All they had, including their church, had burned to the ground. They had buried two of their sons only a short time ago. The mood in the family was one of remorse and confusion. Neither Stan nor Ruby had the faith necessary to sustain them. Their lives were falling apart before their eyes. Today Stan, Ruby, and their children, along with dozens of other families, were being housed in a makeshift shelter in Quilpie.

******

Tommy and Tina sat together on their back porch watching young couples with children playing on the beach. There was a rumor of another volcano in South America. Tina wanted desperately to go, but for some reason she could not convince Tommy and, of course, she would never consider going without him.

Tommy felt a change in the wind, or more precisely, he felt danger. He hadn't forgotten the question Stephanie had asked him: "'Did you hear a voice or feel impressed to leave the volcano before the eruption?'" Tommy knew the truth. Something had warned him and, as a result, he and Tina were still alive. *But what was it?* he wondered. *Was it intuition? Is there such a thing? Was it God? Is there such a thing?*

******

Carl piled his dope into a small mountain on the mirror. In five more hours he would be preaching a sermon on the Return of Christ to a hungry Los Angeles audience. He was going to make a lot of money today. He was happy, and soon he would be happier.

Clorisa knelt by the side of her bed and prayed for God to deliver her from this life. She was sad and angry. She had wanted to stay in Chicago for Zach's funeral, but Carl wouldn't have any of that.

"We don't even know this guy," he said. "Besides, I need you back in L.A. with me. I have a show of my own this week."

"Lord, deliver me!" Clorisa cried from the bottom of her heart.

******

Elisha and Jasmine slept side by side in the dark cold cave. They had been inside for 21 days although they had lost count after the second week. Both Jasmine and Elisha had grown strong in the Lord and in each other. Recently, however, hunger from their three-week fast had taken its toll on both of them. For the last two days all these young adults had the energy to do was to sleep the day away.

Suddenly there was a warm, soft light illuminating the entire length of the cave. A gentle presence spoke Elisha and Jasmine's name, and slowly the two exhausted teenagers began to stir. "You have done well, but now it is time to leave."

Elisha got to his feet first and then helped Jasmine up. She was so weak from hunger that she could barely maintain her balance.

"You must go now. There is much to be done!" the angel commanded.

Elisha supported Jasmine as they both staggered their way to the entrance of the cave. As they approached, the intense sunlight caused them severe eye pain. They fell to the ground and lay silently on the warm, soft sand. "Rest here for a while, and soon I will tell you what to do," said the angel.

******

Leo finished reading his Bible and slowly closed his faded, old book full of multicolored notes. "Three days ago," he said, "Zach Miles accepted Christ into his life, and today he stands in Heaven with our Father."

At this the two demons hiding behind the headstone snarled. "He's a liar!" they croaked. "Zach's in Hell with us. If he is in Heaven, then why hasn't Christ come back? After all, wasn't Zach Miles supposed to be the Last Gentile to be saved?" Not that either of them was in a hurry to go back to Hell to look for Zach. It was enough for them to know that he was dead and there was no sign of Jesus anywhere. They had done their job.

Leo continued, "Zach struggled in life. He fought against God at times, but in the end he realized that our God is a loving Father. He realized that it was his own anger that kept him from being happy in life. Now if there are any among you that are wrestling against God—" as he said this he looked at Timothy. The two demons turned quickly towards each other as two ghastly looks of terror filled their grotesque faces. They looked over to the tree where Philip and Barthemaus were now kneeling in prayer. Rage filled their evil and ugly hearts.

"—The time has come," said Leo. "Put aside your disagreements with God and begin to follow after Him. He knows what is best for your life, and He will never fail you. I'd like us to pray a prayer. It is the same prayer that Zach said only three days ago." Leo began to recite the prayer word for word with much of the crowd repeating after him.

Timothy, too, closed his eyes and silently began to pray to God asking Jesus into his heart. *I'm tired of running,* Timothy thought as he recited the sinner's prayer.

Suddenly the ground beneath their feet began to shake ferociously. Joseph staggered backwards as Zach's coffin fell off its stand. Joseph turned toward Timothy, but to his surprise, Timothy was gone. So was Stephanie. In fact, many of the people that had been standing there were gone, including Valerie and Leo. In panic and fear Joseph fell to the ground as the earthquake intensified. His eyes were fixed on Zach's coffin. The lid had come open, and the only thing in it was a nice, new suit that Valerie had purchased days earlier.

Scott crawled over closer to Joseph. "What has just happened?" he asked in a total state of panic. "Where has everyone gone?" Suddenly Scott saw what Joseph was looking at. "Where did he go?" he asked in amazement and fear.

Joseph looked up towards Heaven as tears streamed down his face. "Dear God, I'm sorry!" Joseph moaned. "Forgive me! Forgive my lack of faith." Joseph lay prostrate and buried his face in his hands as he wailed uncontrollably while the quake finally began to subside.

******

Izuho watched in fascination as the powerful earthquake leveled the Buddhist shrine. Before his very eyes he saw groups of people on the streets of Tokyo disappear. He was speechless. Suddenly a thought occurred to him. Was this the Rapture that Stephanie Miller had asked him about? Has this Jesus Christ returned for His church?

"Jesus, are You the one that saved me?" Izuho asked aloud. "How can I come to know You as my God?" Izuho vowed to find Christ or die trying.

******

Calvin clung to the bars until the room finally stopped shaking. The voice of the prisoner who had been reading the Bible was silent. Calvin looked into his cell and was astounded to see that it was empty although the cell door was still tightly shut.

Calvin wasn't sure what had just happened, but he had a pretty good idea. "Now it begins," he said aloud as he bowed his head and began to cry for the first time since he had been put into prison. "God, what about me? What do you want from me? What do I need to do?"

******

Professor Lisa Taylor was sitting in her living room as the second floor of her beautiful house came crashing down on top of her. Apparently the Rapture had come sooner than she had thought.

******

The ground shook beneath Elisha and Jasmine as they lay on the sand. "What is it?" Jasmine cried.

"It's an earthquake!" Elisha answered as he struggled to pull himself up.

Just then the entrance to the cave began to collapse. Dirt and sand were floating in the air making it difficult to see more than a few feet in front of the cave. A warm glow engulfed both Jasmine and Elisha. "It is time," said the voice. "You must leave here and head east, for the Lord has come, and now you have much work to do." Elisha lifted Jasmine to her feet as the both of them enjoyed the peace and safety of the warm glow for the last time.

******

The Evans family clung to each other as the earth shook. People began to disappear before their very eyes. On their cots were their blankets and clothing, but the people were all gone.

"What is it?" Ruby shouted above the sound of the earthquake and screams of the other people.

"I don't know!" Stan was dumbfounded.

Ruby thought about what she had been taught so many years ago by the Christian missionaries who had come to Australia. In a twinkling of an eye Christ will return and the saints will meet Him in the air. "Oh, my God!" she cried aloud. "Lord, forgive us!"

******

Tina and Tommy were accustomed to earthquakes, but from the beginning this quake was different. It was like the entire world was being shaken all at once. Tina screamed as she observed that the many children who had been playing on the beach suddenly disappeared, all except for their little bathing suits.

Tommy also was speechless by what he saw. He grabbed Tina's hand and pulled her away from the porch. "We have to get to higher ground before the tidal waves start to come in," he said.

They sped down the interstate heading north away from the Pacific coastline. "Where did those little kids go?" Tina asked with panic in her voice.

"To Heaven," said Tommy flatly as he depressed the accelerator. The first tidal wave could already be seen in the distance, and it was going to be a big one. California was not going to have a bountiful harvest of crops after all.

******

Carl ran into Clorisa's bedroom just as the quake started. What he saw caused him to stop in his tracks. As the walls swayed back and forth, Carl tried to focus on the articles of Clorisa's clothing as they lay on the floor. Wasn't this the very clothing she had on not an hour ago? Clorisa's watch and her wedding ring were also lying on the floor.

The room slowed its swaying as Carl stepped closer to Clorisa's bed. He looked down at two shiny objects and bent to pick them up. There in the palm of his hands were two small gold crosses. "Clorisa's earrings," he puzzled aloud.

Carl took the earrings with him and headed into his office. He sat back silently for a few minutes before he began to call upon his servants. After many attempts, he realized that they were all gone. Hours went by as Carl sat staring out of his large office window. His show tonight would obviously be cancelled. In fact, Carl knew he would never be able to deceive an audience again. *Christ has already come back, so what could I possibly preach on now?* he wondered. *Besides, they will all want to know why I didn't go with Jesus.* "Jesus!" Carl growled aloud. He looked at the small gold crosses in his hand and angrily threw them against the wall. Carl turned his attention back to the mountain of white fluffy powder sitting on the mirror in the middle of his desk. He reached into the corner drawer and pulled out a half-empty bottle of Scotch and set it next to his drugs. Behind him, although invisible to him, stood two evil creatures mocking him and encouraging him to take a drink and have a blow. In the corner of the office stood Philip with his head bowed in prayer to God.

Carl leaned back in his chair after taking a long blast off the small golden straw on his mirror. "Well, I guess I need to find a new wife," he laughed. Suddenly Carl felt tightness in his chest. He struggled to breathe as he fell out of his chair, kicking over the mirror loaded down with cocaine. Carl landed on the floor solidly. As he opened his eyes, he found himself staring at a small golden cross lying in front of him. Carl's heart began to pound loudly. The two demons in the room grinned horribly as Philip walked out of the room with his head bowed. Carl's breathing intensified and finally stopped altogether. He died with his open eyes staring directly at the little golden cross in front of him.

John 3:16

About The Author

Cary Bybee has been married to Peggy O'Malley since 1980 and has four children: Christy, Melissa, Carrie, and Zachary. He lives in the Willamette Valley in the state of Oregon and has worked internationally as a scientist and engineer since graduating from Texas A & M in 1988 after an eight-year tour of duty in the United States Air Force. For many years he has been a musician and worship leader in his church. He is the author of *The Last Gentile, Deacon's Horn, The Final Witness,* and *The Library Man.*

Printed in the United States
48577LVS00003B/268